M...
Dea...

Also by Stefan Petrucha

Dead Mann Walking

Dead Mann Running

A HESSIUS MANN NOVEL

Stefan Petrucha

A ROC BOOK

ROC
Published by New American Library, a division of
Penguin Group (USA) Inc., 375 Hudson Street,
New York, New York 10014, USA
Penguin Group (Canada), 90 Eglinton Avenue East, Suite 700, Toronto,
Ontario M4P 2Y3, Canada (a division of Pearson Penguin Canada Inc.)
Penguin Books Ltd., 80 Strand, London WC2R 0RL, England
Penguin Ireland, 25 St. Stephen's Green, Dublin 2,
Ireland (a division of Penguin Books Ltd.)
Penguin Group (Australia), 250 Camberwell Road, Camberwell, Victoria 3124,
Australia (a division of Pearson Australia Group Pty. Ltd.)
Penguin Books India Pvt. Ltd., 11 Community Centre, Panchsheel Park,
New Delhi - 110 017, India
Penguin Group (NZ), 67 Apollo Drive, Rosedale, Auckland 0632,
New Zealand (a division of Pearson New Zealand Ltd.)
Penguin Books (South Africa) (Pty.) Ltd., 24 Sturdee Avenue,
Rosebank, Johannesburg 2196, South Africa

Penguin Books Ltd., Registered Offices:
80 Strand, London WC2R 0RL, England

First published by Roc, an imprint of New American Library,
a division of Penguin Group (USA) Inc.

First Printing, September 2012
10 9 8 7 6 5 4 3 2 1

ALWAYS LEARNING   PEARSON

For my dear pal Steve Holtz. He knows why.

I have seen with my own eyes the Sibyl hanging in a jar, and when the boys asked her *"What do you want?"* she answered, *"I want to die."*[1]

[1] The Cumaean Sibyl referenced here was granted immortality by Apollo, but forgot to ask for perpetual youth and shrank into withered old age. Translated from the Latin/Greek epigraph to *The Waste Land* by T. S. Eliot.

1

Rebirth sounds great, doesn't it? Sounds like hope, possibility, spring. Nope. It's more like that poet T. S. Eliot said, *April is the cruellest month.*

Not that the rest of the year's much better. Take November for instance. Take it on a boring night as a fat rain fell, the drops thick and icy cold, but too lazy to turn to snow. I was slumped in my ratty recliner, getting ready to watch Nell Parker, a dead stripper I'd had an unusual relationship with, on the tube. Sure, I could've shut it off, but there's nothing like seeing the face of someone you want to forget every day on TV.

She'd gotten the gig partly as blowback for the Chak Registration Act; chakz, short for charqui, or dried meat, being the preferred term for us zombie-types. Thanks to an undead-riot caused by a pal of mine, an awful lot of livebloods died. Jane and Joe average didn't like that much, so some pretty Draconian laws were passed. As a nod to the bleeding hearts worried about chak rights, a "good" dead person was given a talk show.

Nell was better than good, she was perfect—smart, pampered, and nothing missing. Her skin was white and silky smooth, not the usual rough gray, her black hair straight and shiny. Oh, they had to work at it. I read the studio was kept below sixty to ensure rot didn't set in. But best of all, Nell was also the only chak with eye color, green, no doubt to match her benefactor's last name, he being billionaire pervert Colby Green. He and his powerful buddies loved chakz any way they could.

Despite the fact that TV was a definite step-up from pole dancing at Green's private orgies, Nell never seemed to appreciate it. She tried to look harmless, knowing that the whole point was to show that all chakz weren't a threat, but there was always a hint of disdain in those emerald eyes. It made me feel like she was looking at me.

The show itself was bullshit, fluff designed to make LBs feel better about imprisoning us. Not that I blame them for that. If a chak gets too depressed, they go feral. That's kind of like going postal, but only if George Romero directed it. Thanks to the new laws, any chak who could speak or write had to take a monthly emotional stability test. Pass, and you're free to enjoy your second-class citizenship for another month. Fail, and they put you in a concentration camp until you do go feral. Then they safely destroy you. They're not clear on how they do the destroying. No one likes watching sausages getting made, or burned.

On the plus side, we all get free cell phones. Not that many of us know how to use them. In theory, they can be used to track us if we go AWOL. In reality, the guard, a volunteer group composed mostly of testosterone types who used to spend their weekends chopping us up with machetes, is charged with chak control, and they don't like sharing with local law enforcement. It's moot in my neck of the woods. Fort Hammer doesn't have the equipment to track anything. All in all, not so much Big Brother as his big, dumb, inbred cousin.

To be fair to Nell, she tried to branch out. She'd done a series of interviews with no less than ChemBet's head of R & D, Travis Maruta, the man who made zombies real. A mousy guy you wouldn't think had it in him to swat a bug, let alone change the world, he went on about how hard he and his wife Rebecca were working to improve the human race even more.

The way I heard it, Rebecca was a second-rate chemist, but a first-rate dominatrix. She'd gotten Travis into some kinky shit that made Colby Green look like a virgin. I doubted either of them gave a damn about anything except getting each other off.

But there are lies, and then there are damned lies. The former would be something no one believes, like if I were to say Nell Parker meant nothing to me. The latter would be a whopper, like my execution. When that needle pierced my soft pink skin, I thought at least nothing worse could happen. It wasn't the first time I was wrong, but it was the last time my skin was soft or pink.

When DNA evidence threw out my conviction, I was subjected to ChemBet's patented, self-perpetuating, neo-magical, electrostatic Radical Invigoration Procedure, *RIP*, for short. I came back with dry skin, brittle bones, sixty percent of my IQ, and none of my photographic memory. And they said I was one of the lucky ones.

Now my memory's like an old dog without a leash. It either lies around doing nothing, or winds up eating things it shouldn't. When I thought Nell betrayed me by going back to Green, it reminded me of what an angry guy I'd been when I was alive. After that, I started thinking she was better off without me. I contented myself with stalking her on TV, but that night, she came on without the fake smile and barely able to speak.

"Dr. Travis Maruta," she finally managed, "was found dead yesterday in his ChemBet laboratory, apparently from a self-administered overdose of an unknown substance. It was November twelfth, the eighth anniversary of his invention of the RIP . . ."

Some chakz would find the news satisfying; others say that real death was too good for him. Some would be too decayed to have an opinion. Me, I was thinking, *Suicide? Maybe the whiny son of a bitch finally realized what he did.*

Big picture, I couldn't care less. Sure, I wished he'd killed himself *before* he came up with the RIP, but blaming Maruta for my problems was like blaming Henry Ford for car accidents. When they switched from Nell to a "real" newscaster, I got bored, turned the set off, and took to watching the shadows on the floor.

I was doing a pretty good job thinking nothing, when a knock came at the door. Answering was Misty's job, my assistant, but she was out with Officer Chester O'Donnell, a boy toy she'd met while I was in jail. When the knock came again, I remembered it might mean money, and that was in short supply. Business, never booming, had gone downhill since the camps opened. Mostly, I'd get some chak hoping I could help him or her cheat on their next test, which I couldn't. Misty ran a little memory class that made more than I did, and she hated charging.

But, seeing as how you never know, I shambled into our so-called reception area. The bottom half of the door wobbled from a third rap.

"Who is it?" I asked.

No answer, but the next knock came faster. With a grunt, I opened the door.

No one was there. Not even a raven squawking *nevermore*. A cold, wet gust of wind slapped my face and set a loose bit of cheek-skin wobbling. I should've had Misty sew it, but the cold weather, while it helped me keep, made me lazy, like a reptile. At least the building was rotting faster than I was. The three story walk-up lost half a wall last week. The rooms across the hall were no longer habitable. A chak or two downstairs were the only other occupants. You get what you pay for, and the landlord stopped charging rent when the building was condemned.

I started thinking the knock was a loose board about to fall, but didn't see any new leaks. And then I looked down.

Six inches from my feet sat a weathered briefcase, cracked and dented as my loafers. But that wasn't the first thing I noticed. That'd be the hand gripping the handle. As usual, an arm was attached, but after that, nothing. No head, shoulders, knees, or toes, just briefcase, hand, and arm.

There's a knock-knock joke in there somewhere, but I don't know what it is.

As I stared, the hand let go of the case, raised its fingers and wobbled the tips as if feeling the empty air. It regripped the handle and squirmed, stub first, dragging itself and the case inside. It crawled through the front room and into my office, leaving a thin trail on the floor. I thought it was oozing the gray stuff chakz have on their insides, but a closer look told me it was rainwater mixed with street grit.

At the center of the office floor, it stopped, like it was expecting me to join it.

I wondered if I'd fallen asleep in the chair. Chakz are tough to kill. Knife wounds, gunshots, even the loss of a limb or two, won't stop us, but our pieces, unless it's the head, don't generally get around on their own. Still, I'd seen a walking skeleton and a laughing skull, so I didn't think it impossible. There was a lot about the radical invigoration process no one knew for sure.

I stuck my head out and looked down the hall, in case it was some joker with a remote. Livebloods don't bother with me, and the only chak I knew warped enough to pull something like this was Jonesey, and he'd been shipped off to the camps after failing his last test, stupid bastard. We tried to help him study. Well, Misty did, I wasn't speaking to him on account of he was the one who caused the riot. Maybe, like Nell, he was better off. He'd already gone feral once, until I slapped him out of it. You can do that sometimes.

Other than the wind, and the rain pouring from the gaping ceiling holes to the mottled floor, there was nothing. No second arm, no torso, no legs or head that'd fallen behind.

I closed the door and turned back, half expecting my

guest to be gone. It wasn't. It was still there, rapping its fingers on the case like an impatient salesman.

Comfortable that it wasn't going to bite, I stepped closer for a better look. Its skin didn't look chak-gray, but my sense of color isn't great at night. It wasn't thin. It had muscles, legit, not baby-smooth like a bodybuilder's. The fingers had less character, but they were thick, rugged. A workingman's arm, if I had to guess. It kinda reminded me of my father's arm, a thought that added to the scene's dreamlike feel.

Christ, I hadn't thought about Larry Mann in ages. I wouldn't say he was a violent man. If I did, I was afraid he'd hit me. But that was crazy. The arm couldn't be his. Its fingers were intact. Dad lost the top halves of four digits when he fell into a circular saw. He was so drunk he didn't even notice they were gone until he reached the hospital.

The rest of him left us about a year after that. Mom tried to lie about it. He'd been a drill sergeant, so she told me he'd signed up for Special Ops, but I saw the papers marked dishonorable discharge. I figured he was out on the streets somewhere, missing his fingers more than he missed us.

Whatever. The arm wasn't in any position to say who it belonged to, or what it wanted. Maybe if I got it a pen? I stepped behind my desk and pulled open the top drawer. Outside, the hiss of wheels on wet asphalt mixed with the rushing rain.

I don't know how the arm could've heard it, maybe it felt the vibrations, but like a demented cross between snake and monkey, it let go of the case, righted itself at the elbow, sprang to my desk and bounded over to the windowsill. The fingers felt frantically along the glass, down to the wood. It was trying to open it, to get away.

"Wait!" I shouted. Like it could hear me. What could I follow that up with?

Don't jump! You've got so much to live for!

I tried to grab it, but it punched a pane, shattering the glass and a good chunk of rotten wood. With a rubbery twitch, it tumbled into the gray. I snatched at the air. The wind sent bullets of rain into my face. I leaned out of the hole it'd left and looked down at wet trash, a rusted Dumpster, and puddles.

2

Through the broken window, I heard a warm, familiar chuckle. It was Misty, laughing good-naturedly at a taxi driver's joke before closing the passenger door. Chester had sent her home by cab again.

November wind and water bitch-slapped the unpaid bills on my desk. The briefcase sat on the floor like a lottery ticket begging to be scratched. Whatever was in it might solve my money troubles. There could be a reward for returning it. But something told me to stay away, not even think about it.

Tough luck about the thinking. When I was ripped they gave me a new set of clothes and a pamphlet. The clothes didn't fit and the pamphlet wasn't good for much, but it did warn that chak bodies could be unpredictable. My left knee, for instance, shivered without warning. Lately, it was thinking I couldn't control. The tired wheels turned in my homicide detective head, but I had no idea how to put the brakes on.

When Misty walked in half a minute later, I was back in my chair. She looked good; meat on her bones, verve in her movements. She was a world away from the starving addict who used to think she could pass for a chak. But everything comes with a price. In this case, it was her increasingly annoying optimism.

Hair and clothes damp, she shook the rain from her umbrella. "What am I going to do with you?" she said when she saw me. The smile on her face kept her from looking disapproving. "You've been sitting there feeling sorry for yourself since I left, haven't you? Moping."

"Mostly. How was the date? Bowling again?"

She leaned the umbrella against the wall and worked the buttons on her thrift store overcoat. "Don't change the subject. If it wasn't for you passing that test, I swear I'd be sleeping with that sledgehammer next to my cot again, waiting for you to go rabid."

"Feral."

"Don't tell me what word to use. You think there's a difference?"

"My mouth can't foam. And don't you tell me you trust that government questionnaire. Not after they took Jonesey."

Her face went a little sad. She'd liked Jonesey, too. "You said yourself he tried to eat you in an alley."

"He got better."

"You're also the one who told me once they go, it's only a matter of time."

"Something I heard on TV."

"Watching your girlfriend again? The one you won't speak to even though she got you out of jail?"

"I heard that a long time ago. *Good Morning Fort Hammer*, I think."

She hung the coat on a stand and came closer, which didn't take much. My office, the front room, the half bath, and the walk-in supply closet she used as a bedroom would all fit in a stretch limo.

She gave me a somber once-over. "Your memory's getting better."

"Because you drill me every day."

She slapped my shoulder. "Every *other* day. You know that."

"It's a fucking game, Misty. Passing doesn't make me safe any more than failing made Jonesey dangerous. Look how many idiots get driver's licenses. That's a test, ain't it?"

"You are one big dead baby, Hessius Mann. I'm trying to hold on to hope here, that's what keeps it from happening, right? Or do you enjoy acting like a piece of furniture? I can't even feel comfortable going out with Chester for a few hours with you . . ." Her voice trailed off.

She had more energy and I was getting slower. We'd become a bad combination. That much was obvious even to me.

"About the boy toy, I've been meaning to tell you . . ."

"He has a name," she said. In a huff, she turned her back, walked off and grabbed a towel.

"So do I. He ever use it, or is he still calling me *it*?"

I was trying to be nice, but couldn't manage it. I could say chakz have trouble with emotions, but really, I was being an asshole.

"He's working on it. It'd help if you'd talk to him. Even *nod* at him."

I could see from a mirror that she'd scrunched her face, sending rainwater from her hair down her cheeks, into the towel. The smile she came in with was gone. Great, now I'd ruined her evening.

I raised a hand to slow her down. "That's what I'm trying to say. I think I misjudged you two. I mean, I thought he needed sex and you needed a favor. Maybe that's how it started, but, it doesn't look that way anymore. You're still going to meetings, and more often than not, you look . . . happy."

The smile came back in a flash. I didn't know whether to feel good or bad about it.

"So I have your permission to date him now, Dad?"

"No, but he's got a salary and a real place. If you wanted to leave . . ."

When she turned back I finally noticed that the ice green blouse she wore looked new. She wasn't unhappy again, but she was serious. "And what would happen to you if I did? We're in this together, remember? How can I think about moving out when all you ever do is . . . what the fuck happened to the window?"

I was wondering when she'd notice.

"Oh, that. An arm punched its way out."

"Your desk is soaked." She rushed toward it with the towel and nearly tripped over the briefcase. "And what the hell is this?"

A few drops of rain fell from her to the case.

"The arm dropped it off before it jumped out the window."

She laughed, and then stopped. "Seriously? Have you been drinking? *Can* you drink?"

"I can go through the motions."

She looked back down at the case. "What's in it?"

"Don't know."

"You didn't open it?"

"If I did, I'd know."

She lifted the case and plopped it on my desk, mushing a few soggy bills in the process. "What if it's a job, something to work on? Better yet, something that pays."

Before I could answer, she flipped the latches.

"Misty, don't . . ."

It opened easily. Whatever was inside bathed her in a quiet blue light.

"Fine. Have it your way, Pandora. What's in it?"

She twisted the case away. "You want to see, get off your leathery ass."

"Misty——" I groaned and shifted, planning to get up. I wasn't fast enough. She picked up the case and headed toward the front room.

"Now you have to walk for it. Shamble for me, zombie-man."

"Don't play with that thing! What if it's poison? Remember the nerve gas?" She stopped. "And if there's any fingerprints, you're ruining them."

Gently, she put it back on the desk where I could see. Inside, it was mostly foam, the edges stained a sickly brown from the dirt and water that'd seeped in. In the center were two glass vials, each nearly filled with a clear, bluish liquid. The streetlight outside the window had given them the glow. We stood there staring like we were watching an interesting movie.

Misty broke the silence. "You really think it could be poison?"

"Doesn't matter what I think. It is what it is. Best guess? Drugs. Drugs is always a good guess. A stash swiped off a dealer by a stupid chak who didn't get away in one piece."

"Wasn't there a chak living down the block that was just a head, torso and arm?"

I prodded the foam. "No arms. One leg. Vernon Gray. They took him to the camps a month ago after he tried to fill out the test with his foot."

She gave me a look. I knew what it meant. "Yeah, I remember *some* things."

"So, what're you going to do about it?"

"Me? Not a damn thing. Cops would never come here, but you could call Chester. Then it'll be the police's problem."

Her eyes narrowed.

"What? You want me to taste it?"

"You're a detective. You could try, you know, *detecting*."

"I am! Handing it over to the cops is the smart move! Stop being so damn cheery and get realistic. It's a brief-case with two glass vials. What else am I supposed to detect? I could yank the foam out and see if there's anything underneath it, but if the blue stuff is dangerous some of it could get loose."

She crossed her arms. "That case was brought to you for some reason. Are you really going to just give it away?"

"Why not? If a bullet's got your name on it, does that mean you shouldn't duck?"

She turned away. "Have it your way. I'll call Chester."

We were stuck in a stupid dance, but I didn't know how to get out of it. I didn't want to drag her down, but I didn't want her dragging me up.

As she went into the front room to get her cell, I couldn't help looking at the vials again. Unmarked, clear glass, real thick. Could be from a high-security lab or a dollar store. Damn.

A frigid blast turned me back to the window. I grabbed the towel she'd left on the desk, balled it up and stuffed it into the broken pane. The effort gave me a view of the roof across the alley.

Something moved.

It was probably a shadow, but I shuddered just the same. If I were the melodramatic type, I'd say it looked more like a figure that'd been watching, and now it'd seen enough. After all, an arm had just brought me a present. Who knew what else was out there tonight?

3

If a killer hides in the dark and no one sees him, does he make a sound?

My eyes trolled the roofs, the brick sills, the broken awnings, all the angles that made up our little chak-slum. It was lively out there, a real Broadway show. Heavy drops sparked the edges of everything, briefly lighting whatever they hit. Other than the rain, nothing moved. But my body wouldn't accept that we were alone.

I called to Misty, "Any luck?"

"Left a message."

She went back to drying her hair, unconcerned.

"Any other way to get ahold of him?"

"What's your hurry?"

I looked at the window again. The towel had reduced the wind to a whistle. Water meandered on the remaining panes, drawing tiny rivers. "Probably nothing. I've just got a feeling that sooner would be better than later. The arm was kinda antsy . . ."

She stuck her head in the doorway. "The *arm* was *antsy*? Was it fidgeting?"

"It wasn't like it could do much else. I was just thinking. You like it when I think, right? If the blue crap's important enough to drag up here, it may be important to someone else, and they may come looking."

She walked in and stared at the open case. "Drug dealers, huh? What kind of dealers would bother with such a fancy case?"

She had a point. It was leather, insulated, the foam neatly cut to match the shape of the glass. The vials had been given an awful lot of care.

"I don't know," I said, but just to contradict myself I started rattling off ideas. "Maybe it's a concentrate, ready to be cut for street sales. Angel dust can be liquid, and there's hashish oil. That's usually brown but it can be clear. Blue? For all I know it's liquid explosive, heisted from a black market arms dealer."

She cracked a grin. Not the reaction I expected.

"Explosions are funny now?"

"No, but . . . an arm stealing from an arms dealer . . ."

I don't have to breathe, but I exhaled through my nose to show her I wasn't amused. "I'm not kidding about getting it out of here. Unless the laws of nature got revised *again*, and nobody told me, at some point that arm had a body. Something split them up."

I closed the case, clicked the latches, and looked for a place to hide it. One pile of crap looked a lot like another. I could shove it under something and never find it again myself. I picked up a pile of laundry, then thought better of it and tried to kick it under the couch. Chak clothes need so much bleach, they're usually rags within a month.

"Maybe he's on Facebook."

"You *still* joking about the arm?"

"No, Chester. He has an account. I could message him."

I was half listening. Under the bureau? "Right. Closest computer's at the Styx."

Her smile widened. "Not anymore."

That got my attention. She disappeared a second, reappearing with a small netbook.

"Gift from my man," she said, flipping it open.

I attempted a whistle, which, thanks to a dry throat, came out like a Bronx cheer. "Forget about you, *I* want to move in with him. He got a storage shed? I don't take up much space."

It was refurbished, probably a lower-end model, but a man doesn't get a woman a netbook unless he wants to stay in touch.

"What're you going to connect to? It's not like we have Wi-Fi."

"I got us cable by splicing into that coax, didn't I? If anyone nearby has a signal . . ."

"In the Bones? Forget it. It's chakz and addicts for half a mile. We're lucky when the cell phone works."

"Got one."

I squinted at the screen. "CB Mobile. What's that mean?"

"Doesn't matter," she shrugged. "It's password protected."

I guess Misty's memory drills were paying off, because I remembered something from my days as a liveblood detective. "Try 'password' or 'admin.' Those're usually the defaults. Most people don't bother changing them."

She clicked the keys and announced, "We're in."

That little trick earned me an admiring wink. "Look at you, Hessius Mann, firing on all cylinders. Feel better than sitting in a chair and moping all day?"

"Not really." The downside of paying attention was realizing when things weren't right. Wi-Fi in the Bones made less sense than an arm out on its own.

I thought about taking the case to the cops myself, keeping Misty and her pal Chester out of it, but that wouldn't have worked. Last we spoke, Chief Detective Tom Booth had promised to spend his off hours figuring out new ways to destroy me. My old boss hated chakz, slept with my wife, and still blamed me for her death. I was three for three.

Ten minutes after Misty sent Chester a message, we heard a car stop outside, another warning that something was wrong. We reached the front window at the same time to gawk at the police car. It was like seeing the Loch Ness Monster in the Vatican. Nothing happens that fast in Fort Hammer, not when you need it, not when you don't.

I had to ask. "Chester patrolling tonight?"

When they'd met, he was a clerk. Two weeks ago, they'd given him his first beat. Must've killed Tom to let someone dating my assistant have a patrol, but since the Registration Act passed and the guard had to be funded, the police had been forced to shift resources.

"No. At least I don't think so."

A uniform got out. He was a little shy of average height, stocky like a longshoreman. His cap was on for the rain, so I couldn't see a face.

As he headed for our stoop, all around him, things moved. Figures shifted in the nooks and crannies formed by the wreckage of buildings, the falling rain giving away their presence and shape.

I knew them. Hell, I was one of them. They were chakz, the ones who weren't as lucky as I was. These were my lesser brothers, who couldn't even remember to get out of the rain, who, more often than not, didn't have an arm to raise an umbrella or piece of cardboard. From here it seemed a few had entrails dangling, but it could've just been torn clothes, made ragged by endless bleaching.

That's the thing. Even the worst of them, the ones who could barely speak, knew that a squad car in the Bones was weird. Even Chester had been warned to visit only in an unmarked car.

It was easy for the cop to ignore them, they looked like bare branches swaying in the trees. He did pause to wipe the rain from his face, giving us a glimpse of dark hair and a handsome face with an aquiline nose.

I nudged Misty. "Know him?"

She shook her head, no. "You?"

"No, but in my case that doesn't mean a whole helluva lot."

Misty tried to shatter the gloom. "Aw, Chester must have sent him."

The rain picked up, falling sharp. I looked to the rooftops again. My best guess was that there was nothing there, and may never have been.

Just the same, I stuffed the case under a recliner cushion. The damn chair was so old and beat up, I nearly shredded the cover. On the lighter side, the big lump didn't make the chair look much different.

Misty watched. "First you can't wait to get rid of it, now you're hiding it?"

"It's an instinct, like a squirrel with nuts. Wouldn't Chester have called first?"

Her face told me she was worried, at least a little. Good.

Hoping to beat our visitor to the punch, I made for the door and opened it. Soaked, the hand-painted sign that read HESSIUS MANN, INVESTIGATIONS flopped into a puddle. The crazy downpour had stifled the hallway wind, but water ran from the ceiling like a fancy showerhead.

I heard shoes splash below, then try to stamp themselves dry.

A male voice called, "Hello? Hessius Mann?"

The tone was too cheery for a Fort Hammer cop, and there was no trace of an accent. I don't trust people without accents. They're hiding something. And he'd asked for me, not Misty. Chester never used my name.

Before I could stop her, Misty answered, "Up here."

"Great. Stay put."

Right, all one big happy family. I first saw our new buddy in silhouette. His cap was on, water dripping from the rim. I also noticed his holster was unclipped.

All the little details, on their own, meant nothing, even the holster, given the neighborhood. And when you add things up, you can be wrong.

As he rounded the top step, lightning flashed and we saw each other at once. Like I said, my body can be unpredictable. Right then, my startle reflex decided to work. I jumped nearly a foot.

Our visitor's face dropped. He reached for his gun. Misty gasped.

An image of myself pushing her out of the way flashed

in my head, but before I could act on it, he stopped himself and gave us a broad grin.

"Thought you were a chak," he said.

"I am."

"Yeah, of course, but, you know, I thought you might be feral."

I gestured at the gun. "Bit of advice? If I were, you *might* stop me with that, but you'd have to empty the clip and hit all the right spots."

Truth is, one feral isn't much to worry about, and he looked like he knew it. The salesman grin didn't waver. His eyes twinkled like it was something he could get them to do at will.

"Got something for me?"

"Depends who you are."

He turned to Misty like I was the stupid kid and she the adult. Again, not unusual. Lots of cops ignore chakz. "Jack Gambrell. Chester sent me. I was over in Collin Hills when he called."

Collin Hills was a gated community on the far side of Buell Park, the closest a cop would get to the Bones. That much made sense, at least.

"Badge?" I asked.

Happy Jack kept ignoring me. If he was going out of his way to do Chester a favor, my question might've seemed offensive.

Misty asked the next question for me. "Why didn't Chester call to say you were coming?"

Happy Jack shrugged. "His battery was dying, cut him off in midsentence."

She laughed. "He's always forgetting to charge that thing."

He laughed back. I didn't.

We stood there until he got tired of waiting and pushed his way in. "This about some kind of vials in a briefcase?"

His head turned like a lighthouse beam. He scanned the walls, the floor, the desk, first one way, then the other. "We've been seeing liquid PCP. Maybe someone swiped a delivery."

"That's usually brown, or yellow. This stuff's blue," I said.

His gaze settled on me. My knee twitched, like it wanted to run and it didn't care whether I came along or not.

"You used to be a cop, didn't you? So what'd you do, hide it? Good thinking. Chester said you were a smart one."

I half expected him to put a sugar cube in my mouth and pat my head.

He was also digging himself in deeper, talking like he'd heard about me in passing. Among the Fort Hammer blue, I was as famous as Charles Manson, one of their own executed for murder. And when they tried to convict me of blowing up an abandoned hospital not so long ago, my ashen face was plastered across the papers. Was this guy even local?

"So where'd you put it? Or am I supposed to stand here all night trying to guess?"

On the other hand, if I was wrong, and made a stupid move against a real cop, I'd be hauled off to the camps. Well . . . I'd been wondering how ol' Jonesey was doing.

I stepped forward. "Sorry, pal, a little slow in the attic. It's right over here."

Soon as I was close enough to him, I faked a stumble and grabbed his gun. It was bigger and heavier than I expected, not standard issue, more like a magnum on steroids.

Misty screamed. "Hess, are you crazy?!"

Jack's hands were up, but he was still smiling. That alone made me want to shoot him.

"You don't want to do that."

"Who are you? Last I heard it was illegal to impersonate a cop, let alone steal a squad car."

"Hess, please, please, give him back the gun. Jack, it's okay. He's a little off today," Misty said, moving between us.

She looked terrified, not of me, but for me. If I wasn't so busy keeping the gun leveled at Jack, I'd have been touched by her concern.

"Get out of the way! He's no cop."

"Whoa! Easy, there, fellow," Jack said, like he was talking to a horse again. "You got it all wrong. I'm exactly who I said I was."

Sometimes it's as hard for me to hold on to a conviction as it is a thought. I was actually wondering if I was wrong about him when he opened his mouth again.

"Give me the case and we can forget all about this."

I tightened my grip. "You're saying you won't tell anyone I grabbed your gun? No charges against me?"

"That's right."

"That sound like a Fort Hammer cop to you, Misty? Dropping charges against a chak? It's illegal for me to even hold a weapon."

"He could be lying, Hess."

"That's what I'm saying."

She rubbed her forehead like a migraine was coming on. "No, he could be lying about not pressing charges."

"Oh."

Jack went into a song and dance. "Hey, hey, hey. I only came by to do my buddy a favor. Can we all calm down a little?"

When he started to lower his arms, I pointed the barrel at his face. "Chester your buddy? Tell me, smiley, how do I know him?"

He glanced at Misty. "You really should put this thing on a leash."

She massaged her temples. "I've thought about it. Hess, if the nice police officer gets the answer right, will you please, please, please give him back the gun?"

"Sure." But this time *I* was lying. "So . . . how do I know Chester? We meet in grade school, fight together in the war, get teamed for a patrol, what?"

I didn't think it could, but Jack's grin actually went wider. "He's your . . . brother?"

You could hear the "wrong answer" buzzer go off. Misty, finally getting with the program, backed away, giving me a clear shot. "You son of a bitch. Where's Chester?"

"Fine, you caught me. But you still want to give me that case."

"Is Chester all right? Did you hurt him?"

"Hurt him? I never even met the guy. The case?"

"Hess, you can't just give it to him."

I thought about it. "Why not?"

"Hess!"

"If Chester *is* okay, it might not be a bad idea. The only way Jack would know to come here would be if he'd been monitoring your phone or the netbook. Maybe it was his

Internet connection we tapped into. Add a stolen cop car, and you've got a pretty complicated operation. Whatever this is about, it's bigger than me, and I don't even like it all that much when things are smaller." I gestured at Happy Jack with the barrel. "If I give you the case, how do I know no one will start thinking of Misty and me as loose ends that need tying? Got a supervisor I can talk to?"

He shrugged. "Can't do it. If you already think you know too much, would knowing more really be a good idea?"

"Right. In that case, we'll all head over to police HQ together."

"That's a long walk. It's raining."

"We'll take your car. On the way, you can entertain us with the witty story of how you nicked it."

I pulled the briefcase from under the cushion. Jack rolled his eyes.

"Shit. I'd have found it easy."

"So I ruined the chair for nothing. Make for the door."

But HJ didn't. "Last chance. You might not care about a bullet or two, but your friend will. Give me the case, or she'll wind up bleeding."

"Did I miss something? I know my memory's bad, but near as I can tell, I'm still the one with the gun."

"Yeah, but not the only one."

He flicked his wrists. Two small black objects flew into his hands. Derringers. The good news was that they're not repeating, one shot each. The bad news was he was already squeezing a trigger.

I threw myself into Misty. There was a firecracker pop and the wall behind us spit plaster. Soon as I caught my balance, I fired back. Big mistake.

Chakz are weak, light, and have brittle bones. In terms of recoil, a Walther P99 is the most I can handle. This monster nearly took my hand off. The kickback knocked me off my feet. The gun flew through the air and across the floor, where it disappeared under a bookcase.

And Jack had one shot left.

I rose in front of Misty, holding the case between us.

At long last, he lost that stupid grin. "Fuck, fuck, fuck! Put it down!"

"Thanks for letting me know it's more valuable than I thought," I said. I held it out. "Back off, or I throw it out the window."

He pointed his gun up. "Don't. Just . . . don't."

"What's the blue stuff worth? What *is* it?"

With his free hand he pulled out a cell. "We can work something out. I'll get you someone to talk to."

"Maybe later," I said.

Using the briefcase as a shield, I pushed Misty along. She was stunned, but by the time we reached the stairs, she was running under her own steam and I was the one having trouble keeping up. One of my ankles pretty much came off a while ago. She glued it back on, but it never sat quite right. Now I have a limp.

Three stories down, the last step nearly collapsed beneath our weight. We half jumped onto the wet, windy streets.

My first thought was to take the patrol car. The doors were open, but no keys. It was in such bad shape even a Fort Hammer cop wouldn't be caught dead in it. One of the headlights had been smashed, the grill was lopsided, making it look kind of like a winking face with a drunken smile.

"Now what?" Misty asked.

"Keep running!"

We did, carrying God knows what, God knows where. Whenever I fell behind, I told her not to slow down for me, but she did anyway.

The livebloods have a few nicknames for chakz; gleets for those still oozing, danglers for obvious reasons. Since the passage of the Chak Registration Act, they had a new one. Thanks to a quirk of the ripping process, it was only the smarter chakz, the ones who still had some mind to lose, that tended to go feral. It was only the smart ones that could fail the test, only the smart ones they bothered rounding up.

The rest, left to rot, were known as goners.

As I dragged my sorry leathery ass along the broken sidewalks and barren streets, the goners, the lesser dead, dripping from rain and God knows what else, were all around, rousing themselves long enough to watch us go.

A spiteful wind drove the rain into our faces, eyes, and ears. It didn't just hit me, it got inside me, pooling in the hollows of my body, block after block, until I finally began to wonder why, if the case was so damn important, Happy Jack hadn't followed.

4

The Styx, a downscale cyber/coffee shop, sits on the edge of the Bones, marking the line between the land of the living and the land of the dead. Druggies, thrill seekers, and chak-haters cross over at will, feeding their addictions, doing damage, or both. For tourists, the Bohemian crowd, or anyone who wants to look but not touch, the Styx was close enough.

We stopped under an awning that vaguely protected the entrance. Misty caught her breath, shivering puffs of water vapor bursting from her lips. The cold was fine for me, but she'd fled without so much as a coat. Her new blouse was plastered against her skin like spandex, and her teeth chattered louder than the rain.

I shook and stomped, trying to lose the water weight I'd put on during our run. Body integrity not being what it used to be, chakz don't dry so much as drain. Water dribbles into the damndest places. I doubted the barista would appreciate my dumping a tub-load on his nice clean floor, assuming I'd be served at all.

Between the storm, my stamping, and her chattering teeth, we barely heard her cell phone ring.

"Ch-chester?"

From what I could make out, no, he *hadn't* sent anyone. He'd been called in on a drug raid across town, got her message two seconds ago. He didn't know about any missing squad cars. He'd be there in fifteen minutes, ten, if he speeded.

"Speed," she said before hanging up.

"Let's go in," I told her. "Better to be around people."

I led her into a poorly lit space done up in shades of brown, thanks to all the once polished, now sticky, wood. The only other splotches of color came from framed posters and glowing screens. As for being around people, I'd spoken too soon. Thanks to the arctic monsoon, the place was practically empty, a pity for more reasons than one. In a crowd, the barista might not have spotted me right off. As it was, he was gawking in an unfriendly way.

A quick glance down told me why. I was standing in a growing puddle. All my stamping hadn't done much good. At least old people can wear adult diapers.

"Order something pricey so he doesn't get pissed," I whispered. "I'll head to the bathroom and try to freshen up."

She grabbed my arm. "You're not leaving me alone."

When she squeezed, more water ran down to the floor. She let go.

"Okay. I'll get a double latte. But hurry back."

I looked around. There were maybe six people, all sitting at rigs, happily stuck inside their own heads.

"Looks safe enough," I said. "Besides, I've got the McGuffin." I patted the briefcase.

Stylized emoticons on narrow doors against the back wall indicated which was for the ladies, which for the gents. Some places have separate chak facilities. No such luck here. I entered the men's room, stuck my arms over the little metal sink and squeezed them out best I could. That left the rest of me. From the looks of it, if I put a foot up on the sink, I'd rip the thing out of the wall. I made for the stall, hoping to drain myself into the toilet without having to look too much at what was in it.

Some detective. I hadn't even noticed I wasn't alone. A guy in a raincoat was standing next to the air-dryer trying to blend into the wall. I knew he was a chak right off. First, no liveblood can be that quiet. Second, half his right cheek was gone. What was left of his face bore a slight resemblance to that old actor, Jimmy Stewart.

Realizing I'd seen him, he gave me a sheepish nod. "I . . . I think I passed."

Given the state of the toilet, all sorts of ugly ideas popped into my head. I knew what he meant. He thought he'd been taken for a liveblood. Kind of a Holy Grail among the less self-aware. Hard to believe, given his face, but maybe he walked in sideways. At least he was smart enough to talk.

"Good for you," I said, twisting my leg above the toilet.

"How about you? You don't look too bad."

Water sluiced down my pants, plopping into the bowl. "Not today, thanks to the leaks. Geez, I stayed on the bottom of a pool overnight once and didn't sop up half this much."

"Did he say you had to stay in the bathroom, too?"

"Eh?"

"The barista. He said I had to stay in the bathroom. Is it crowded out there?"

If he hadn't been smiling like an idiot, I might've told him the truth. "Um . . . a bit, yeah."

He nodded. "I knew that was it." He picked up a Styrofoam cup precariously balanced on the dryer. "Nothing like a hot cup o' joe, huh? You drink?"

I flushed, then twisted the second leg, hoping there'd be some end to it. "Maybe some water if I want to sound LB on the phone. Other than that, don't see the point. Had a friend who used to like espresso, though. Said it worked for him."

He raised his cup to his lips. "Well, it works for me, too."

Having done what I could about the excess moisture, I shifted out from the stall, trying not to hit Jimmy Stewart.

He seemed upset. "They're letting you sit inside?"

I shrugged. "Oh, not me, pal. I'm with a liveblood."

"Chakking up?"

That's what they call it when a liveblood gets his jollies with the dead. Kind of like necrophilia with an animatronic corpse. Weirdly, it wasn't *un*common. Most chakz need the cash and couldn't care less what a liveblood did with their orifices.

"No, nothing like that. She's a friend."

"Huh. Well, praise Kyua."

Kyua. I'd heard the word before. It was one of those catch-all words, used for all occasions, like *fuck,* a verb, an adjective, a noun. Some version of Japanese for *cure.*

It could mean literally, a cure, or Maruta, the man who "cured" death, or God, salvation. It started out as a joke among the smarter chakz, but we're not all that smart, and some of us took it literally.

Jimmy Stewart raised his head and took a gulp from the cup. Light brown liquid, mixed with white foam, dribbled from a crack in his neck. I don't think he noticed.

"Good luck to you, too," I told him.

Misty'd sat at the table farthest from the counter. She was looking damp, but shivering less. A blanket was over her shoulders and a steaming mug of something in her hands. She'd signed on to one of the machines and was so busy typing, didn't notice me until I was practically on top of her. Apparently I'd gotten most of the water out, because the trail I left looked nearly human.

"Barista put you back here on my account?"

Still intent, she was kind enough to shake her head. "I sat here because we can see the door, but whoever comes in won't see us right away."

"Good." I slid the case under the table and nodded at the screen. "Checking your friends' status?"

"No. I left the netbook at the office, right? It's got a camera. I'm trying to see if I can pull it up."

Impressed, I slipped into the chair next to her. "You should be the detective."

"Actually, Chester suggested it when he called."

"Okay, *he* should be the detective. Um . . . he isn't yet, is he?"

She stopped typing to look at me. "Not yet . . . Oh, my God . . ."

I leaned in closer. The image was pixilated because of the crappy light, the view askew, from a low angle. The netbook must have been sideways on the floor. But I could see our reception room and a chunk of the office.

Happy Jack was still there, lying on the floor, shoulders bunched up, arms twisted in front of him, hands dangling, like he'd fallen asleep while giving himself a hug.

"Is he dead?" Misty whispered.

I squinted and moved my kisser closer. The son of a bitch was still smiling. His eyes were motionless, though, despite one being jabbed by his pinky.

"If it takes one to know one, oh, yeah," I said. I touched my yellowed fingernail to a spot above the body. "What's going on in the background?"

Papers were floating around. At first I thought it was wind, but then the whole desk shifted. An unpaid electric bill landed on Happy Jack's face, covering his eyes.

"Somebody's rifling the place," I said. "They're looking for our door prize. Can you zoom out, clean up the picture any?"

Misty waved her hands helplessly. "I don't know how."

A blur flit by the lens, too dark and fast for the camera to focus. It may have been someone wearing robes. For that matter, it could've been a werewolf, or Voldemort. Unsatisfied with whatever it found off camera, it flit by again.

"Can you record this? If only in case someone decides to blame us for killing Happy Jack?"

She shook her head. "It's not like I had time to read the manual."

The feel of a hand on my shoulder made me jump.

"Till Kyua comes." It was Jimmy Stewart, from the bathroom. A big coffee stain covered the lower right of his otherwise gray neck. I motioned toward the same spot on my own neck.

"You got something there, brother."

He patted me and headed for the door. Judging from the windows, the rain had slowed. By the time I turned back to the computer, the image had gone blank.

"What? The battery run out?"

"Weren't you watching?" Misty said, upset. "Whoever it was kicked my netbook and it went flying. Damn. I only had that thing for two hours!"

"You get a better look at him?"

She shook her head.

In my mind, at least, the figure looked the same as the one I'd spotted on the roof. Unless ChemBet had some new products I hadn't heard of, a chak can't move, jump, or climb that fast. Definitely liveblood. One helluva liveblood.

5

Chester O'Donnell was impressive against the coffee-house gloom. Ginger-Irish, red curly hair, freckles, cherub cheeks, he was Ralph Malph from *Happy Days*, but with gravitas. Misty flew into him so hard, his grunt made everyone turn. Laying her head sideways against his chest, closing her eyes, she looked, for the first time in a while, as if she felt safe. It made me feel like chopped liver. Well, chopped liver if you left it outside for a week.

I couldn't blame her, but I did anyway. Not that I had romantic notions, but when I'm deluding myself, I like to pretend I can protect her. If breathing some nerve gas on her a month back hadn't put that fantasy to rest, watching her relax in his arms did. Plus, he was alive. *They* were alive. I should be a picture on her mantel at best.

I'd been thinking of disappearing on her, let her move in with Chester. The only thing stopping me was that I was sure she'd waste a lot of time trying to find me. That was one of the reasons she deserved better.

Chester showed some intelligence right off. Gently peeling her away, he said, "I want you out of here, now. I sent a car to the office. If they're not there, they will be soon. We'll head to the station, sort things out, then you come back to my place for the night. *Just* for the night, if that's how you want it."

I faked a cough to remind them I was there. Misty looked at me. Chester did not.

"What about Hess?"

He shrugged. "Sure, him, too. But definitely just for the night."

"Actually, I wasn't thinking about me." I lifted the briefcase. "I was thinking about the star of the show. Want a look-see?"

He glanced at all the caffeine-fueled eyes watching us. "Save it for the station. Let's go."

The crazy-rain had packed it in, but left a bastard child in the form of frigid mist. It was cold enough for me to feel the warmth from the squad car engine as we approached. I sat in the back with the mystery case, where the perps go, separated from the good guys by a metal grate.

As I settled onto something sticky, two headlights went dark down Masters, a side street. Maybe the driver was parking, or maybe I was on some kind of postmortem detective roll.

I rapped on the grate. "What time did you call in the shooting?"

Chester started the car. "Soon as I was off the phone with Misty. Why?"

"The man who attacked us was in uniform, driving a squad car. Hard not to consider the possibility the police are in on this."

I could see Chester's eyes flare through the rearview. "*You're* accusing the police?"

I put my hands up in surrender. "*Some* of them ... maybe *one* ... just a thought. Where else do you get a police car? It was pretty scratched up. Missing any from the garage?"

He pulled away from the curb, wordless. Misty eyed me like I'd spit in his mother's eye. And then I remembered. His uncle used to be a cop until he was brought up on corruption charges. He was found guilty and serving time. I may as well have spit in his mother's eye.

Miffed, he kept his eyes on the road. Misty kept pointing at him, mouthing that I should say something to make nice.

Shit. I wasn't built for social pleasantries when I was alive. At the light, I shifted in my seat and cleared my throat. I guess I did it a little too hard. It felt like a piece came loose and tumbled into my gullet.

"Chester, uh ... Officer O'Donnell ..."

I hoped he'd stay true to form and not look at me, but with the light red, he turned and eyeballed me. It wasn't physically uncomfortable, the way a deep emotion was for a chak, but I didn't like it.

"I didn't mean anything. And ... I know, I haven't been exactly talkative around you, mostly because I figure you don't want to hear from someone like me, but I wanted to say, you know, with Misty and all ... thanks."

I could practically feel my hands clasped behind my back as I looked down and kicked at the floorboards. What was I, eight?

Chester surprised me. Looking as uncomfortable as I felt, he said, "Ah, I dunno if I've been brainwashed from listening to Misty, but for what it's worth, given what I know about the court system, I don't think you killed your wife."

You think I'd be pleased to hear it. Instead, I got a quick, vengeful wave of nausea. I tried to come up with a response, but the silence got awkward and thankfully, the light changed. Green. Go.

When he turned right down Masters, I was almost relieved to be feeling paranoid again. Down the block, a black stretch limo sat at the intersection, the highlights on its finish glowing red from the next traffic light. A limo's something else you usually don't see in this neck of the woods. Not a big nightclub area. Could be richies cruising for drugs, already so blotto they didn't realize how conspicuous they were. But it was strange enough to be strange.

"Which way you going?" I asked.

Chester answered quick, eager to change the subject himself. "Through the park, past Collin Hills. Cuts a few minutes off the trip."

It's great when the right choice is obvious, but there was a lot going on that didn't fit into that category. I was still wondering if I should've given the case to Happy Jack. Technically, Chester was right, the park was faster, but it's also more isolated. The main road, more lights, more people, was safer. I was debating whether to risk hurting his feelings again and say so, when the point became moot.

He flashed his lights and bleeped the siren.

"What is it?" Misty asked.

"Asshole behind us has his headlights off. I should pull him over," Chester said.

Out the back window, a big shadow, maybe five yards behind, dogged us.

"Wait . . ." I said, but that was moot, too.

Instead of pulling over, the aforementioned asshole hit the gas and rear-ended us. We all flew forward, me more than the others, since I hadn't put my seat belt on. It's not always safer for a chak. Shoulder straps can dislodge bones, crack ribs, or worse.

Chester found himself hugging the steering wheel. The world in which he lived, the one where people did not ram police cars, had changed.

"What the fuck?"

He was looking back when a squeal of rubber snapped my head forward. The limo ahead was making a wildly sharp turn. It stopped, wobbling like a boat on water, its big stretch-ass blocking most of the road.

Have to hand it to him, Chester was fast. No sooner did I stop leaning forward from the impact, than I was pulled back by the car rushing ahead. It looked like he'd broadside the limo, but with a bump we were on the sidewalk, a clear path ahead.

At least two steps ahead of me, Chester tossed the radio mic to Misty. I was starting to like him. "Call it in! Give them our location!"

As Misty fumbled with the controls, the briefcase shuddered and flopped to the floor, reminding me it was there. The thought of having it damaged made Happy Jack nervous, so I wrapped myself around it like I was a dog and it was my master's leg.

"Easy on the GTA shit!" I barked. "This could be explosive!"

Chester jabbed a thumb over his shoulder. "Tell it to them."

Headlights on now, our pursuer zoomed onto the sidewalk to follow. Farther behind, the limo backed up and turned, a whale trying to maneuver in a bathtub.

A tired voice came over the radio. "Miss, please calm down so I can understand. Is the officer there?"

Misty, of course, screamed. "You calm down! There are two fucking cars chasing us!"

Chester grit his teeth and put his eyes on the road ahead. "Tell her we're heading west on Masters, into Buell Park, and we need backup."

A few blocks ahead, I spotted the park entrance. Much as I hate backseat drivers, I said, "Not the park. You'll crack up in there. Stay on the main road."

In response, he said what I was thinking. "Thanks for the advice, but shut the fuck up."

It was stupid of me to second-guess him during a chase, an amateur's mistake. In the half second he'd taken to answer me, we nearly hit a hydrant. Unlike the movies, it wouldn't have snapped off and sent a geyser into the air. It would've shredded the radiator and brought us to a quick halt.

The bump as we slammed back onto the street set the squad car bouncing. My jaw nearly came unhinged. The corner of the briefcase slammed my upper leg. It would've been agony for a liveblood. I could only hope that when the chase was over I'd still be able to walk.

The car behind us, some sort of notchback sedan, was catching up. The stretch limo was less than half a block behind and picking up speed. Maybe the park was the right move. The limo, at least, would never manage the paths. Which begged another question.

"Who is *stupid* enough to use a stretch limo for an ambush? The same geniuses who stole a squad car?"

This time, Misty said it: "Hess, shut the fuck up!"

But it wasn't my trusty assistant that finally put a cork in my mouth, it was physiology. The fast, bumpy ride hit my system like a heavy junk-food meal. All of a sudden, I was dizzy. The sickly yellow streetlights dovetailed with the asphalt blacks and building grays, turning the world into blurred puke. Focusing on our pursuers didn't help. Their tinted windshield was a mirror, surrounded by the weaving and bobbing dark.

The next thing I made out was the wrought-iron gates of Buell Park, getting bigger fast. Our front wheels hammered the incline leading up to the entrance. I don't know how Misty and Chester took it, but my shoulders crunched down toward my chest so hard, I swear I was an inch shorter.

Past the gate, we swung right onto a narrow paved path. Overgrown bushes and hanging branches scratched the finish like a mob of jilted girlfriends with keys. Nothing was big enough to stop us, though, except what looked like a tall mound of trash about a hundred yards ahead, blocking the path.

Fort Hammer sanitation isn't the best, but the park was usually cleaner than that. Then I noticed the trash was moving. Goners. They probably came to the park thinking the trees would shield them from the rain. Even birds and squirrels figure that much out.

In short order, the headlights revealed limbs and torsos. There were at least three or four of them, but it was hard to tell exactly how many, what with them all huddled together. The tallest had a long, bearded face, kind of like Abe Lincoln. More together than the others, he'd seen us coming and was trying to move the group out of the way, like a momma duck herding her young out of the path of a tractor trailer.

"Slow down!" I shouted.

He didn't. Just chakz, right? A little heavier than say, cornstalks, but like the branches, not enough to stop us.

But Misty screamed, "Chester!" like she meant it.

Even then, he didn't slow down, but he veered. Turning the wheels on the icy path sent us into a skid. For a second, I thought we'd slam the goners. Instead, still spinning, we barreled into an over-full trash can. Making lemonade out of lemons, Chester steered into it, transforming the skid into a sharp left.

I guess the driver behind us didn't have anyone like Misty there to remind him of his better angels. He plowed straight into the chakz. Lincoln's torso flew into the windshield. Arms stretched the width of the car, his head hit the frame above the glass. His legs, and the bodies of those he'd been trying to protect, were bashed by the grill then pulled under. The car went forward and over them.

"Son of a bitch!" I screamed.

Like I said, chakz aren't easily destroyed. We're kind of like that last piece of dog crap on the bottom of your shoe, that one little bit you just can't get rid of no matter how hard you scrape the edge of the curb, or scratch with a stick.

The sedan carried the torso forward, but left behind a pile of pieces that twitched and writhed like a meaty, gray lasagna bubbling in the oven. They were in shock, but as soon as they sorted themselves, they'd realize what'd happened. Then there'd be nothing to do but go feral or wait until a trash collector carted them off.

As the sedan shrunk in the rearview, I saw it brake, sending the torso flying. Like half a Superman, the arms twisted as it spun and fell.

There was a loud blast and a flash. I thought they were lobbing grenades until I realized that Chester had decided to turn on the lights and the siren.

"I want the backup to see us," he said.

Yeah, if they were in the area, they'd spot us faster, but I had to wonder how that weighed against the fact that we were now a perfect target. I didn't have to say it. The bullets made the point for me. The first few lodged in the frame, but one hit the rear windshield in a sweet spot, sending a diamond rain my way. I ducked with the case. Chester took his right hand off the wheel and pushed Misty down.

Funny, when I held the case up at the office, Happy Jack's gun went to the ceiling quick. Didn't these guys know what it was? Were they from another group? How many people were after this damn thing?

At the park's center circle, blue and white flickered on the bronze of General Buell's statue. Chester took the turn a little tight. The car skimmed the stone base, making an awful racket as the metal fender spit sparks. But we made it to the other side. And you know what they say about driving into a park—you can only go halfway, after that, you're driving out.

The sedan had less luck, catching the statue's base. That slowed them down, gave us some distance. There were bumps. We may have run over more chakz, maybe not. I was too busy twisting my head back and forth, trying to figure out if we'd crash or get shot, to tell.

The exit came into view. Essex, a lovely, wide, well-lit avenue loomed beyond it. Unlike the entrance, there was no incline, just a curb. We hit it so hard, the grill pressed to the street and chewed pavement for half a foot before the suspension remembered what it was for and lifted us back up.

There were no more bullets, so Chester pulled his hand back from Misty to steer. He rubbed his fingers, made a face, then looked at something red and sticky on his thumb and index finger.

"Misty?" The fear in his voice didn't do much for me. "You okay?"

"There are people shooting at us and you ask if I'm okay?" she screamed.

Hearing her was reassuring, but she'd been hit and didn't even know it. With all the shaking and twisting, it'd be easy to confuse a bullet for a hard slam against the inside of the car. It also takes a few seconds for the sensations of pain and burning to reach your brain. Could be a flesh wound, could be serious. No way to tell. Not yet.

Worse, a new bullet hole in the lid of the trunk told me the sedan was back. With Misty hurt, I decided to do something stupid. I grabbed the case and opened the door.

"They want the case, I'll give it to them. You get Misty out of here."

Before either of them could express an opinion, I folded myself around the briefcase and tumbled out.

Having just left the park, we weren't moving very fast

yet, so I thought the fall wouldn't be too bad. Wrong. Doing about twenty, I went into a sideways roll that ended when my back slammed something hard. I couldn't see what I'd hit, but given the way I was sprawled on the sidewalk, facing the street, it must be a building.

I probably had a broken rib. They're a pain to Krazy Glue. I managed to get to my feet. The case was cracked, but intact.

I jogged back toward the street. Doing as I asked for a change, Chester floored it. The squad car fishtailed, then squealed forward, the open rear door flying shut.

The sedan was coming. I waved my arms at it and screamed, "I've got it! I've got it!"

They drove right past me. Son of a bitch. I limped into the middle of the street, holding the briefcase over my head.

"Hey! Assholes! Here!"

No go. The squad car's siren and flashing lights won the beauty contest. Trying to sacrifice myself, I'd made the perfect escape. Shit.

I climbed up on the hood of a parked car. If I was stuck watching helplessly, I may as well have a decent view. Essex was long and flat enough for me to see another set of flashing police lights headed our way. Chester and Misty would reach them in less than a minute.

But the sedan hadn't given up. Brief stars appeared along the open windows, the pop-pop-pop of gunfire echoing back my way. Misty had already been hit. Christ, if anything happened to her.

No longer hampered by the park, the sedan caught up. It was kissing the squad car's rear fender, the cavalry still blocks away.

Chester swerved left and right, trying to ruin their aim. It's hard to drive like that. You have to look back and forward at the same time. You're bound to miss something.

And he did.

A small figure, maybe four feet tall, stood in the road. It was a child, wearing a long coat, looking a little like Madeline from the kids' books, one of those twelve little girls in two straight lines. She was nowhere near the center of the street, but Chester's last swerve left him headed straight toward her.

A professional race car driver might've managed to miss the kid and keep going. But Chester did what I would've. He panicked, turned the wheel sharply and slammed on the brakes.

The squad car flipped.

The sedan, so close behind, smashed into the right side of its underbelly, making it spin on its side.

"Misty!"

I dropped the case on the hood of the car, jumped down and actually ran. My bones didn't mesh quite the way they should, and I was probably tearing muscle, but it didn't matter.

Smoke twirled from the squad car's engine. The sedan skidded and stopped. The doors flew open and two men in black suits, ties, and white shirts, jumped out. They moved toward the sideways car, but hesitated when the smoke from the engine flared into a small fire.

I was screaming as I came up. "You sons of bitches! You bastards!"

The fire bigger every second, the police closer, they jumped back into the sedan and sped off. I never got a decent look at their faces.

Madeline, the girl Chester had swerved to avoid stood there, the blue siren and yellow flames glowing on her small form. As I rushed past to get to Misty, I got a closer look at her face. Half was bone. Beneath the coat, her left shoulder looked broken or missing.

She was a chak, a raggedy.

Child-chakz aren't as uncommon as some would like to think. When ChemBet's process was new, parents who'd lost a kid to illness, accident, or worse were allowed to jump to the head of the line. They were happy to have their sweeties back, until they lived with the results a while, the waxlike skin, the sunken eyes, the weakness, the rot, the tendency toward depression, and savagery.

Most tried to love their postmortem kids, but we're not all saints. Some dumped them after a month, left them to fend for themselves. Outraged at the growing number of undead waifs, the blogosphere dubbed them "Annies" as in Orphan Annie. Language has a way of changing on its own. Annie begat Andy, leading, as sympathy waned, to raggedy. By then no one was surprised when any chak was abandoned, no matter how old they looked.

The kid was too close to the fire, so I slowed down enough to say, "Get the hell out of here."

What was left of her nose turned up in the air, but she didn't move.

I didn't have time to explain the nuances. "Out! I said out!"

She hissed like a cat and made for an alley.

Did Chester know what she was? Would he have swerved if he did?

I pushed into dry heat and the smell of gas. Grabbing the center of the chassis where the metal was still cool, I scrambled to the upturned passenger door. Balancing as best I could, I yanked it open. Smoke poured out. I heard Misty coughing, saw her arms flail in the haze.

She was alive.

Chester, not so much.

Car bottoms have no airbags. The impact had crunched his side of the roof, forcing his head into a position only dead things can manage.

I tried to keep Misty from seeing him, but she was struggling too hard for me to do a very good job. No sooner did I have her out, than she tried to climb back in.

"Chester! We have to get Chester!"

"He's gone," I told her.

"No, he's not! He's right there! His head's hurt!"

She pulled at me so hard, the tail of my jacket flew out and nearly caught on fire.

I pulled back, harder. "No, Misty. He's dead,"

It was as if my saying it was more real than seeing it. She stopped struggling, went limp, and shrieked his name. She screamed it over and over as I dragged her back from the flames, blood from her wound seeping onto the gray skin of my right hand. And all the while, all I could think was that I wished I'd never opened my damn office door.

6

Light and heat and plenty to go around. The light was from the recently arrived squad cars blocking the street, the heat from the burning wreck, flames covering half its underbelly. The jaws of life nowhere in sight, four men in blue risked their lives pulling Chester's mangled body up across the passenger seat and out. I recognized them, worked with them. Now I wished I could remember their names. One was Darnell, I think.

The body was laid on the street, the young, handsome face covered with someone's jacket. They didn't bother trying to put out the blaze with the rinky-dink extinguishers kept in the cars. That would have to wait for the fire trucks.

I took Misty to the side, as if that would help. Already exhausted, her screaming had slowed to a chugging sob. My more immediate concern was the wound. Hoping I looked apologetic, I tore the shoulder of her first new blouse in ages for a better look. The bullet hadn't penetrated, just left a long, angled gash. She might need a stitch or two to prevent unsightly scarring, but she'd live.

The cops had nothing against Misty, so I was about to call one over when another car arrived. It seemed bigger and louder than the others, but that could've been my mind playing tricks. Out stepped Chief Detective Tom Booth, square jaw clenched so hard it looked like he wanted to crack his teeth. He was my old boss, the man who slept with my wife, Lenore, and was still convinced I'd killed her. Lately, he'd left me to rot in the Bones, but our relationship was complicated.

Despite the carnage between us, his eyes found me. His looked like he was about to form some words, my name, an order to arrest me, or maybe a colorful invective. But one second there he was, the next, a blob appeared in the corner of my eyes and my whole field of vision went paper white. The color faded briefly into a sort of periwinkle, then settled in on yellow and red. The gas tank, cracked and weeping, had, at that moment, decided to blow.

Debris flew around us. More smoke would follow, so I pulled at Misty.

She resisted. "Just leave me," she said.

There wasn't any energy in her voice. Her arm felt cold, even to me. If she'd been a chak, I'd worry about her going feral. That's when it happens, when you give up. As it was, I think she was going into shock.

Booth, in some ways a decent man, would've called her an ambulance, but with everyone dealing with the blast, I couldn't bring myself to trust him. I dragged Misty out of sight, into an alley between a deli and a pharmacy.

We'd crashed on the other side of the park, liveblood territory, nowhere near as bad as the Bones, but the economy had taken its toll. The buildings were smart and stylish, but looked as if whoever had built them were long gone and their descendants had no idea how to maintain them. Still, there was a clinic about a block away. With any luck, they kept their needles and thread sterile.

Struggling with her weight, I propped Misty against a brick wall.

"Can you walk?"

"I don't want to."

"Not what I asked."

I put my right arm under her good shoulder, hefted, and moved through the alley. We came out on Damon Street. The clinic was across the way.

As soon as we hobbled through the doors, a curly-haired male nurse rushed up, all googly-eyed. "My God!" he said. "Were you in that accident?"

Before I could stop him, he put his palm to my face. Realizing his mistake, he snatched it away. Must've been his first night.

"Too late for me," I told him. "Not her, though."

A taller, more tired but less frazzled woman, the doctor, I figured, came over, and helped us get Misty into a chair. I knelt beside her.

"Looks like you're in good hands for the next ten minutes or so. I've got to get the case and hand it over to the police."

A spark of energy took her. She grabbed my sleeve. "Hess, what if it's meant for you?"

Was she delirious? Gently as I could, I took her hand from my sleeve and laid it on her lap.

"Remember what I said about that bullet with your name on it? The sooner I'm not the only one who knows where it is, the better I'll feel about both of us. I'll be right back."

She said something else I didn't make out. The bleary-eyed doctor started asking her questions, so I moved away and kept going.

I'd gotten here all right, but the first half block back was tough. My limp was more pronounced, the movement of my hips jagged. I'd done some damage when I rolled out of the car. Supporting Misty's weight had made it worse. After another half block, it felt like a branch snapped inside me. A bone shifted back into place and I was once again what passed for normal in my world.

The case was where I left it, on the hood of a parked car. I picked it up and headed toward all the bright shiny lights at the accident scene, which now included a fire truck.

Sticking to the cool dark near the buildings, I moved up along the side of the accident, wondering what to say to Booth and how to say it. I decided to leave out the part about the arm. Hallucinations were a sign of mental problems, mental problems were a sign I might be going feral. With a cop down, he might listen to me, but that didn't mean he wouldn't try to find an excuse to have me shipped off to a camp.

At least I *thought* he'd hear me out.

As I neared, thanks to a chak's propensity for blending into the gray, he couldn't see me, but I could see him. He was surrounded by six or seven officers, all eager to do what they could to find the cop killer. The wind slapped the fabric of his coat against his torso like a plastic bag against a statue. He usually looked angry, but tonight a downright loathing lurked in his eyes. He looked like he'd been forced to swallow something big and shitty, and was struggling mightily to keep it down.

"Forget the sedan and the limo," he said. "Find the girl and the chak. I want them in custody within an hour."

In unison, the men's jaws dropped. Chester O'Donnell, one of their own, was dead. Everyone knew he was seeing Misty, that she was my assistant. Several had seen the sedan speed off. The orders didn't make sense. They stood there for so long, stunned, he had to say it again. "Find Mann and the girl. Arrest them on suspicion of murder. Go! Tonight!"

What the fuck? Booth wouldn't go after the wrong perps with a cop down, no matter how much he hated me. There's a myth, Greek, I think, where a poor bastard steps on an invisible temple and winds up turned into a bush or a plant as punishment. An *invisible* temple. I was beginning to understand how he felt. The gods must be sadists.

I pulled back, faded the rest of the way into the dark, then ran. I had to get Misty, figure out our next move, but being wanted by the police was too much for my body to process. Then my ankle acted up, clicking with every step, like it was about to crack.

I crashed through the clinic door. An old woman in midcough screamed. A puffy intern's eyes shot up from his e-reader. Figuring I was feral, he came for me, wobbling on elephantine legs. Thankfully, he was slow enough for me to maneuver around.

"Misty?" I yelled.

I rushed past admitting into a wide space with curtained beds. Pulling back the first curtain, I saw a pug-nosed kid laid out. He was maybe sixteen, had a bullet or knife wound in the leg. He was blue, unconscious.

A caffeinated doctor leapt between us, waving his clipboard in the air like I was a dog he could scare off. "Get out of here!"

I snatched the clipboard, turned it around and handed it back to him.

"In a minute, pal."

Misty was behind the curtain of the second bed, alone. There was a little more color in her face. The stitching on her arm looked finished, but the loose ends dangled, waiting to be cut.

"We've got to go," I said. "The cops are after us."

She didn't even ask why. "I don't want to. Let them take me."

"Misty, no. There's a lot going on here and I don't know what it is. You wouldn't leave me. I'm not leaving you."

A lab coat hung on the wall. I grabbed it, wrapped it around her and pulled her to standing. Out front there was some kind of hubbub going on. Either the intern and the doctors were arguing about how to deal with me, or the police had arrived. With Misty wounded, the clinic would be the first place to check.

I steered her toward the rear of the building, scaring more patients in the process. Pushing open an emergency exit, I set off a lame whine of an alarm, but we were out. Despite the cold, Misty wouldn't hold the lab coat on. I kept having to stop and wrap it around her again. Other than getting us someplace safe, I didn't want to think about her emotional state, but I couldn't help it. She looked broken, helpless. Electric syrup pumped through my veins, tearing them open as it went, making me shiver.

Once they realized we'd left the clinic, the cops would probably focus on the park and the Bones, knowing it'd be stupid for me to try to hide in an LB neighborhood, so that's where I stayed. I needed a direction, though, an idea, and Misty wasn't in the mood to offer suggestions.

After maneuvering some alleys that were cleaner than my office, I spotted an ancient Chevy Nova all by its lonesome, begging to be stolen. I don't usually steal cars, or anything else for that matter, but whistling for a cab in the middle of the street here wasn't going to work. Most won't pick up a chak anywhere.

A fallen brick took care of the driver-side window. I put Misty in the passenger seat, the briefcase in the trunk, and climbed behind the wheel. Next, I pulled off the plastic column covering the ignition. It wasn't until I was staring at the three pairs of wires that I realized I'd forgotten how to hotwire a car.

I grabbed a few, to yank them free, but picked the wrong ones. Nasty sparks rolled into my fingers, making my arm vibrate until I let go. The car filled with a gross smell, like a bad hamburger cooking on a grill. There were black scorch marks on my fingertips, but I didn't feel much of anything that resembled pain.

"Red pair's usually the battery, brown's the starter," Misty mumbled.

I eyed her. "Now you tell me. What do I do with them?"

She sounded like she didn't care. Part of her must've
or she wouldn't have kept talking. "Twist the red together, then touch the brown ones for a second. Careful
you don't . . ."

Another set of sparks, more burning. That time, I felt it.

"Ow. Careful I don't touch the brown ones, right?"

She gave off a weak laugh. That was something, anyway. Almost worth the burn.

The engine roared to life.

7

I doubted there was enough gas to reach any of the major shantytowns where most chakz lived. Besides, between the weekly LB raids involving machetes and rice grinders, and the guard passing through to hunt for chakz who hadn't shown for their tests, they had enough troubles of their own.

The closer option was a darling of a cheap motel on the southern outskirts of town called the Deluxe Econo-Sleep, false advertising on all three counts. If a liveblood with a penchant for chakking-up preferred his necrophilia in a bed instead of an alley, it was the place to go. On the plus side, the police treated it like it was in another dimension. We might even get a nice view of the desert out the back, if the windows weren't painted over.

It was past midnight when I pulled onto the buckling asphalt of the parking lot. Out front, a blue oval hung from a tilted steel post. The neon that used to spell the name was long gone, angry rust stains dripping down the center. I was expecting it to be quiet, but there were barely any spaces left. Love, or something more contagious, was in the air.

Misty wasn't perky, but she was on her feet, walking with me to the office at the end of the L-shaped building. Inside, there was a short line and a familiar face, or I should say half face. The raggedy was here, the girl Chester swerved to miss, arm in arm with a paunchy, slimy-skinned pederast.

I'd say it was funny how the law worked for chakz, but I've yet to laugh. If she died six years ago aged twelve, technically she was eighteen, the age of consent. That's how the courts saw it anyway, mostly thanks to perverts like billionaire Colby Green, current owner of Nell Parker.

Misty grabbed my arm to keep me in place, but it took all I had to keep my mouth shut. Of course she didn't recognize the kid, she was just a blur in the windshield at best. Probably better that way. At least this explained why a raggedy was in that part of town. She'd been meeting her john.

But here we both were, and I like coincidences about as much as I like child molesters. I wasn't about to let either go. Hearing the room number the clerk gave them, I reached for my digital recorder to get it down, but my pockets, like Mother Hubbard's cupboard, were bare. I'd left it in the office. Whispering the number to myself over and over, I let Misty fill in the motel form.

At least we didn't raise any eyebrows. Between her clothes, and my good looks, this was the only place in the world we'd pass for a couple. The only problem was that they rented by the hour. I knew she had Chester's credit card, but didn't want to mention it because one, it would remind her about Chester, and, two, it could be used to track us.

We still had some money from the last case, and between us, enough cash for three hours. When I forked over my share, the bespectacled night manager, who looked like a watermelon with suspenders, a greasy head and gray stubble, gave us an impressed whistle.

"Last guy I had to argue with to pay the full hour. Only wanted fifteen minutes," he croaked. "Bless your endurance, both of you. Making a video or using some kind of pills?"

I grabbed the pen from Misty and scribbled the raggedy's room number on my hand. "Neither."

He smiled, showing shreds of some kind of food between his teeth. "No offense. Just asking. I could use some pills myself."

"I'll let you know if I find any."

Our room was on the second floor. A thick odor of bleach swept out as soon as I opened the door. The sheets were clean, though sterilized would be a better word and they weren't Egyptian cotton. The cloth was so thin, the deep depressions and wildly shaped stains on the mattress made it look like a relief map of a mountain range.

"At least it's germ-free."

Misty, moving faster than she had since the ambush, headed for the window and tried to open it. "The only way this place would be germ-free is if you burned it."

I smiled. Not that it was funny, but she seemed a little less shell-shocked. I pulled the cushions off the couch, laid them on the bed and motioned for her to lie down.

"I doubt anyone uses the couch."

She sat on the edge of the bed. "I don't know if it's worth it anymore, Hess."

"What? You don't like the room?"

"No, I mean, anything."

I parked myself beside her. "You just got hit in the head with a baseball bat. Not a good time for making plans."

"Y'know how you get, staying in your office day after day, doing nothing, like you're ready to just say fuck it all and give up completely, go feral?" she said. Her eyes bored into me. "And don't bother telling me that's not how it is."

"All right."

"Well, except for the feral part, I finally think I know how you feel."

I wasn't sure that was true, but I wasn't about to argue the point.

"Okay, yeah, I've been on the darker side lately. Used to be I held on to the crazy idea I might find Lenore's killer, but that's done with, other than proving it to Booth and the police, and frankly, I don't care about that. But, I haven't gone feral, have I? I figure a lot of the reason is you, the promise we made. We take care of each other, right? Keep each other from falling in the toilet?"

"Hess, it's just . . . never mind."

I hesitated, wanted to pet the hair on her head, but didn't. "Baseball bat, remember? It's going to hurt a long time, but until it slows down, no decisions, no big investments. Lie down, pretend you're somewhere else, someplace you can rest."

Soon as I stopped talking, thumps from the wall behind the bed filled the room, shaking a torn picture of a crying clown. I wouldn't call them rhythmic.

"Well, *try* to rest," I said. "You heard the man. The racket won't last longer than fifteen minutes."

I stood up.

"Where the fuck are you going now?"

"The ark of the covenant or whatever, is in the trunk. I don't want it near us. I'll take it maybe a few miles into the desert. Take less than half an hour. Make sure you're here when I get back."

She didn't lie down. She remained sitting, hands folded in her lap. "Will do."

There are sins of commission and sins of omission. I hated the first when it came to Misty, but it wouldn't be the first time I didn't tell her everything. There were two things I wanted to take care of, the case and the raggedy.

The case put everyone in danger, so I handled that first. I drove a mile or so past the motel then headed off-road into the desert. The Chevy's rear-wheel drive got me a few yards into the filthy sand before the back started wobbling. Worried I'd get stuck, I got out and walked, my feet doing near as badly as the tires.

I thought about opening it. Some squeaky pain in the ass part of me wanted to pull out the foam and see if there was anything under it, but I shut it up quick enough. The less I knew the better. And I had to get back to the raggedy in less than fifteen minutes.

I found a sad-ass clump of trees that didn't seem to realize they shouldn't have tried growing in a desert, and wedged the case behind two branches so it wouldn't be visible unless you came right up on it.

Back at the motel, I grabbed a tire iron from the

trunk. Then I stood there like an idiot, trying to remember the room number. I'd almost given up, when I happened to glance at my hand. Room 154. A short walk.

I didn't pause long enough to listen at the door. You'd think the manager would want to keep the locks working in a place like this, but it swung open with a nudge. Seeing me, the pederast at least had the decency to be embarrassed. Had something to lose, I figure, wife, job, whatever. The raggedy, who didn't, was pissed. She gave me a catlike hiss like the one she made at the accident scene.

I used the crowbar to pry them apart. Figuratively, meaning I threatened to do some damage if the liveblood didn't get out. Flushed red and panting like he was going to have a heart attack, he grabbed his pants, didn't bother putting them on, and made for the door.

The kid glowered at me with sunken eyes. "I was getting paid!"

I got it. Chakz don't care what livebloods do with their orifices. I could well be robbing her of enough cash for a decent place to stay a night or two. I reached into my pocket, planning to give her some bills. Her face lit up until we both realized I was out of money.

She rolled her eyes, favoring the missing side of her face. The exposed tendons had a weird sheen, like plastic. Reminded me of that travelling corpse exhibit that shows you how the body works.

"Great. You can't even remember what the fuck is in your pocket."

"How old are you?"

"Twenty-seven."

My turn to roll my eyes. "Not so great with the math,

huh? Ripping's about eight years old. You can't have been more than twelve when you died."

She wrapped herself in a blanket and stood. One shoulder slumped, like part of the bone was gone. "*That* you remember. Fine. Sixteen. Five years since I died from multiple myeloma, four since my parents stopped looking at me."

"Then you're still illegal."

She grabbed her clothes from the floor and headed for the bathroom. Other than the face, I didn't see any rot or damage. "Give me a break! I'm trying to save for a cheat sheet so I can pass the next test."

Now I actually felt guilty. There was an active black market in exam answers, but they were pricey. From what I hear, sometimes they worked.

"Not doing so good?"

She stepped out and grabbed her coat. The anger had faded from her face just a bit. "Last time I made it by one question."

"Look, I don't have any money right now, but I can help you study. Well, not me, but Misty can. She's good at that. Got me through the last few times."

"Who the hell is Misty? Who are you? What do you care? Why are you here? What are you, my guardian angel?"

"Remember me from the accident?"

She paused, like maybe my question meant she was in trouble. "Yeah."

"Someone pay you to be there, too? Wait for a car?"

Her forehead was like a smooth piece of marble until her brow knitted, "Do you realize how stupid that sounds? Here, chak, here's a dollar, stand on the corner until you scare someone into flipping his car? That's what you ruined my gig for?"

"When you put it that way, it does sound like a long shot," I said. "But that's not my only question."

She looked at the clock. "I've got the room for another three minutes. Go on."

"A friend was driving."

The lines in her brow grew deeper. "That was a cop car. A chak friends with a cop? No wonder you believe in long shots."

"Fine, friend of a friend. Point is, he didn't have to brake. He could've driven right into you, left you with just an arm to hold your teddy and drag your torso around. But he didn't, and now he's dead. Not dead tired, not dead like us, really dead. You were standing there a while when the second car pulled up. Did you get a good look at the guys who came out?"

"Tick-tick. Couldn't you have just asked?"

"I like to set the scene. See how you react."

"Am I reacting okay so far?"

"So far. Did you get a look at them?"

She shrugged her good shoulder. "Happened quick. I think they wore black, kind of like in a movie. You know *Reservoir Dogs*? Like that. One balding, I think. There was something shiny up on top. The other had light hair, maybe. That's all."

I'd seen how they were dressed, so she wasn't lying. The balding part and the light hair sounded familiar, but I couldn't place it.

"See that? Your memory's not so bad. What's your name? Where can I find you?"

"Why?"

"To help you study."

She smiled, looking girlish for a second, until the skin around the exposed bone crinkled, ruining the effect. "The guy who can't even remember what's in his pocket? No thanks. My ride's gone, though. Can you get me back to the city?"

I walked her out to the car. She eyed it up and down.

"Looking for something?" I asked.

"Is that thing safe to drive?"

"All of a sudden, it's about safety?"

She hissed and climbed in.

Wishing I had a few bucks, or a toy to give her, I dropped her at one of the smaller shantytowns, going as far as I dared with the needle tapping E.

The ride back gave me time to think. With Chester dead and the police after us, the smart move would be to leave. Not like we'd be leaving a lot behind. It wouldn't be easy, though. Legally, wherever we went, I'd have to check in to keep up with the testing. Even if they lacked the equipment to track my cell, the police could find me through my chak registration. Fake IDs were tough to come by. Then again, I might be able to avoid the test for a month or two, and by then the whole briefcase thing could blow over.

Or I could try to solve the case, literally, figure out what the blue stuff was, why the arm gave it to me — maybe get Misty killed and myself immolated, or worse, in the process. Fuck that. She'd already lost too much. A slim to nothing chance at justice wasn't worth her losing more.

I was patting myself on the back for deciding to take it on the lam when a picture popped into my head: Tom

Booth's face, with that sickened look like someone had forced him to swallow a live kitten. I tried so hard to wave it away, I wobbled into the wrong lane. But the face stayed until I admitted what it meant. Booth was doing something he didn't want to do. It *wasn't* his idea to go after us. The order must've come from above, far enough to cow him.

How high was that?

Fucking moments of clarity. Now I was terrified that if I put enough together about this mess, even by accident, I'd have to do something other than run. And that wouldn't be fair to Misty.

A quarter mile later, the gas ran out. Served me right for playing taxi. Luckily, the motel wasn't far, but I'd been on my feet a lot lately. I was nearly falling over myself when I saw the parking lot and realized something was wrong.

The lot had been nearly full. Now there was only one car, one with a siren on top. It sat crooked in front of the entrance, empty, its rear end facing me. Thanks to the budget cuts, patrolmen mostly travelled one to a car, but if they'd already found Misty, they'd have called for backup. I sure as hell didn't want to go up against any Fort Hammer cop, but I wasn't about to let anyone stuff her into a holding cell.

As it turned out, official backup wasn't going to be the problem. One headlight was cracked, the grill lopsided, looking like a winking face with drunken smile. It wasn't the true boys in blue. It was Happy Jack's car. He was dead, so it was either friends of his, or it'd been stolen again. By the ninja?

On my way to the room, I looked through the lobby

window. The bespectacled clerk was missing. Not a good sign. Too worried about Misty to check on him, I bounded up the steps. The door to our room was half open. Not even thinking to peek first, I pushed it open and stood there like an idiot.

The room was small, even for a cut-rate motel. I could take everything in at a glance, but it still took a beat or so for me to make sense out of what I was seeing. Misty lay on the couch cushions I'd put on the mattress, but she wasn't resting. Her eyes were wide open. Duct tape covered her mouth. Plastic strips tied her hands and ankles.

8

Unlike Jack, our two visitors hadn't stolen uniforms to
match the car. They still wore black. The raggedy's description was accurate enough. The taller one was mostly
bald. A mix of chestnut and white made a low-hung
crown around the back of his head. With the rounded
cheeks and spherical nose, add a few dabs of greasepaint,
and he'd make a great clown.

The other was fair-haired, narrow eyes set closely in
the center of a flat face. They weren't vacant like chak-
eyes, more sunken, like a pig's. His arms were too thin to
be healthy, and his hands trembled. Not his features, but
what you might call his mien reminded me of Misty, not
now, but when we met. He was an addict.

Both had guns. Not crazy big-ass guns like Happy
Jack, normal .38s. I wondered why they hadn't brought
the sedan, then realized why: police radio. They were
keeping track of the hunt.

"Guess what we want," Chuckles the clown said.

I took a step in. I was still ignorant enough to try to turn my back on whatever was going down. If they let Misty go, maybe I could keep it that way.

"You can have it. Been trying to get rid of that thing all night. Trust me, I don't even want to know what it is."

Flat-face waved his gun. "Great. So where is it?"

"If I hand it over, you'll let us go? You won't kill her?"

Chuckles shrugged. "*We* won't."

"I'll take it. Three miles up the road, in a tree branch a hundred yards due east. You can't miss it. So, if you found us through the radio, I take it the cops are on their way?"

Flat-face looked like the question pissed him off. "Nah. They won't help you. They're still in the Bones. Our boss sent us here, figured you might show. You're all ours."

"Fine, fine. Just don't tell me who he or she is, okay?"

Chuckles twisted his round head and made a face like I was joking. "You don't recognize us?"

That surprised me. I didn't. Part of me tried, by reflex, but I drew a familiar blank.

"No."

"He's lying," Flat-face said.

"Look, boys, I swear I have no idea who you are. Much as I might've enjoyed playing *Maltese Falcon* in another life, so to speak, right now I just want to hand the case over to whoever, so me and my friend can disappear."

"Maltese what?" Flat-face asked.

"An old movie," Chuckles explained.

Flat-face seemed irritated that there was something I

knew that he didn't. "So, you think you're one of the smart ones?"

"I'm trying," I told him. "How do you want to do this? Both of you come with me to get the case, we leave my friend tied up until we get back?"

Chuckles had other ideas. "I go with you and my associate stays with your friend. Anything happens to me, something happens to her."

I'd stepped close enough to get a good look at Flat-face's clammy skin. Definitely an addict. "How about you stay and your friend goes with me?"

That pissed off Flat-face all the more. "Think you can take me, chak?"

I hadn't even thought of that. "I couldn't take either of you. I'd just rather have the cooler head stay with my friend. She's had a rough day."

Chuckles was thinking about it, but Flat-face got a weird smile. "I can be sensitive! No deal."

I didn't like it, but I didn't have a choice.

"So let's go," Chuckles said.

"Just a second," I said. I knelt by Misty and tried to smile confidently. I have no idea what it looked like, probably a scene from *Night of the Living Dead*. "I know I've been making a habit of leaving you lately, but I'll be back soon and this'll be over."

Her expression didn't change. I rose and turned to Flat-face. "That was her boyfriend you blew up tonight. Let her rest, okay? Read a book or something."

He patted my cheek. "Don't worry. We'll be fine," he said.

I followed Chuckles to the squad car.

"You don't trust your friend with the case, do you? Why should I trust him with Misty?"

"Because I have the gun."

I headed for the passenger side before he stopped me. "You drive."

"Suit yourself."

This time, the keys were in the ignition. The engine chugged and sputtered, misfiring like it had a bad plug or worse. I tried not to think about that. I tried not to think about lots of things, but Chuckles had already put a nasty thought into my head. I *knew* these guys from somewhere. Who were they? Who was ordering Tom Booth around? What was in that damn case and why had that piece of work brought it to *me*?

The cop car managed the sand a little better than the Chevy, so I took us to within ten yards of the tree. The single headlight caught the edge of the briefcase, telling me it was still there.

"You want me to get it for you?" I asked.

Chuckles eyed me. "You're really handing it over, just like that. You don't want to leave your girlfriend with my associate any longer than you have to."

I nodded. "So, would you mind hurrying it up?"

"Nope, I wouldn't."

He got out. His back a black slate, he trotted over to the case, the cuffs of his shirt showing bits of white where the fabric folded. A few feet from the tree, he stopped and looked around. He stared into the dark ahead of him, then back at me in the car. I don't think he'd seen anything. It looked like he'd just had one of those feelings.

He gave the case a hard tug, then seemed to remember it was somehow fragile. Using both hands, he gently tugged it free. One foot against the tree trunk, he balanced it on his bent leg and clicked the latches. The headlight caught the vials, giving his smiling face a blue glow that proved me right about the whole clown thing.

Satisfied, he closed it, then he took his sweet time walking back to the car. Maybe it was to annoy me, or maybe he was daring whatever he'd imagined might be in the dark to do something.

I opened the window. "Come on already."

"Shut up and pop the trunk."

Stupid. I should've kept my mouth shut. I could practically hear his feet drag as he went around to the back of the car. I bent down and pulled the latch. A few minutes and we'd be back in the motel. Hang in there, Misty.

After what seemed forever, I heard him put the case in the trunk, then saw the lid slam through the rearview mirror.

Instead of getting back in, like he had all the time in the world, the bastard flipped open his cell and hit a number. There's always a bit of sadist in a hired goon, but the real pros were better at hiding it than this idiot. As he waited for an answer, he leaned a hand against the car and stretched his back, putting his neck forward to the dark.

"Got it. No troubles. He's playing it smart. Boss said he wouldn't be a problem, didn't he? The girl? Just cut her . . ."

Shit. I twisted around for a better look. Cut her what? Cut her free? Cut her throat? I'd never find out.

The next sound he made was a wet gurgle. Head down, he dropped the cell phone and grabbed at his neck. His clowny hands tried to cover a long gash in his throat. Without my even seeing, someone had cut him a second smile. Blood spurt from the wound into the darkness.

Now I saw the figure, and thought I recognized it from the webcam. It moved as fast as it did in the office, all but flying toward me in the car. I threw the transmission into reverse and floored it. The tires spun helplessly in the sand as the figure grabbed the door handle. When the tires found purchase, the car lurched, but the ninja didn't let go. Instead, it flipped itself onto the hood.

I could see through the windshield, it was cloaked, hooded, but not in black. The cloth was a deep red, just bright enough to make me wonder how the hell it'd hidden in the dark. As I turned the wheel trying to shake it off, it rolled with the changes in momentum, moving too fast for me to get a good look at the face. If I had to guess, I'd say it was a mask.

It was still holding on as I spun onto the street. Still in reverse I gunned the engine, fighting to keep the car on the road as it went backward. At about forty, I slammed on the brakes. The car squealed, twisting right. The figure hurtled over the roof. Through the mirror, I saw it hit the ground and spin along the yellow double line.

I didn't wait to see more. I put the car in drive and raced for the motel. Chuckles had been killed in mid–phone conversation, leaving Flat-face to improvise. Even money he'd figure I'd betrayed them. The question was, would he kill Misty outright, or do the smart thing and keep her alive to use as leverage? He didn't strike me as smart.

I nearly crashed the car into the building, but there

was no one around to see. I bolted into the lobby, thinking I'd tell the manager to call the cops, but he'd been stuffed behind the front counter, looking like he'd fallen asleep in a funny position, two bullet holes in the center of his shirt.

And yeah, when I got back to the room, it was empty.

9

A cell phone's beveled rectangle stood out on the cush-ion like the monolith among the apes in *2001*. I snapped it up and nearly went berserk trying to find the redial. It wasn't fancy, but it was more complicated than the free-bies they issued chakz, lots more buttons. When I finally got it, someone answered: "How smart a chak are you?"

The voice was ocean-deep, modified electronically, the sharper tones eliminated by the pitch shift. It sounded like a drunken toad. When I didn't answer right off, the toad repeated the question, so slow I heard his lips smack between words.

"How smart a chak are you?"

"Not smart enough to avoid getting stuck in the mid-dle of this. Where's Misty?"

He ignored the question. "Someone thought you'd know what to do with the case. Any idea who brought it to you?"

"No. Where's Misty?"

Another smack. "Any theories?"

"No." The only thing I did know was that by the time he reached me, there wasn't much left of him. But why share everything with an anonymous toad?

"If you find out, I'd really like to know." I think he believed me.

"Same here. Where's . . . ?"

He cut me off. "Do you know who this is?"

That game again. "No, but you know me pretty well, right? You told your boys I wouldn't be much trouble. So, maybe you'll believe me when I say I didn't kill your man. We were attacked."

"He's dead?"

Stupid, stupid, stupid. He didn't know until I'd told him. Dizzy with frustration, anger, and fear, I lowered myself onto the mattress. It was like sitting on a relief map of the moon.

"Yeah, unless he can survive on his own with a severed jugular. I'm telling you it wasn't me. I'm no trouble, remember?"

"Who, then?"

One wrong word, I'd lose him, and maybe lose Misty. "I didn't ask for a name. A freak in ninja robes, someone fast, well trained." I felt like I was trying to describe Bigfoot or the Loch Ness Monster. "Whoever it was, they were better trained than the fake cop you sent to my office, and that guy was pretty good. You should've gotten him a better car, though."

"He wasn't mine. My men picked up his car later."

"Then that makes at least three groups after this stuff."

"How so?" asked the toad.

"I usually get a fee when I work, but under the circumstance, tell me where Misty is and I'll share my deepest thoughts, okay? That is, if you know where she is."

There was a buzz and a click, like he'd swallowed a fly. "I do know, more or less. I'll tell you depending on how the conversation goes."

"More or less?"

"Nothing in life is certain."

"Except for death and taxes, right? And these days it's just taxes. Fine. If the cop doesn't work for you, that's two. He was killed by the same ghost who got your boy, which means they don't work for either of you. That much math I can do."

"A zombie telling a ghost story. Interesting." There was a pause. "Unless you killed them in both cases. Convince me otherwise."

"Geez. Think about it. Even if I did manage to overpower a liveblood with some serious muscle tone, why the fuck would I go after your guy while Misty was in trouble? If you know me, you know that, being dead, I don't care about much, but one of the only things I do care about used to be in this room. What would I have to gain?"

"Maybe everything." An electronic hiss came from the cell's speaker as the voice shifter tried to compensate for the silence.

"What?"

"You don't know what's in the case?"

"Two vials of blue liquid. They could be the plans for the Death Star or the one true ring. I don't care."

I started pacing. Every minute I played word games with the toad was another minute Misty was alone with Flat-face.

"Such emotions, from a chak. Do they hurt the way

they did when you were alive, or is it more like a cut? Is it a throbbing or a stabbing pain?"

Of course it hurt. My whole body was pulsating in a sickening way. There was something familiar about the line of questions, too.

"Another fucking sadist! What is this, a club?"

"You're confusing me with my employee. I'm only trying to figure out whether to believe you or not. She's alive. Safe depends on your definition. Her host is regrettably unpredictable."

I squeezed the phone like it was a neck. "I'm through with this shit. Call your man now, tell that flat-faced bastard if he does anything to her, I'll shove those vials down his throat and pull them out the other end."

"Then you still have them, despite the attack. Does the anger hurt less than fear?"

More, but seeing as how he tricked me into telling him that much, I stayed quiet until he spoke again.

"Let's assume I believe you. You'll need to get out of the area soon. A senator staying in one of the rooms called 911 a while ago. I'll give you some coordinates and have my associate meet you there with your friend."

"Coordinates?"

"Latitude and longitude."

I clenched the phone so hard I nearly broke it. "I know what coordinates are! I just don't know what to do with them without a map!"

The toad tried to talk some sense into me. "Take a breath, detective. Oh, that's right. Never mind. Do whatever it is you do to calm down. Find a pen and write these numbers down. You can punch them into the GPS in the squad car."

Detective. The voice shifter hid subtleties like a sarcastic tone, but I was pretty sure it was there. I scribbled the numbers on a napkin and pocketed the cell. I gave the room a quick once-over, found nothing except a stale stench in the bathroom that even the bleach couldn't hide, and headed out.

The empty motel was sullen, the only sound the wind slapping the few raindrops still clinging to the gutters back into the air. Wherever they hit, my skin went briefly numb. I looked around enough to notice that the doors to two of the rooms were open. I didn't want to see what was inside. Flat-face had left quickly. He'd probably stolen another car and didn't want to leave any loose ends.

Assuming the toad hadn't lied about the police, I should get out first and worry about directions later. With the squad car's one headlight off, I pulled onto the road. After a minute of driving dark, some red pimples flashed low against the cityscape. I headed off-road, stopped, then waited until three squad cars rushed by, leaving the road behind them empty.

Satisfied they hadn't seen me, I took a look at the GPS. It may as well have been the instrument panel for a jumbo jet. My fingers kept missing the right spots on the touch screen. In no time, I had the thing talking Russian, then German. When I finally got the coordinates in, the damn thing announced:

"Biegen sie links ab in hundert Metern."

Looked like I'd be following the little yellow line on the map screen.

It wanted to take me straight through Fort Hammer, but I respectfully disagreed. If someone spotted a chak driving a police car, I doubted they'd think it a good thing. The GPS voice said, *"Neuberechnung!"* so often it started to sound angry.

Over the course of half an hour, it took me east, where the increasingly quiet roads were lined by wet junk pines and the occasional oak. I'd call it a forest, but that sounds more organized. This was nature's version of Fort Hammer, a gangly mess that'd been put out of its misery ages ago but still hadn't realized it.

In short order, the badly paved road gave it up to a muddy, winding path. The growth was so thick on either side, it looked like a tunnel. It didn't get more private. After the third twist, the headlight illuminated a fallen oak. I thought about ramming it, but it was big enough to total the car. If I did find Misty . . . *when* . . . when I found Misty, we'd need wheels to get out of this wasteland. According to the GPS, I was either half a mile or half a kilometer from ground zero. Shit.

I unplugged it, hoping the battery would last, opened the trunk and picked up my good buddy the briefcase. Just to make sure, I took another look at the tree trunk. Some of the moss-covered wood was rotten, but not enough to matter. It came up to my waist. Like it or not, I was one of the walking dead again.

Taking marching orders from the Germanic GPS, my shoes, which had seen better days, crunched on thin ice, sometimes slipping, sometimes breaking into a frigid puddle. At least it wasn't raining anymore.

Minutes later, a light finger-poked the gray. It was too low to be a plane or the moon, so I turned off my cyberguide and headed for it. As I got nearer, the dark surrounding the glow acquired shape, forming into something like a single-room shack, maybe a hunting lodge. I didn't see any power lines. A look at the cell told me there was no signal. Mr. Toad and Flat-face wanted to be sure no one could listen in. Either that, or this was their magic forest home.

Another shape rose from the gloom, a green Subaru. That meant there was another way in and out. Stupid GPS. By the time I reached the car, I could tell that the light inside the cabin came from a Coleman lamp, typical camping gear. Remembering my mistake at the motel, instead of heading straight for the door, I made for the window, hoping to get a look inside before I knocked.

It was a little higher than my shoulders, so most of what I saw were shadows cast on the ceiling. A woodpile sat nearby. It looked as sturdy as the shack, so I grabbed the handle of an old axe whose business end was embedded in a log, and pulled myself up.

Not being an optimist, I imagined a series of bad outcomes: Misty dead; the Red Riding Ninja leaping from the window to cut me up like year-old salami; the cops arriving.

But I had no clue what fresh hell was coming.

Flat-face and Misty were in the rough center of the room. She was tied in a chair, and he was hovering over her. There was a long scratch on his face, two lines of blood trailing from it, almost like tears. That wasn't completely unexpected, it was a hostage situation. Misty would fight back. But both of them looked crazed, sweaty, in a way that didn't fit.

A table sat nearby, pulled close for convenience. Its surface was so dark it seemed to sop up the Coleman's light, making the silver foil the size of a gum wrapper glow. In the foil were a few small, off-white nuggets with jagged edges.

As I watched, Flat-face forced a smoke-filled pipe into Misty's mouth. He clamped her nostrils with his other hand. The seeping smoke crawled up the side of her nose, wafting into her watery, bloodshot eyes.

He spit as he spoke: "Suck it, bitch, suck it!"

Misty, bruised, twisted her head feebly, but did as she was told. Sweat, tears, or both, streamed down her cheeks. When he pulled the pipe away, I could see that her eyes were completely black, the pupils fully dilated. It wasn't her first toke. That first one must've been tough for Flat-face. It was probably how he earned that scratch. Each one after that, well, it had to be a little easier.

He howled like he'd just slammed the pigskin over the goal line: "Yeah!"

You'd think that would've been enough to drive me feral, but that's about giving up, and I had something very definite I wanted to do.

I let the precious briefcase fall and grabbed the axe handle with both hands. A thick splinter lodged in the dry meat of my right hand, but the axe came free nice and easy. It went through the rotted window frame pretty easy, too. So did I.

I even landed on both feet.

Still hunched over her, he didn't straighten. He did drop the pipe and look at me with those tiny, bat-shit-razy eyes.

"Oooh! A mon-ster!" he said, lips curling into a smile. "What a big bad . . ."

I slammed the flat end of the axe into his head. I felt the bone in my forearm bend, but not break. Why not the blade? I don't know, really. Maybe I was figuring on keeping him alive, but most likely it just happened to be how I was holding it.

Flat-face was no fun. He fell right over.

"Son of a bitch!" I shouted. "Stupid fucking . . ."

He was dead before he reached the floor, but that made two of us, and I was still pissed. I smashed the table and the wall. As if he could still hear me, I kept talking: "I'd have given it to you . . . handed it right over, asshole . . . if you just hadn't . . . why'd you have to . . . ?"

The next swing, stronger than I planned, dislodged my shoulder. No pain, but the out-of-place bone made it easier to stop. I got a look at myself in a wall mirror and understood why someone like Tom Booth might have a hard time believing I was innocent of murder. I dropped the axe.

I turned to Misty. She was staring, not at me, but at what was left of Flat-face.

I rushed over to untie her. With my shoulder out, it was slow going. I tried to block the gory scene behind me, but she, wide-eyed, shaking, kept shifting her head for a better view.

I had no idea what to say to her, about what I'd done to Flat-face, about the crack burning through her, about anything. For a while, the only sound was the hissing of the Coleman lamp.

No sooner did I have the ropes off than she bolted to her feet. Her body wavered like a branch in a heavy wind, but her eyes stayed fixed on the bloody corpse.

I fumbled for words. "Misty, I had to stop him . . . after I saw what he was doing to you. . . ."

Noticing I'd smeared some of his blood on her wrists,

I wiped my hand against my jacket, leaving a five-fingered stain.

And then she asked, "You going to eat him?"

I thought she was accusing me. "That's the drugs talking."

She shivered like she'd been dunked in ice. "No," she said. "I *want* you to. Hess, I want you to eat that son of a bitch." She aimed a shaky finger at him. "Eat him!"

I staggered back. "Misty, you know chakz don't . . . you know, I'm not . . ."

"What do I know?" she said. She slammed her index finger into her chest. "What the fuck do I know?"

She ran, not bothering to avoid stepping on Flat-face on the way out. The last part to leave was her shadow, cast long and large by the hissing lantern.

10

I followed, called her name, pushed my way through thicker and thicker wood. Now and then, a sliver of ice green blouse poked through the mangled gray, but it was smaller every time I saw it, until, finally, I didn't see it again.

Foot-long pangs, radiating from my shoulder down into my ribs, made me stop. It was no use. I'd never beat her on foot even if she wasn't fuelled by crack cocaine. Finding a thick bastard of an oak, I threw myself into it, mostly out of rage, until the shoulder popped back into place. At least I think it was back in place. It hung a little looser, but everything seemed to work.

Now what? Come back when it was light, look for footprints? Right. By then she'd be dead or in Disney World. The high would fade. Once she stopped sobbing her guts out, she'd keep running or head someplace familiar. That wasn't much to go on. I'd met her on the streets, in the Bones, and she'd never said where she'd been before that.

Big picture, there were two possibilities: she'd stay straight or she'd find more drugs. She might decide she'd come too far to head back, or pure spite could keep her from giving Flat-face the postmortem satisfaction of knocking her off the wagon. In that case, she'd try to find someone to talk her down. That was no help to me. I didn't know anyone from the program other than Chester.

And then, what help would I be if I did find her? Spiritual support was never my forte. I mean, what could I say? Sure, your lover's dead, your body's full of poison, and the dead guy you're living with turned out to be an axe murderer, but cheer up, things could be worse?

If it wasn't for possibility two, I'd have left her alone. But she could just as easily end up thinking she didn't have any reason left to just say no. In that case, she'd need money, but we'd spent all we had. There was some cash in the office. She'd realize the danger, but calling a junkie self-destructive is redundant. She could waltz right into the arms of the toad, the police, or the ninja.

For starters, I headed back to the Subaru. There weren't many roads around here, and with a little luck, I might find her trying to hitch a ride.

On my way, I stopped at the cabin to peer in at my handiwork. Looking at what was left of Flat-face, I couldn't bring myself to feel bad about it. Then again, if I'd been a sadist, I'd have taken some pleasure in it, but I didn't do that, either. That was something, wasn't it? I told myself I had to save Misty. Was it my fault his skull was thin?

Crap. Another sin to carry.

Pandora's briefcase, now my *only* pal, sat lopsided against the cabin, looking like she knew I'd be back to pick her up. My biggest reason for trying to ditch the case had run off in a drug-fuelled haze. Not that I wanted to keep it, but now I didn't want all those assholes looking for it to have it either.

I clicked it open to see if anything had broken. Last I'd looked, the two vials were perfect, pristine, but they'd been through a lot since. One had what looked like a hair clinging to the narrow neck. I ran my finger against it, gently, but it didn't move. It felt sharp. It was a crack, not as thick as the glass, nothing seeping yet, but a crack. Another few bumps and whatever was inside would be out.

Pandora. Now there's a story that never made sense. A teenager can't keep from peeking in a closed box, surprise, surprise, and releases all the ills of the world. Then, she closes it just in time to keep hope inside. What the fuck? All the evils out, hope still trapped? Even the ancients needed a good editor.

I closed the case, carried it to the Subaru, put it in the passenger seat and wrapped the belt around it nice and snug. The keys were still in the ignition, the tank half-full.

I was cruising the dirt road, looking for Misty, seeing nothing but dark, when the cell phone they'd left for me back at the motel rang. I doubted that with two of his men dead I'd be able to again convince the toad of my good intentions. I turned it off so the sound wouldn't bug me, then found myself missing the voice of the German GPS.

A few hours later, I was no closer to finding her on the

road. That left the office. Once I scratched it off the list, the list would be empty. I was back in the Bones, a few blocks from home, when the dirty yellow haze that passed for dawn arrived. The day promised to be colder, the patches of ice thickened.

I ditched the car in an alley between a wrecked walk-up and a deserted pool hall called *Balls of Fire*. It was the hangout of our few local LB crackheads. Misty always recoiled at the sight of the place, but times change. Praying I wouldn't see her there, I stuck my head in through one of the glassless window frames.

Six or so skeletal figures lay strewn around the pool tables, broken cues, and other mementoes of a lesser sin. One had an arm missing, another's face was full of sores. I knew at a glance they were all livebloods. Don't ask me how, I just did. If they were chakz, they wouldn't stand out from the garbage in quite the same way.

I didn't see her, but I called out, "Misty!" in case anything moved.

Nothing even raised its head. I tried to feel good about that.

Hoping to avoid any eyes that might be looking for me, I stuck to the alleys and vacant lots. I did run into two danglers, but lacking mouths, they wouldn't be able to talk about it later even if they did recognize me, unless they remembered how to write, and I doubted that.

Expecting someone, hell, maybe *everyone*, to be watching, I stopped at the building next door and turned toward the roof. It was up there I'd spotted the figure. If the vantage was good enough for Red Riding Ninja, why not me? It was a plan.

Living up to its name, the rear fire door had long ago

been burned off its hinges. Inside, a skylight put a dull square on what was left of the stairs. Between missing steps, broken railings, and fallen pieces of wall, it took more than I expected to make it all the way up, but I managed, at least until I reached the roof. There were so many holes looking down into the lower floors, I felt like a drunken tightrope walker. Red was hot shit.

I found what I thought was his spot, near a chimney. It faced east, so the sunrise would make it harder to see me, and provided a decent view across the alley and into my home sweet home.

The place was ransacked, not that it looked all that different before. The sight of my ratty recliner, smashed and on its side, gave me a weird pang. I'd left pieces of myself in that old chair, literally. The desk was intact, but askew, as it had been on the webcam, the drawers missing. If Misty hadn't somehow beaten me here, Red had found the false bottom where I kept our measly savings. I hoped the amount was too embarrassingly small to take.

A thin black rectangle, less than a foot wide, lay sideways against a wall. Misty said the ninja kicked the netbook. Had it been overlooked? Ridiculous. I was probably looking at a hunk of plasterboard pretending to have a shape. I leaned out for a closer look. That's when the iffy support beam holding my weight decided it'd had enough. It didn't snap, but I wound up swaying out over the alley, snatching at the chimney to keep from falling thirty feet down into a Dumpster.

That would have hurt. The old thing had been down there so long, it'd all but recycled itself. The wet mess inside had rotted into a mushy soup. Most of it, anyway.

Something lay atop the ooze, barely distinguishable from its surroundings, like a zombie Waldo, gray as a corpse, about the length of an umbrella.

From here it looked like an arm.

I could've been hallucinating, I could've been wrong, but if that was the sucker that started it all, I had to check it out. The office, the building, the streets, all looked deserted. Yeah, looks can be deceptive, but I headed down anyway, a little too fast for safety's sake.

Arriving in the alley, I braced my feet against what used to be its blue metal side, gripped the frame and hauled myself up. One look and I didn't want to go in. Close up, the gunk looked like something I could sink into. It was an arm all right, though, *the* arm, muscles that looked like Dad's, the thick fingers he wished he'd had.

Whatever voodoo science that gave it its get up and go, had got up and went. It was swollen from the rain, really dead. I pulled closer. Had it been *that* gray when it knocked on my door? Had it been gray at all? I seemed to remember it being pinker, but that'd be crazy.

A bit of white at the end of its index finger looked like a paper scrap. Turned out it wasn't at the end of the finger, it *was* the end of the finger, exposed bone, the flesh scraped off. Maybe some rat had gnawed on it. They'll eat anything.

But there were no little teeth marks. The finger had been worn to the bone, like the arm had done it on purpose, scraped its own skin away. On what? Why?

Then I saw it, scratched into the metal, four letters, one word, *KYUA*.

11

Misty was gone and all I got was this lousy clue. *KYUA*. The imaginary god of the zombies.

Did the arm get the joke or did it, like Jimmy Stewart in the coffeehouse restroom, have faith and expect the same of me? Faith was Misty's bailiwick, what she said kept her sober, at least it had this morning. She tried to explain it more than once. The closest she got was telling me about this Hindu book, the *Bhagavad Gita*.

It was basically a chat between God and Arjuna, a poor sap fated to start a huge war among his family. Only he doesn't want to. Vishnu takes Arjuna aside and explains the universe, the whole ball of mortician's wax. Once Arjuna supposedly understands, he accepts his role and starts the war. Let the bloodbath roll.

Thing is, I never believed Arjuna really understood. I figured at best he got sick of all the yapping and said fuck it, shut up already, I'll start the war.

Assuming I was looking at the netbook and not an

optical illusion, she may have had time to put some contacts on it. Could be a way to find her. It could also be a way to get D-capped. Sure, from above, the office looked barren, but someone had been watching everything else so far. I took a leap of faith, as in, fuck it, let the bloodbath roll.

But I was no Arjuna. After climbing three flights and wading through the icy hallway puddles, my bravado wore off. I stood in a corner like a toddler doing time-out, went dead for half an hour. There wasn't a peep, not a single car driving by, not even an electric hum. The silence was as unnatural as I was.

I went in.

I didn't check for the netbook right off. Instead, in a rare sentimental moment, I prodded the broken recliner with my foot. The useless frame whimpered like a wounded dog. If I had a gun, I would have put it out of its misery.

Most of our belongings had been scattered, but against the wall, right where I'd spotted it, was the netbook. If it was a genuine miracle, the battery wouldn't have been drained and the AC adapter missing. If there was a way to get it going, it wasn't here.

Next, I checked the desk drawer, surprised to find the money still there. That meant Misty hadn't been here and it wasn't worth Red's time. It put a few hundred in my pocket, enough for a new adapter, anyway.

I grabbed my thrift store coat and went through the pockets. My digital recorder, my memory crutch, was gone. I tried to remember what was on it, but if I could do that, I wouldn't need the damn thing. Then for some reason, I started cleaning. I gathered what I could of

Misty's things and put them back in her bureau, in case, I don't know.

I was busy stuffing some of my dryer clothes in a plastic garbage bag when a weird tingle caterpillared along my spine. I didn't see or hear anything, but I went to the door. The sign with my name lay flat on the floor at my feet. The hall oozed nothingness.

"Misty?"

Nothing answered, but I didn't trust it, so I headed for the window and tried to open it. It was a contest to see which would give out first, the frame or my fingers, but the wood creaked up enough for me to climb out.

Bag in hand, I clambered down the fire escape. I doubt it was up to code when the building was new. Now, it was more paint than iron, my meager weight nearly pulling it free from the mortar. In the end, I fell, but by that time I was low enough to hit bottom in one piece.

Short-lived victory. I spent the next half hour wandering the alleys trying to remember where I'd left the Subaru. If I hadn't left the case in it, I'd have given up and taken a bus. Once I found it, I tanked up, bought some supplies at the Quickie Mart, then swapped the plates with an out-of-state van. Why the hell someone would drive to Fort Hammer from out of state is beyond me, but there you have it.

Next, I hit a big box electronics store. The security guy wouldn't let me in until I showed him my money. I spent too much on a new recorder that didn't look like it'd work and an adapter for the netbook that looked like it might. The cash about tapped, I headed for the second-most abandoned place I could think of, the warehouse district.

The feeble afternoon sun was being bullied by some massive gray clouds, the ice on the road serious. As I wheeled among the giant corpses of Fort Hammer's forgotten retail trade, I skidded more than once. The buildings looked so rickety I was afraid one whack would bring the whole block down. Even chakz didn't bother making shantytowns here. The only guy who'd used the place in recent memory had been a serial killer. And while he was trying to cut my head off, at least he'd shown me which warehouse still had electricity.

I found an outlet, plugged in the netbook, and turned it on. As I waited for it to boot, I pulled out my favorite piece of luggage and set it on the hood. No reason not to look now. The glass vials were the same, that single hairline crack on the one. I gently turned the other, sideways, upside down. It wasn't viscous. The liquid moved easily. The color was rich, lighter than cerulean, the crayon a kid might use for an ocean if he'd never seen one. I put both vials on the passenger seat, and turned to the briefcase.

There was something stuck in one of the hinges, a bit of pink nylon ribbon, smaller than a fingernail. I pulled it off, then tugged at the bottom layer until it threatened to tear. I got the sense it'd always been part of the case, that both were made just for those bottles. Drug trade gets pretty sophisticated, but I wasn't thinking local distributor anymore.

I worked my way around the edge of the foam, pulling, getting the same resistance. When I tried the top, though, one corner peeled away revealing something underneath; the end of a plastic card—a credit card or driver's license.

Ever try lifting a dime from the floor with wet fingers?

The wrinkled pads of my fingers kept slipping over it. My nails were too short to get under. I could shred the foam, but might need the case for the vials.

I fished the proverbial last dime from my pocket and used it to pry the card up. I had to see only the corner of the stylized double-R logo, for Revivals Registration, to know it was a chak ID. If a cop or guardsmen asked and you didn't have one, into the camps with you. And they asked whenever they could.

The embossed name on it—William Seabrook—had to be fake. Seabrook was the author of *The Magic Island* back in 1929, the book that supposedly introduced the word *zombie* to Western culture. Somebody had a sense of humor. The number was intact, but there was no picture, the plastic split where it was supposed to be. It'd be easy to put a new one in. This was exactly what a chak would need to escape the camps and start over. Maybe the arm was what was left of an escapee.

The thought of shredding the foam gave me an idea. Everyone was looking for a briefcase, right? I pocketed the card, then tore off enough foam to wrap the vials in, secured them with duct tape and shoved the results into a cinder block. To make it look good, I wrapped the case in two plastic garbage bags along with a couple of bricks for weight, and sealed the whole thing up with duct tape. Then I found a great big vat full of water, tied a rope around the handle and dropped the sucker in.

By now the netbook had booted, so I checked Misty's contacts. She'd had the thing only a few hours, but there were two. One was Chester, and the other a first name, Mary. Her sponsor in the program. There was a phone number.

I had the toad's cell and mine, but wasn't stupid enough to use either. There was a pay phone nearby. I'd used it to call Misty once, when I was bound with a leather strap around my neck. Don't ask. And I had just enough quarters for a one-minute call.

After three rings, a female voice, ravaged by cigarettes to the point where it sounded like a cartoon, said, "Yeah?"

"Mary?"

"Yeah?"

I'd have swallowed if it would have helped. "Hessius Mann. I'm looking for Misty."

"She's in the can. I'll get her . . ."

Something like relief flooded my bones. The other big addict in my life, Dad, tried getting sober, but it never stuck. He used to joke that he'd quit so often he should be getting better at it. Misty, bless her, still wanted to take care of herself. And if she was with a friend, she was safer than I was. Which meant now was not the time to stick my nose in.

"Wait. I don't want her to know I called. I just want to know if she's all right."

A phlegmy laugh. "Well, she ain't all right. She's been fucked over, good."

"Right. I know. I mean to say, are you helping her out?"

"Trying. You the dead Mann?"

"Yeah. If she told you half of what's been going on, you know there's trouble. I don't think she needs more."

"Shouldn't that be up to her?"

"I'm not talking emotional stress. Cars are blowing up. People are dying. You tell me, is Misty in any kind of shape to deal with that now?"

Silence.

"Good. I just want her to be safe while I try to work this out."

"Life ain't safe."

"You're preaching to the choir. Tell her I'll be back in touch when I can. Tell her not to try to get ahold of me. Tell her . . ." my voice trailed off.

"To have faith?" Mary offered.

"No reason to talk crazy, but you get the idea."

"Yeah."

"And Mary?"

"Yeah?"

"Someone else calls from a public phone, don't answer. It's not going to be me. And it'll probably be someone willing to torture or kill you."

"Fuck."

I hung up, thinking it was the smartest thing I'd done in days. Now all I had to do was figure out who was after the vials and find them before they found me.

The GPS from the Subaru had my office, the motel, and the shack on it, so all I had was the card and that fucking word, *kyua*. The card was as big a mystery as the arm, and while I knew what *kyua* meant to me, I didn't know what it meant to the believers. That's what the Internet is for. I went back to the car, left the netbook open next to me and started driving, hoping it would beep or fart when it found itself a Wi-Fi signal.

As it turned out, there was no sound. But, as I cruised a liveblood business district, a pop-up told me there were five networks available, two unsecured. I connected and started the browser.

The first thing I saw wasn't good. The local news feed

on Misty's home page featured a mug shot, probably taken during a stay in holding. Harsh lighting washed away the haggard skin texture, but the dry hair was a giveaway. If you saw this guy laid out in a coffin, you might think he was sort of handsome before the mortician went and ruined him.

It was me, my mug right below a big headline: CHAK WANTED IN POLICE KILLING. That didn't surprise me as much as the fact that I'd made it this far without being picked up. Maybe *fate* was saving me for something worse. They mentioned Misty, but didn't have a picture.

I Googled *kyua* and got about two hundred thousand hits. Most told me that the word was a) Japanese for *cure*, which I already knew, and b) the name of a nineties horror film. Chakz didn't generally have Web pages, so I wasn't expecting any sermons or religious blogs. I did hope some overachieving grad student had decided to do a study about nascent chak-culture or some such. Mostly, I wanted to know if there was any kind of organization involved, something I could tag to the arm and the vials.

With so many chakz shipped off, what lame communications I did have with the so-called community had broken down. Jonesey worked hard to keep his hand in, that was his thing. Once he was gone, for me, it was mostly watching Nell Parker on TV. She visited some of the camps, but only to show how nice they were.

I followed some links, found photos of an abandoned cat found in Tokyo, for instance, but one reference stuck out. *Kyua* was the nickname of a local chak-camp, about five miles north of Fort Hammer, near a town called Chambers. More than that, it wasn't the inmates who gave it the name, it was livebloods. I was surprised I'd never heard of it, wondering if I had but had forgotten.

Camp Kyua, provided some more focused results, including a blog by the self-involved Kafka228, a liveblood clerk who handled chak intake forms at The Chambers Observation Center, the camp's official name. He thought himself too smart for the room and wildly underemployed. He was also deeply amused by how *eager* some chakz were to get into Camp Kyua.

"They seem to think it's Disney World!" he wrote. "I think some actually failed their tests *on purpose*. Wish it were this easy to get rid of roaches in my kitchen."

An anonymous comment read, "If there were no kyua, chakz would have to invent one." Another: "Kyua cures those who cure themselves." Which, as the real Kafka pointed out, was kind of redundant.

Why the rush to get in? That was the kicker. From what I could piece together, ChemBet, the folks who brought you tomorrow's zombies today, used this camp to cull "volunteer subjects" for testing.

So, a bunch of my fellow corpses had gotten it into their decomposing heads that Camp Kyua was a good thing. Given how hard we are to destroy, the smart ones figured ChemBet was hunting for a way to *really* kill us, quickly and easily. I could see it. Given the mangled results of failed efforts, that's not an unwelcome thought, Still, not something I'd *volunteer* for. The not-so-smart ones thought it meant that ChemBet was trying to *improve* the RIP, *really* bring us back to life.

So, the "cure" meant life or death. *Praise Kyua*.

And I was still hoping the blue stuff was relatively harmless, like an addictive drug or an explosive. If this crap was ChemBet's, it had to be worse. And so was my situation. ChemBet had real power. I'd already figured I was royally screwed, but every time I thought I had a handle on how deep the screw went, it twisted in a little more.

I thought about the briefcase I'd so carefully wrapped in plastic. I thought about the arm, moving on its own. A bit of conversation slipped into my head:

What would I have to gain?

Maybe everything.

The toad, whoever he was, was worried I'd try the stuff myself. Right. Given all Travis and Rebecca Maruta's great work to date, I'd sooner saw off my head with a Spork. It also meant I couldn't hand it back to them. These were, after all, the folks who'd fucked up *death*.

There also had to be a story behind that arm. Since it'd cost him, Misty, and myself so much, I wanted to know what it was.

Camp Kyua was ground zero. If there were answers, they'd be there. Under normal circumstances, getting in shouldn't be a problem, but my corpse-kisser was plastered all over the net. I had a new ID card. I just needed a new face.

At the warehouse, the women's room still had a mirror. Looking at my photo was one thing, but I had to fight my instincts to give myself a good hard look in the flesh. That was one thing going for me. Livebloods didn't like looking at us too much either. Can't blame them. Even if we're dressed nice, you can never be sure what might pop out from where. Think seeing someone's flabby gut poke from a T-shirt is freaky? Imagine desiccated intestines slipping over a belt.

But I had to change myself at least a little. Makeup could work, but I didn't have any. That left the last refuge of the fashion conscious, self-mutilation. If thine eye offend thee cut it out, and replace it with something that matches your hair.

The few chakz who'd gone that way had generally died as teens, and were now trying for echoes of lost angst. Some idiots filed their teeth into points, which *really* made the LBs love them. One girl, featured on Nell Parker's show, had carefully razored the skin from her hands, creating a kind of muscle-glove effect. Others just carved at themselves idly. None of them kept from going feral long enough to start a trend.

My attachment to my body wasn't as strong as when I was alive, but it was all I had. I could take a knife to some of the skin, but the wounds would never heal. Break my nose?

I was pissed enough about it all to grab a brick and give myself a half-hearted whack that hurt more than I expected. I clutched my proboscis, danced around, banging into stalls and wall, using all the invectives I had at my disposal. After all that, another look in the mirror told me I'd only scraped the tip, exposing some cartilage, a pebble of white on a little gray hill.

That left getting some makeup.

12

Having seen myself on the net, I wasn't thrilled about leaving the warehouse again. But, Halloween wasn't two weeks old. One of those seasonal costume stores might still be open. I cruised until I found a quiet strip mall that had what I wanted, a costume outlet complete with a witty banner reading, EVERYTHING MUST GO — AS DO WE ALL!

The display window was full of overturned boxes, scattered masks of clowns, ghosts, and witches. Livebloods didn't dress as zombies anymore, for obvious reasons, but there'd be plenty of greasepaint and fake wigs.

I had my hat and trench on, and it was cold enough so that pulling the collar up didn't look out of place. Across the street sat an empty lot with a few sad chak shacks. That meant, I hoped, if I was spotted, my condition wouldn't be too much of a surprise.

I was about to go in when I learned it wasn't just the net. My face was also on the TV the pimple-faced clerk was watching. Next to that was a bank of security monitors, covering the merchandise. If he so much as glanced at a security cam while I was shopping, he'd see one picture right next to the other.

I looked at the chak shacks again. A Subaru would look suspicious parked there, so I walked over. A few goners sat inside a doorless ad hoc square of tin and cardboard, the smell of their decay thicker than the walls. Misty used to tour the Bones, bleach bottle in hand, cleaning up anyone she could, but these days it was like spitting in the ocean.

I stuck my head in and held up a bill, hoping one would remember what money was.

"Anyone want to make five bucks? Buy yourselves some bleach?"

They all picked up their heads. A few could only hiss, but two managed something sounding like, "Yes."

One was a blond woman with a swollen gash down the center of her face that looked like a big flat worm. The other was a door-wide guy, relatively intact, but having trouble keeping his eyes open. I started with the girl.

I explained what I wanted as carefully as I could, but she wasn't as smart as she looked. Then again, I didn't notice the back half of her skull was missing until she had my money in hand and was walking across the street. She never made it into the store, just sort of staggered to the front of Sam's Liquors, sat down and tried to eat the cash.

I was running out of money, but I pulled out another bill and turned to option two. After checking the back of his head, I went through my instructions again.

He nodded and said, "Yeah, yeah," like he was listening. That was a good sign.

Better yet, about twenty minutes later, he came back with a big bag.

I hadn't asked for all the candy, but it looked like he got the rest right.

"Thanks, buddy," I said.

"You're welcome," he answered. He smiled widely, showing a few corn-kernel teeth, pleased he'd remembered his manners.

"Make sure you buy some bleach, you big lug," I said. I repeated it, slowly, holding my nose for emphasis. "Rot, you know? Big stink."

He smiled again. "You're welcome."

I shoved another bill in his hand.

"Bleach," I said loudly. I pointed to the others. "For everyone. Understand?"

The smile vanished. He nodded again. "Bleach."

For Misty's sake, I walked him back across the street and gave him a push toward a convenience store. He waddled, slowed, but then picked up some steam that took him inside. I could've stayed and helped more, I suppose, but I could also end up cleaning rot out of chakz until Judgment Day.

Back at the warehouse, I swapped my usual clothes for a moth-eaten sweater, stained sneakers, and mottled pants. The big guy had done well. Inside the bag, there was a fright wig, greasepaint, spirit gum, latex wounds, vampire blood, a wad of scar wax, and scissors. I was starting to think he'd actually buy that bleach. Whether he'd use it on the rot or try to drink it was another question.

I had to make at least one, big, obvious change, something to act as a distraction from the rest of my face. I covered my left eye with the scar wax, rubbing what was left of the waxlike crap past my temple. A little black greasepaint made my right eye sink even more. In honor of Jimmy Stewart from the Styx men's room, I used the spirit gum to stick a nice open wound along my neck.

The fright wig was tougher, the frizzy long hairs didn't look remotely real. Trimming made it worse. I tried pouring vampire blood on it, to tamp things down. By the time I was finished, it didn't look exactly like hair, but neither did mine. The result vaguely resembled an oozing scalp. I twisted my head, let my arm dangle, and practiced exaggerating my limp.

Christ, I looked like an asshole.

Finding a bare wall that may have once been white, I stood against it, held the toad's cell phone camera at arm's length and kept snapping until the flash card filled.

Phase two would tell me if any of this gaudy shit actually worked.

I drove back into town, found a big-box store with a help-yourself-just-give-us-the-money photo section, and staggered into the fluorescents doing the funky corpse. The aging greeter uttered a muted hello with about the same energy the goner had grunted, "Bleach."

So far so good.

The sheer size of the place let me keep my distance from the shoppers and minimum-wage clerks. Even if someone saw through the disguise, I'd have a shot at getting away. I did tense up when I noticed I was shambling in front of a wall of TVs showing my face.

No one was around to notice except a chak in a turtleneck standing in the laxative section. Either he'd gotten lost or had swallowed something he shouldn't have. He gave me a second look then tsked so loudly it sounded like one of his teeth had snapped. He didn't say anything. None of his business.

I made it to the photo-printer, fumbled with the tiny data card, but managed to get it in the slot. I picked the best shot, took the receipt and pushed my last bill at the cashier. Too busy chewing on a chocolate bar, she didn't give me any change. It ticked me off, but I didn't think I should make a fuss.

The hardest part turned out to be cutting the damn photo down to size and slipping it into the fucking ID card. That took nearly all morning.

All I had to do now was present myself for a test at the right center, and fail. The state didn't like to waste fuel, so it was a good bet they'd ship me to whatever camp was closest. Camp Kyua was nearest Chambers, a town that used to be a trade hub, and was now mostly known for sitting on Settler's River without being swept away. I reached their chak center around noon. It was a squat brick building with few windows that once served as a DMV.

Inside, a faint chemical smell, like Lysol, hit my nostrils. No surprise. All chak centers were equipped with decontamination stalls—showers, pretty much, mostly water, twenty percent antiseptic. If you passed the test, the shower was voluntary, but highly recommended. If you failed, well, then pretty much everything was mandatory.

I slogged with deliberate slowness through the silver poles and black nylon ribbon, scraping my feet on the remains of arrows taped to the linoleum. Chakz aren't much for lines. We're not impatient, most of us just don't understand them. We'll wander toward anything shiny, or stand in the same spot for hours blocking things up.

So I was a little surprised that the line wasn't bad, meaning it looked like a line, mostly. It occurred to me that the testing process self-selected the smarter ones. You had to get here and follow the arrows, which already made you better off than some. Goners were supposedly too decayed to go feral, but I had to wonder if the LBs left them alone because there was no way to monitor them all effectively.

There was a gap between the last two chakz. A woman, hunched over so far her chinbone touched her navel, was where she should be, but ten feet behind her stood a lipless man, if you could call it standing. While she was bent forward, he curved sideways, his spine twisted into a nearly perfect half-moon, like he was standing on the sloping deck of the Titanic right before it split in two.

Not wanting to draw attention by cutting ahead, I gave him a nudge.

"You on line?"

He pivoted toward me, then back toward the distant bag woman. His eyes went a little wide at the space. "Yeah, sorry. Thanks."

Since that was a reasonably coherent response, I decided to ask, "Do you know Kyua?"

He put a finger to his bare teeth, telling me he did, but didn't plan on talking about it. Kyua helps those who help themselves. Looked like I was in the right place. Every five minutes or so, the line moved, but he didn't, and I'd have to nudge him again.

Things went on like that for a while. My mind was knocking around aimlessly when a voice from behind whispered, "If someone bigger shoves you, do you shove back?"

I whirled. A raggedy was behind me, looking up expectantly, half her face missing, the muscles exposed. Not *a* raggedy, *the* raggedy, the one I'd seen twice already, at the accident site, then at the motel. Had she seen through my shitty disguise?

Before I could open my mouth, she repeated the question. "What are you, a goner? If someone bigger shoves you, do you shove back?"

"That some kind of metaphor?"

"No, idiot, it's a test question. You're smart enough to nudge the guy ahead of you, I thought maybe you'd know the answer."

Maybe she didn't recognize me. I shrugged. "I'm not sure. The usual, ethical answer might be something like, only if I had to, to protect myself. But if they're looking for a tendency toward violence, then the right answer might be no, never, or only if they're not a liveblood. Go with that."

She lowered her head and moved it back and forth, like she was trying to memorize what I'd said. "Yeah, yeah. Okay. Thanks."

I'd forgotten to alter my voice, not that I'd be any good at it, but I risked a few more questions. "You from Chambers?"

She scanned my face suspiciously. Not wanting to give her too close a look, I staggered back a little, hoping it looked natural.

"Why, are you?" she said.

I nodded, lying. "Haven't seen you around town. Then again I'm not good with faces, whole or half. What brings you?"

"What do you think? My test. Took me days to walk here."

So she'd picked Chambers, too. "I heard rumors some of the chakz that get here plan to fail on purpose. You one of those?"

She shook her head. "No fucking way. But if I do fail, might as well wind up at Kyua, right?"

The conversation was interrupted. The hunched-over bag lady had been seated for her test at one of three desks beyond the end of the line. Now she'd bolted to her feet, her back so curved, she nearly slammed her chin on the paperwork.

"No, no! You bastards! Bastards!"

A few chakz behind me groaned and gnashed their teeth. It was kind of an involuntary reaction, but if it went on too long, some would go feral. There was a quick nod from the tester and two guardsmen in khaki uniforms grabbed her.

They couldn't straighten her out without breaking her, and that would only rile the chakz more. Instead, they lifted her sideways, still bent over. Hands scratching and legs kicking, she looked like a petulant piece of furniture. They took her beyond a blue door where they kept the decontamination showers and the holding cells. I assumed the door was soundproofed because we didn't hear her once it shut.

Chak Centers being one of the few places where public smoking is still allowed, the tester tamped out her cigarette with a shaky hand and put up a sign reading, NEXT WINDOW.

I looked back at the raggedy. "Not everyone feels the same way about the camp."

Her shrug looked strange with one shoulder gone. "Everyone's got an opinion." She nodded for me to turn around. "You're up."

Another desk had opened up. I lumbered up and plopped my card in front of a forty-something woman with coiffed hair. Kafka228 herself, for all I knew, looked at the card, at me, then back at the card.

"None of my business," she muttered. I sat and she started with the test.

"Can you tell me your middle name?"

"Sorry, I don't know. Billy?"

"Close enough. If someone shoved you, would you shove them back?"

I managed a grin. "You bet!"

That part was easy.

The rest wasn't. About an hour after my shower, they shoved me, the raggedy, and a bunch of others, onto an old school bus. It had undergone a few modifications since it trucked around the kiddies: there was a stainless steel gate between the driver and the passengers, and the emergency exit in back had been welded shut.

Things seemed to be going as planned for a change. Despite my appearance, I almost felt like a detective on a case.

Then about five minutes into the trip, it dawned on me we weren't going north. We were headed south, away from Camp Kyua, toward God knew where. The raggedy noticed, too.

"Crap!" she shouted.

I agreed.

13

There was nothing to do but enjoy the ride. At least no one felt like singing "99 Bottles of Beer on the Wall." We made a few stops at other registration centers, each one farther south, dashing any hope I had that we might turn back. Every time, more not-so-happy campers were shoved on by the guardsmen.

Soon, the bus was so crowded we were stacked, two or three chakz high. I wound up in a twisted position that would have killed a liveblood, buried on a seat I couldn't see, head shoved sideways against the window. Every time we hit a bump, and there were lots, it felt like my skull or the glass would break. Eventually the glass did crack, not enough for me to climb out, but enough to let the November wind freeze the fake vampire blood on the dome of my skull.

The pickups done, we headed away from so-called civilization. After about an hour of steady uphill progress, the bus creaked and slowed. Unable to move my head, I turned my eyes toward what was left of the window. It was night, but the moon was out. Through the spiderweb crack in the window, I saw a tall gate, chain-link with barbed wire up top. There weren't any signs warning that it was electrified, but the still-smoldering palm and charred fingers of the disembodied hand poking through the chain-link gave that impression.

My fellow passengers grunted and moaned, sounding more like undead cattle than a threat to public safety. I barely heard the bus door sigh open. A smell you couldn't miss, like overcooked bacon, pushed away what was left of the air.

We didn't walk so much as fall out, keeping our cramped shapes as we hit the ground. Even after I extricated myself from the lump of entwined torsos and limbs I couldn't stand at first. When I straightened, all kinds of things snapped, crackled, and popped inside me.

Aside from the bacon smell coming from the fence and the familiar chak version of body odor, my nostrils met something more immediately dangerous, a strong stench of rot. As I looked around, I could hear that German GPS saying, *Sie sind angekommen.*

You have arrived.

Chak-camps were the result of lots of talk, but no planning. Most were repurposed stables, racetracks, country fairgrounds, that sort of thing—big spaces used to holding lots of garbage. I had no idea what this place was when it was alive. It looked like they'd just found a field and tossed it up, which meant they were running out of space.

The wind blew colder and harder, not that it helped the smell, so I guessed we were on some kind of plateau. Carbon-arc searchlights made whatever they touched briefly brighter than the moon. As far as I could see, the whole place was one great big fence, sprinkled with guard towers, their spindly steel legs glinting whenever the lights kissed them. Other than that, no buildings, no shelter, only a wide view of mud piles and trash.

I wondered where the other prisoners were, until the mud piles moved toward us. The Bible said God made man from mud, and here we were, going back to it. It was around then I thought of ripping off my disguise and letting the bus driver take me to the police. But a metallic click told me he'd locked the gate. I turned in time to see him hop back into the bus and drive off.

Was this it? No sign-in? No orientation? I didn't expect it to be like it was on Nell's show, comfortable, with shelter and recreation, but I expected *something*. On the brighter side, a week here and I'd feel like I'd done my time for axing Flat-face.

Hell, a *day*.

Chakz are never colorful, but what got off the bus wasn't nearly as gray as what was coming toward us. At first, I thought they might greet us, give us the lay of the land. Instead, they started checking our pockets.

A one-eyed man with a single tooth yanked a locket from the raggedy's neck. He held it up and announced, "Pretty!" right before she clocked him in the jaw.

"Give it, Grandpa, now!"

I wanted to help, but there were hands, many missing fingers, all over me, fishing through my clothes. If they grabbed my wig, they'd yank it off and I'd be exposed. Then again, the guards were probably used to seeing body parts slough off. And where else would they put me, prison?

I pushed a few away, trying to be gentle until I felt someone snag my recorder. I snatched it back, pinching the hand that held it. A woman with a mud-caked beehive hairdo yowled, "We share everything!"

"No," I said. "We don't."

She grabbed again, but I held on tight. I was ready to start a real ruckus when a short guy with Superman biceps ambled up from the shadows. What I saw of his face looked pretty complete, even had some white stubble. I almost took him for a guard, but he wasn't wearing khaki. The pants hitched up too high reminded me of a semiretired handyman my late wife Lenore and I used to hire.

He put two fingers under his tongue and blew. A harsh whistle erupted from his mouth, something I couldn't do when I was alive. Everyone stopped moving.

"If it's important to them, let them keep it." He spoke with lazy authority, like an experienced foreman on a construction site. "One item each. Johnny, you give that girlie her locket."

But old Johnny had already lost that fight. He was in the dirt, tugging his single tooth to see if she'd loosened it. I didn't know who the raggedy was, or why she kept turning up, but I was starting to like her.

The beehive woman scowled. "We share *everything*."

"Let him keep it, Cheryl. We'll figure out some way he can pay."

Cheryl let go and snarled at me, "You'll pay."

"I got a feeling I already am," I told her.

She looked like she was about to utter a clever comeback, but someone shouted, "Bottle cap!" and she toddled over to check.

After shoving the recorder back in my pocket, I stepped toward our protector, deeper into the camp. I had to slow when the stench grew stronger, but he seemed like a man worth knowing.

"Thanks, pal," I said. "I use it to remember things."

He couldn't care less. "You look like you're in one piece. Can you work?" He pointed to a pile of something against the fence. "Got wood, nails, hammers, and permission to put up a building."

"Sure. It's something to do at least, right? We could use a shelter."

He shook his head. His jaw wobbled as if it wasn't properly attached. "Not for us, for the supplies."

"What supplies?"

He counted on his fingers. "Chain-link, posts, sledge-hammers, stuff the guard uses to extend the fence. Oh, and sometimes fuel for the flamethrowers."

"You're fucking with me. They expect us to help expand our own prison?"

He shrugged and spoke slowly, like English wasn't his first language, or there was something wrong with his throat. "They don't expect anything except for us to go feral. This is an overflow camp, understaffed, over-crowded. They just wait, then come out with the throwers and burn us, real slow if they have to conserve fuel. Five, six a day. They wish it was more. But like you said, the work gives you a focus. Makes it harder to go," he said. "A little harder, anyway."

Boy, did I get on the wrong bus.

Mr. Fixit had been mostly in shadow, but when the searchlight passed this time, I got a lightning view of his face. He looked much better in the dark. What skin he had was covered with black patches and oozing holes. The exposed muscles were dark red puddles, with bits of bone showing like potatoes floating in a stew.

It was rot, lots of it. It was a miracle his jaw stayed on at all.

"Christ," I said.

"Oh, the face. Is it bad? No one wants to tell me, and it ain't like I've got a mirror."

I didn't hang around to hear the rest. I stormed up to the base of one of the guard towers and banged on the steel leg.

"Hey! Hey!"

My fists made vague thuds, so I rapped with the recorder, hoping I wouldn't break it. A searchlight stopped on me. I'd gotten their attention. The deafening klaxon that followed made me realize that wasn't a good thing.

A wheeled side gate squeaked open. Two guardsmen trotted my way. The one in front was a square-jawed kid, his face a mix of fear and determination. His eyes looked deader than mine. The other looked more like a weekend hakker, the sort who used to chase chakz with a machete for fun. His khakis fit him about as much as he fit this place.

I held my hands up, to show I wasn't a threat, then tried to make my face look pleasant. That was always an uphill struggle; I had no idea what it looked like with my disguise.

"There's a ton of rot out here, pal ... uh, sir. A little bleach can go along way. Any way we can ... ?"

I didn't finish the sentence, and at first wasn't sure why. Everything went slo-mo, then it lost definition, color, grayscale. From there the world slipped into a series of wild geometric shapes, some black, some white. I stumbled from a white circle into a black rectangle and collapsed.

When I saw the silhouette of a rifle, I realized the second guard had come up behind me and slammed me on the back of the head. From the look of the silhouette, he was about to do it again, but I couldn't bring myself to care. It all felt even more distant than usual, like it was happening to somebody I didn't know, and if I did know them, I wouldn't like them very much.

The second blow never came. Two hands grabbed my shoulders and dragged me someplace darker. When the spinning stopped and some of the textures came back, I made out the face of the raggedy.

"You are one fucking idiot," she said.

"Someone once told me it never hurts to ask. Guess they were wrong." I forced myself to sitting.

She pointed to her hair. "Wig's falling off."

I said, "Thanks," and tried to adjust the hair, but my arm wasn't quite working.

"What were you, like a vain cancer patient when you died?" she asked.

She still didn't seem to recognize me. I didn't think it meant the disguise was good, just that I wasn't the only chak with memory problems.

"Something like that," I said.

She put her hand to the wig and pushed it into place. It felt like part of my scalp *had* come free.

"I gotta tell you, forget bald, bone would look better than that thing," she said. She tapped the exposed bone of her cheek. "Keeps the LBs on their toes, too."

"Thanks for the fashion tip. And the rescue."

Once everything stopped pulsating, I checked myself and didn't find anything missing. My rib cage didn't feel right, but my body never does. There wasn't much I could do about it here anyway.

I stood on wobbly legs and caught another whiff of rot, not as bad as the stench from Mr. Fixit, but close, maybe somewhere on the girl. At least it wasn't summer. Even if it was from her, given the cold, it might be a month before it got too bad for her.

Eventually, morning, or something like it, came, blandly proclaiming that the days here wouldn't be very different from the nights. I tried talking to a few fellow inmates, but the conversations didn't go far. Most could be summed up along the lines of:

"This is it?"

"Yeah, this is it."

It was like being stuck in a really big, really crowded elevator, knowing you'd never get to your floor. If I had half a brain, I'd give up on ever figuring out what was going on at ChemBet, accept this as payment for sins past, but if I did that, I'd have nothing left and I would go feral. Much as I hated the thought of a D-cap, what I'd seen of burning looked worse.

I didn't want to wind up like the others here, either. The half-moon fellow who'd been in front of me on line back at the Chak Center was here, too. He spent a lot of time sitting on the ground, shaking his head, and talking about how Kyua had deserted him.

"What did you expect?" I asked, hoping to get a rise from him.

"Kyua," he answered. "Kyua."

If there wasn't much keeping me going, he had less.

Not that you could say any of us were emotionally stable. I wondered if the guards ran a pool.

Fixit said there were five to six ferals a day, but the first I saw happened about forty-eight hours after arrival. It wasn't half-moon, it was Cheryl, the "we all share" woman who wanted my recorder. That wasn't a surprise. The surprise was how quickly she was handled.

True to form, she'd nabbed a newbie's pocketbook and dragged it off to a little corner, as if none of the rest of us could see her. She shook it and rubbed it, the expression on her face somewhere between a child on Christmas morning and Gollum with the ring.

Try as she might, though, she couldn't get the golden clasp that held it shut to open. She poked it, squeezed it, but her thumb and index finger lacked the physical dexterity to work it. She pounded it against the ground, then gnawed at it, breaking off half a tooth.

I'd been watching the whole thing—there wasn't much to look at here—but it wasn't until she screamed that everyone else paid attention. Not a standard scream, this was long and low. It started from the bottom of her lungs and threatened to bring her throat up with it. Her gnashing teeth gave it a bit of vibrato. Then, without even inhaling, somehow, she found the breath to moan.

Ten seconds later, that was it.

Some go in bits and pieces, in and out for a month or so. Others, it's a finger snap. Which is exactly what Cheryl did. She grabbed the index finger on the hand that wouldn't open the purse and snapped it off.

Her next mournful bellow seemed to lift her to her feet. She shambled toward one of the towers and gnawed at the leg, breaking more teeth against it.

I hadn't seen it happen yet, but I knew what was coming next. I thought I was far enough away from her, but when the klaxon sounded, rattling my chest, the others pulled me even farther.

That same gate rolled open, the same two guards rushed out. Only this time they were carrying flamethrowers. Dad, while still an army man, once told me all about flamethrowers. Say what you like about waterboarding, but the military hasn't used flamethrowers since 1978. That was partly due to the horrible death they inflict, but also because they're cumbersome and the fuel tank makes for an easy target. One shot and you're off in a ball of glory. Even if you survived and got captured, the infuriated enemy pretty much always executed you.

They brought them back though, just for chakz. It wasn't cruelty, more a matter of pragmatism. Ferals tend not to sit still for D-capping. Bullets don't stop them, unless you use enough to shred them. And so on, and so forth. So what could you do, really? Softhearted liberals grumbled about the morality, but shut up when asked if they had any better ideas.

Cheryl either heard the guards coming, or smelled the fuel that dripped from the nozzles and left fiery dollops in the dirt. They moved fast, but she still had enough time to whirl in their direction.

When they opened up on her, she was swamped by a hot, yellow and orange sideways waterfall. Ten yards away, the heat pushed me back even more. When I looked again, she was a silhouette in the flame, walking slowly, as if strolling along a beach. She made it three feet, went to her knees, then fell forward. There wasn't enough left to move anymore, but they kept it up for about five minutes until a final *thok* told them the skull had popped.

When the flames stopped, all that was left was a wobbling husk of charred bone in the center of smoldering earth, smoke twirling from the extremities. Call me superstitious, but I wasn't sure she was really dead. I'd seen one too many talking heads to think it that easy.

They left her there. And when they didn't give us so much as a shovel to clean her up, I knew better than to ask for one. It was then I finally noticed that all the mud piles that weren't moving were piles of blackened bones.

Within an hour, I decided to take Mr. Fixit up on his offer and help him build that shed. Something to do, right?

I kept my distance, hoping to improve my odds of not catching whatever was eating him. We put in a few hours, more the next day, which saw seven ferals burnt to toast.

As we worked, I made rough marks in the planks, trying to make some look like circles, others rectangles. You'd think it the sort of thing a psycho would scrawl on his cell wall.

On the third day, the raggedy came up and asked, "Why do you bother?"

She was smart. Maybe she could figure it out. I pointed my chin toward the scratches. She eyed them a while.

"You're keeping track of the guards?" she asked quietly.

I nodded. "Something to do."

She pointed at me. "You figure a way out of here, *swear* you'll let me know or I'll tell everyone right now what you're doing."

I shrugged. "You got it."

But I didn't have an escape plan and I wasn't sure I should try it if I did. My last scheme, after all, was what got me here. This was more a hobby. I was hoping to figure out who was lazy, who was late, maybe eventually figure the best time to make a break for it. If I succeeded with that much, I might move on to the whole "how" thing.

But I didn't get the chance to complete phase one.

The next day, the frame was finished and the first wall of our shed went up. Taking a break, Mr. Fixit bent forward to straighten a kink in his spine, and his jaw fell off. Just like that. One minute it was there, the next it wasn't. Plop, gone, like it'd rolled out of his pocket.

I've seen a lot, but when he stood up, I had to turn away. Scores of tightly packed maggots were writhing in the holes where his jaw had been. It was one of those times I really wished I could puke. The poor bastard didn't even realize anything was wrong until he saw the expression on my face and tried to talk to me.

Tongue flapping half in the air, awful noises came from his throat. "Ggrggll shahhhshhh?"

When I shook my head, he tried to repeat it. "Ggrggll shahhhshhh?"

The third time through, he realized he wasn't making words. Wondering why, he reached up with his hand and felt nothing but dry flesh and squirming bugs. Then he started looking for his jaw on the ground, like he expected to clean it off and stick it back on. Misty was a whiz with Krazy Glue, thread, and needle, better than some doctors I'd seen, but this mess was beyond even her.

Fixit kept looking. He thought he found it, but when it turned out to be a rock, he stomped his feet. It wasn't tough to guess what we were all thinking would happen next. Only, he didn't go feral, not at first. That honor went to half-moon guy, the one disappointed in Kyua.

He'd been sitting with a small group, the raggedy among them, that'd taken to watching us work. After all, we were pretty much the only entertainment. When Fixit started stomping, half-moon realized he didn't like the show anymore and couldn't change channels.

There are moans and there are moans. Chakz still moan when we're annoyed. Half-moon didn't sound gone, more irritated. But he kept it up long enough for the others to try to calm him down. He pushed them away, threw his hands in the air, and wailed. That was enough of a warning for the raggedy to back away. The next chak who came near him was rewarded with a long raking scratch across the side of their face.

The klaxon sounded. It was official. The gate wheeled open. The flamers rushed in and we gave them room. Half-moon was swallowed by twin streams of searing agony, Kyua and all. He didn't buckle to his knees like Cheryl had. He kinda twisted and broke in two.

Meanwhile, Mr. Fixit was vocalizing like crazy, making noises like a mad cow. It sounded like he was still trying to communicate, so I turned from the burning to see if I could make it out. He lunged at me, pushing that wormy face into mine, tearing my clothes with his stubby fingers. He tried to chomp on me, but with that lower jaw missing, couldn't.

More afraid of the rot than his scratches, I pushed him hard. He staggered, spinning like a top as he went. When he stopped, he was facing one of the flamers who was still busy barbecuing half-moon. To a feral, one victim's as good as another. Fixit trundled toward the guard like a puppy moving through molasses.

The professional flamer didn't see him coming, but his hakker partner did. He shouted a warning, but couldn't be heard over the rush of burning fuel and crackling bones. By the time the klaxon sounded again, it was too late.

Catching him off guard, Mr. Fixit slammed into the flamer, sending him to his back. A burning geyser shot skyward from the thrower. It twisted left and right, raining fire. Burning patches appeared on our clothes. Some were smart enough to put them out, others only watched the pretty flames.

The klaxon always got a Pavlovian response, rattling us, but the second alarm, coming so soon, did something more. A good ninety percent of us wobbled and shivered in unison, and not in anticipation of being fed. They grunted rhythmically. After a few, slow, steady beats, the noise morphed into something closer to moans.

I didn't feel like moaning myself, but I've never been much of a joiner. It looked like the raggedy was also keeping her act together. She stared at the others as if they were nuts, and backed even farther away.

Chakz going feral en masse wasn't a topic they covered on Nell's show, but I'd heard about it. Until now, I'd chalked it up to one of the many urban myths surrounding the life-challenged, but I've been wrong before.

For instance, before the Fort Hammer riot, I thought ferals were incapable of acting in an organized way. But when hundreds massed on the city plaza, it sure as hell looked like they were moving in patterns. Mass suicides had been known to occur in the living, so why not mass savagery in the dead? You couldn't find a nicer spot for it.

The flamer was on the ground, freaking out as Fixit nuzzled his pink cheek with his maggot-filled face. If that wasn't ugly enough, the fuel tank, dented in the fall, had sprung a leak.

"Get him off! Get him off." His screams sounded more like sobs.

With a pop, a round tear appeared in Fixit's shoulder. A bullet hole. If they thought anything less than an exploding bullet was going to make a difference, they were idiots. Then again I never got the sense that even the paid guardsmen earned more than minimum wage—and you get what you pay for.

The gate squealed open again, revealing two more flamers, both baby-faced. The crowd's caterwauling grew, like a game show audience really disappointed by the prizes. The newcomers took it slow, trying to size things up, but not the downed flamer's hakker buddy. That pinhead pointed his nozzle at Mr. Fixit, like he thought he could aim the foot-thick fire accurately enough to pick the chak off without hurting his pal.

I imagined him saying, "Hold still, Lennie, I'll light that cigarette for you!"

I'd sat for a lot since I'd been here, but there was only just so much sheer stupidity I could stand. I ran up, waving my hands, screaming.

"Asshole! Squeeze that trigger and his fuel pack will blow!"

It wasn't polite, but I'd made the point. The second flamer's eyes widened like he'd suddenly remembered how fire worked.

In for a penny, in for a pound. Once I was close enough, I gave Fixit a hard kick, sending him rolling. Unfortunately, the jackass figured I'd given him the distance he needed, and opened up. The heat barreling through the air alongside the flame was enough to throw me off my feet. I landed on my back, my clothes smoking. I crawled away, like a caterpillar on speed, nearly hitting the prone flamer on my way.

He looked at me, absolutely terrified. A single maggot squirmed below one eye.

"Easy! I'm not feral!" I said.

I don't think he believed me because he started screaming, "Feral! Feral!"

That's when I noticed that the weeping fuel along the dent in his fuel pack had caught fire.

"Fuck!" I said.

I could've run, left him to blow. He was the enemy, so to speak, but he wasn't a sick fuck like Flat-face, and I hated seeing anything burn. I clawed at the straps, trying to get them off. Screaming in frustration at my stupid, useless fingers only helped convince him I'd gone Romero.

Somehow, I managed to release the straps. I yanked the tank off, got to my knees and swung the whole mess toward the storage shed Fixit and I had been building.

And what did I get for my troubles? There was a sudden pressure in my lower back, followed by a little explosion below my rib. A sniper bullet had sailed through me. No good deed goes unpunished.

Out of reflex, I grabbed at the hole with one hand and dragged the downed guardsman away from the shed with the other. I don't doubt the sniper would've fired again if the fuel pack hadn't exploded. The concussive blast took every chak in sight off their feet. The shock even stopped the fucking moaning. Nothing like a good slap in the face to get your attention. Sometimes it works.

Seeing the blast, the other flamers yanked off their own throwers like they were, I don't know, a chak riddled with maggots. I was only half standing to begin with, so I had less of a trip back to the ground. The heat seared my fake hair and it felt like the Halloween scar-glop I'd used to cover my eye had melted into my skin.

Afraid to even touch my eye, I looked down at my gut. The wound was oozing, but I wouldn't call it blood. Best guess was that the bullet had missed my internal organs. Then again, I didn't need them anyway. Lungs, maybe, so I could talk, but otherwise, not so much.

"You saved my life," a voice said.

The guardsman was looking at me, no longer quite so terrified.

"Looks that way," I said.

He got up, and then put his hand out to help me to my feet. I figured that was going to be it in terms of returning the favor, but he said, "I'll get you some bleach, needle, and thread for that. You need anything else, let me know."

I didn't have to think about it.

"A transfer, if you can manage it," I said. "One for the girl, too."

14

They had me sign some paperwork. I think it was because they wanted to see if I could write my name, so I tried not to misspell Seabrook. According to the form, I'd shown "unusual proactive behavior"—*unusual*, as the flamer explained, being what they were looking for at the Chambers Observation Center. We were being watched more than I thought. The raggedy? Well, that was a gimme. On her form it only said, "unusual."

It was bright and cold the day we were transferred. When the last bus of the day rolled in, fifty new chakz tumbled off. The incoming were increasing. When the bus left, it was only me, the raggedy, and the driver.

She sat across the aisle from me in the middle of the bus, close but not too close. Outside, a group of curious campers gathered to watch us go. She watched through the window, giving back the same dull expression they gave us.

Not looking at me, she asked, "Feel guilty leaving them behind?"

"I did get them some bleach and a few folding chairs," I told her.

"Some favor. Two went feral when they couldn't un-fold the chairs," she said.

I shifted in my seat and tried to look the other way. "Even if I overpowered the guards and got the gates open, they're all too far gone to know which way to run."

The bus rolled downhill. The camp finally vanished from sight. Can't say that relaxed me, but my sense of doom was less impending, until my travelling companion twisted my way, put her elbows to her knees, and asked, "How long have you been wearing that lame-ass disguise? You're that detective chak, right? Hessius Mann, the one the cops want?"

I guess I looked surprised, because she rolled her eyes. "Please. Maybe the LBs don't like looking, but half the camp knew, and like you said, they don't know much."

I raised the eyebrow that wasn't covered by scar putty. "And no one turned me in?"

"Most didn't care. The rest thought it'd be wrong to help the livebloods."

"And when did *you* spot me?"

What there was of her lips curled into a smile. "First time I saw you at the test center. I remembered you from the accident and the motel. You cost me some money, but you were the first person who's tried to help me out in a long time. Not easy to forget that."

"I hope that question I helped you with wasn't the one that got you in there."

She shrugged. "It's not like they go over the answers before they drag you off." Her expression grew puzzled.

"I thought you were getting me out because you were afraid I'd tell. You thought you had me fooled?"

"Guess I'm as good a detective as I am a disguise artist."

Her perplexed expression deepened. "But, if you didn't think I'd spotted you, why'd you get me out? Have a kid or something that looked like me?"

Funny, Nell Parker had trouble figuring out why I'd tried to help her, too. For that matter, I had trouble with it. Out of habit, I blew some air between my dried lips.

"No. No kids, no nephews, no nieces. I figured I owed you for kicking out your john, and pulling me away from those guards. Plus, you keep turning up, like a bad penny. A friend of mine would say there must be a reason for that. If you *are* going to keep turning up, at least this way I have the illusion of control."

She stared at me like I was crazy. "That is one crappy reason."

"You got a better one for anything you do?"

She shook her head, no.

I leaned across and nudged her shoulder. "You know my name. You got one?"

Her head listed, as if a muscle was missing. "I like Bad Penny."

"Bad Penny it is. You believe in Kyua, Penny?"

She sneered. "The only difference between Kyua and Santa Claus is that I used to believe in Santa."

On the way north, we made a few stops at registration centers, picking up one chak here, another there. The seats filled, but slowly. Only one caught my attention. At the Chambers test center, a tall chak got on, and when I say tall, I mean he could have played Lurch in *The Ad-*

dams Family. He wore a pressed suit and clean clothes, like he'd walked out of his own funeral. But it wasn't the clothes that made me stare. There was something about the way he carried himself that seemed, well, self-possessed.

Instead of numbly filing to the rear of the bus like the others, he stopped to help a one-legged man into a seat. Chakz helping chakz isn't unheard of, but there was another little detail. Before he sat, he unbuttoned his jacket, like he wanted to avoid creasing the fabric. He looked *intelligent*.

Once we were moving, I tried to get his attention, but he was too far away. I made a note about him with my recorder, then spent the rest of the trip wondering how Misty was, if she was climbing those twelve steps, or looking for a down escalator.

Unlike the overflow camp, the Chambers Observation Center was exactly the sort of thing I'd seen on Nell Parker's show. Instead of some fences and gates thrown up, there were buildings, created for the purpose of housing chakz. Not that they were built to last, but there were rows of them, with corrugated steel walls, composite doors, and actual windows that you could open and close. There were even a few brick-and-mortar structures, no doubt for the livebloods managing the place.

The outer fence was electrified, but there was a sign, and no charred limbs. Inside the fence? More fences, not electrified, but forming a dirt-floored maze. Within its confines, chakz ambled about. Some leaned against posts, some sat on benches. One was even reading a book. It was upside down, but still.

At first glance, the COC was nicer than most of the

hovels free chakz inhabited, on par with the larger shantytowns, minus the danger of weekly hakker raids.

Everyone on the bus was plastered to the windows as
we stopped in front of one of the brick-and-mortar jobs.
Exposed to the elements for I don't know how many
days, I was eager to get inside. But, I was in the middle
and had to wait forever for the others to shuffle out.
When it was finally my turn, I nearly barreled into the
tall chak with the suit.

"Sorry, buddy," I said.

He motioned me ahead. In a deep voice, he said. "No
problem."

It almost made me feel human.

Soon as we were off, two women in bright orange
worker's overalls took Bad Penny by the arms. I started,
and the kid was suspicious, but they weren't guards. They
were gentle, and explained to her that they had separate
facilities for raggedies.

The rest of us were divided by sex, then into groups of
four. I kept near Lurch, hoping we'd wind up in the same
area. Along with a bone-thin gleet with more tics than an
infected dog, and some sort of ooze coming out from a
hole in his face that wasn't his nose, we were the last
three.

A male worker marched us out into the fence maze.
The building walls held another sign of civilization; regu-
larly spaced bulletin boards. Most of the posts were
schedules prepared by the livebloods, regular exams and
so on. A few requests for volunteers caught my eye, as
did some of the "social events" in the main hall—art
therapy, disco dancing, a clothing swap.

These were all laser printed except one. Handwritten,

if you can call a Jack the Ripper–style scrawl handwriting, it said: "Kyua Prayer Group Every Night 8 P.M. Take part in your salvation."

Noticing I was eyeballing the sign, the worker recited, "Residents are free to enter the hall nine to twelve and three to nine."

"You got Ping-Pong?" I asked.

I was joking, and he laughed, but he also said, "Yes, we do."

I doubted there was much of a line.

He took us to our room and left us there. There was a slop sink, cots, chairs, and a couch facing a wall-mounted TV. With static on every channel, it looked like I wouldn't be watching Nell anytime soon, but at least I was where I'd planned on being for a change.

Not that I wanted to go snooping around right off. Bad Penny had rattled any confidence I had in the disguise. If anything, the LBs here were paying closer attention. Besides, after sitting in the dirt for days, I liked the idea of being comfortable for a few hours before getting into more trouble, so I chatted with my roomies.

Lurch was Franklin Gilmore, a family guy who'd once had a penchant for fast food and heart attacks. A misreading of his Do Not Resuscitate order led to him being immediately ripped. The twitchy guy was Palmer Hudson, former stockbroker.

Gilmore found a corner to lean against, I sprawled in one of the chairs. With the television off, Hudson's erratic pacing was the only entertainment. His constant twitching aside, one of his eyes was swollen, not like someone with a thyroid condition, *really* swollen, like an egg next to a marble.

The Hudson show went on. Pacing not enough, he rapped his fingers on the coffee table in a way that completely defied rhythm. Then he kicked over a wastebasket and started slapping his hand against a wall.

"Nervous?" I asked.

Gilmore wobbled, like he'd chuckled.

I didn't think there could be anything more irritating than Hudson's jerky movements until I heard his nasal, whiny voice. He shook his head, six or seven times, then came out with a rapid-fire stream of words. "Nah, nah, nah. I'm calm, perfectly calm. I'm a fucking Buddha. I always get calm in a place where they cut you up in tiny pieces and then experiment on the pieces."

"Cut? What makes you say that? Place looks pretty nice to me."

He practically screamed. "Isn't it *obvious?* We're lab rats!" The end table had a pen and pad on it. He grabbed the pen and stabbed the pad. "Lab rats they want to kill. Only they can't, so they try again." He stabbed the pad over and over, faster and faster, boring ink-stained holes into the paper. "And again and again and again!"

When the tip finally cracked, he stopped.

"Oh," I said.

Even if he knew something, he was too damaged to be much help. I hoped he didn't get ahold of another pen, or a knife.

Gilmore rose and shook his gentle giant head. "That's not what I hear, friend."

Hudson whirled. "Yeah, friend? What do *you* hear, friend? Crap about them looking for a way to cure us, friend? This is a fucking Nazi death camp, friend. The only difference is they haven't figured out how to kill us yet."

Gilmore frowned, but stayed calm. "They already know how to kill us. D-cap."

Hudson made a noise like a woodchuck throwing up. "Cheh-cheh-cheh. Right. Ever see a chak with a hole in his chest, major organs missing? He's still moving, ain't he?" He brought his hands together and squeezed them tight. "Can't just cut the head off, you gotta crush it. Even then, the pieces move. They're like legless bugs. That's us, fucking godless abominations."

I wondered what "special" attribute got him chosen for Camp Kyua. I was guessing it wasn't his social skills.

"He's right about the head," I said. "I've seen a few."

I hoped some validation would slow him down, but Hudson was shocked, like he hadn't said it himself first. "I'm *right*? Shit. Shit. Shit."

His right leg started dancing. Gilmore and I watched in silence for a while, hoping he'd run out of steam. This was worse than college. Fucking roommates.

I stood and tried to make eye contact. "Hey, maybe I'm wrong."

Hudson leapt up on the couch. "Wrong, wrong, wrong, wrong!"

At last, he stopped. His body, anyway. His skull was moving like a bobble head in a windstorm. Finally, he bounced out to find more room to pace.

Gilmore nodded at the door. "There's something wrong with him."

"I noticed."

"It's not just the spasms and the talking. He's different."

Gilmore settled on the couch. I was standing now, but

his head still came up to my shoulders. "I think I know what you mean," I said.

He turned his head toward me slowly. "If you ever decide to twist his head off, I'll sit on him for you."

I laughed, but had to ask, "You serious?"

"Were you serious about seeing those heads?"

"Sorry to say it, but yeah. Guess that gives them lots of reasons to experiment on us. Unless you think they're really looking for a cure?"

He pursed his lips. "I don't know, but what I like to believe, is that Kyua found the answer before he died."

I furrowed my brow. "Wait. Are you talking about the boffin, Travis Maruta, or the god? He's Kyua, this is Kyua, the cure is Kyua."

"The boffin."

"Where'd you hear that?"

"My daughter is a big fan of conspiracies, UFOs, that sort of thing. She'd read it somewhere. I always thought that stuff was ridiculous. But don't make fun. She visited me sometimes, before I failed the test."

"You must've been a good father, better than mine, anyway," I said. "She read anything else?"

He shrugged. "That they're hiding the cure to keep us down."

I shook my head. "Doesn't make sense, brother. If ChemBet could *really* bring people back to life, they'd be rich."

"I didn't say it made sense," he said with a little shiver of emotion. "But it's hope. My daughter gave it to me, so I plan to keep it. She said if we get enough of us into the testing facility, one of us may find it. We should all take a vow to try and bring it out. Maybe you'll be the lucky one. You have to believe in something, right?"

I gave him a smile. "Maybe, but every time I tell myself to cheer up, that things could be worse, I cheer up, and sure enough, things get worse."

He laughed, and his body calmed a little. "There's a chak here running Kyua meetings. I hear he's really smart. I saw you looking at one of the signs. Would you like to go to the meeting with me?"

I'd been planning to do just that. Now I'd have someone big to hide behind.

"Sure," I said.

Thankfully, it was time for the meeting before Hudson came back. Walking behind Gilmore, I followed a group through the maze and into the main hall, another temporary building, but with a tall roof. The first thing that surprised me was that there were about a hundred of us there. The second was that they were all smart enough to sit in folding chairs and face the same way.

"Praise Kyua!" the man behind the podium said with a shit-eating grin.

Son of a bitch.

Thinking I was impressed, Gilmore nudged me. "They say he used to be a politician."

I shook my head. "No. A motivational speaker."

I should know. There, at the front of the room, yakking about divine love and rebirth like he'd been born to it, was my old pal Jonesey.

15

Jonesey was a chak's worst enemy. He perpetually struggled against the darkness, kept a good thought, and tried to act "as if" the best were true. That sounds great, until you add in the fact that he was also the charismatic loon who organized the Dead Man March that caused the riots that caused the Chak Registration Act.

At the time I didn't think it was possible to have a zombie protest, like getting cats in a row, but I knew that having a bunch of walking corpses stroll down main street wasn't a good idea. Worried about Jonesey going feral, like an idiot I passed out a few of his brochures. Turned out I was wrong about the impossible part and right about it being a bad idea. When push came to shove, one chak went feral, then another and another and another. The livebloods, matching crazy for crazy, attacked in earnest, and everyone went wild.

Not that Jonesey ever considered for a moment that all these chak camps were his fault. He just kept acting "as if" right up until he failed his test. But here he was, eyes still sunken, goofy grin eternal. The only difference was that his old flannel shirt had been replaced with clean gray overalls that matched his skin. I was surprised he got the shirt off. He'd worn it so long, I thought for sure it'd melded with his skin.

For all my slack-jawed gawking, he didn't notice me. It wasn't my brilliant disguise, or the crowd. I could've been standing on a table with a Hessius Mann sign plastered on my chest and Jonesey wouldn't have blinked. He was too into himself to notice anything, in some sort of charismatic, ain't-I-hot-shit trance. He ambled along the short width of the podium, stopping now and then to shake his head at the foolishness of the world. Silly thing, the world.

Noticing I was the only one still standing, Gilmore tugged me into a seat.

Jonesey turned to the crowd and slammed his palms onto the fake wood.

"Life from death!" he cried out. "Whoa. That is one long mother of a trip to take without a map."

When the echo of his voice stopped, you could hear a pin drop. Then again, the audience was used to keeping still.

"And the LBs hate us for it, right? We're *other*, big-time. Not just from another country. It's not like we're going to open delis and integrate ourselves into the culture. It's not like we're bringing some strange new beliefs that'll undermine the basic tenets of the American way of life. We *are* American. We have no other country to go back to. So we can't leave. And that makes them hate us all the more."

His voice had more timbre to it than I remembered.

"But we are from another country in a way, what Shakespeare called the undiscovered country. Death. Ask for directions and they'll say you can't get there from here. But we did, didn't we? We got this far." He nodded enthusiastically, answering his own question. "Oh yes, we did."

A few chakz parroted the nod. Gilmore did it, too.

"Only, it wasn't a choice, was it? We didn't do it by ourselves. We didn't head back under our own power. I didn't, did you?"

A few groaned, "No."

"No, it was done *to* us. No one asked. We were just brought back, brought here. We don't understand how. We don't even know how long we're staying. We don't know much at all. If only I knew now what I knew then, right? But there is one thing we *do* know, one thing we know for a fact. We know it in our bones. And what is it?"

He scanned the crowd like a teacher expecting a raised hand.

A garbled sound came from up a chak up front: "Paghhr mbrgll!"

Jonesey pointed at him like he was Einstein. "That's it! That's it exactly! We know *it can't be forever*. Truth of the universe. Forget death, forget taxes. Nothing is forever. Nothing. Everything ends. Everything."

His fingers were a little stiff, but he did his best to wave them around, including this and that in his everything. "This wood, these chairs, those walls, everything. What's inside, what's outside, the sun, the stars, everything."

He dropped his hands dramatically. "But what does that mean to us? It means that even *death* dies. Even death. Look in the mirror. We're the proof. We killed death. We kicked death's ass. We're his conquerors. We sure as hell look like it, don't we? Don't we?"

More nods from the crowd.

"Yes, we do. Zero to our bones, spiderweb minds, ashen hearts. We all *look* like what we are, people who kicked death's motherfucking ass."

He pounded the podium with each word, then all at once, he dropped his smile. "But if we didn't ask to be brought here, how'd it happen? What brought us to the fight? What's carried us this far? The radical invigoration procedure? Some machine that filled our inanimate sacks with electrostatic magic? The liveblood technician who pushed the button on the machine? Maybe. Maybe. The man who built the machine? Dr. Travis Maruta, praised be his name? Maybe. But who brought them? Who brought Dr. Maruta? Kyua."

His voice rose to a shout again: "Kyua, Kyua, Kyua! The source, the cure, the core! And why did Kyua bring us here? Why did Kyua do this to us?"

Because Kyua sucks? —came to mind, but that wasn't where he was going. This camp had been good to him, I'd give him that. Out in the Bones, his enthusiasm had been stuttering at best.

Jonesey answered his own question: "To test us. We've been tested, we're being tested, and Kyua willing we will soon be tested again . . . in ChemBet. And we will pass. Sooner or later, we'll all pass. How can anyone think for a second that Kyua *won't* bring us the rest of the way, put sinew on our bones, cover us with new skin, make us breathe not just to speak, but because we need the air? Sure, we're the walking dead, making our way through a dark forest. But how far can you walk into a forest? Halfway. After that, you're walking out. Kyua walked us in, Kyua will walk us out. Kyua is in our bones. We carry Kyua, we bring Kyua to Kyua. Kyua is here, Kyua is coming, Kyua is eternal!"

At that point, I didn't have the slightest idea what the fuck he was talking about. I doubt anyone else did, either, but they all seemed to like it a lot. The sound of their approval wasn't like liveblood applause, quick wet hoots and hollers. This was slower, more about grunting and jostling whoever was next to you.

And that was it. Jonesey was done talking. The meeting was over.

Some chakz stayed seated, confused about what to do next, others shuffled out, but a decent-sized crowd made its way up front, to bask in the presence of the big J himself. Chakz with questions?

When I didn't budge, Gilmore nudged me. "He speaks well."

"Yeah. Uh . . . what did you think content-wise?"

"I think my daughter would like me to believe him, so I'll try. You?"

I didn't want to tell him I knew Jonesey. "Long story. If you don't mind, I'll stay a while. Maybe you should head back to the room to see if Hudson left anything standing."

"Hudson," he said. With a vague head shake, he rose.

Once he was out of sight, I made my way toward the chak-pack at the podium. They were all talking. As I got closer, I made out a few words. Most were off-topic, but still.

"Think I left the stove on . . . left the stove . . ."

"Have you met *Kyua*?"

"When . . . he . . . come . . . ?"

"Did you get milk?"

"Are you him?"

I waited as long as I could for a gap in the noise, gritted my teeth and called out, "Jonesey!"

He'd been smiling beneficently, but the sound of my voice put a curious expression on his face. He looked up and stared straight at me, until a noseless woman grabbed him, twisted his head around and gave his cheek a peck.

Was she actually *kissing* him?

"Asshole!" I said, louder.

He pulled away from her, looked my way again and rattled off a string of words. "Guest . . . mess . . . rest . . ."

It was the memory game he played. It worked well enough. Despite the corpse bride trying to kiss him on the cheek again, he got there. ". . . chest . . . Herbert West. Hess. Hess? Is that you? What, are you in disguise? Are you hiding?"

When they saw his widening smile directed my way, the little crowd parted for me like the Dead Sea.

I stepped closer and grunted. "Trying."

He pulled free of the kisser and whispered, "Right. The cops want you. What're you doing here?"

"Looking for information. Figures I'd find you, instead."

He clicked his teeth. "Same old Hess. Keeping it real. I'm so sorry about Chester. How's Misty taking it?"

"A real piece of work kidnapped her, forced some crack into her. I got her out of it. Now she's with her sponsor and I . . . don't know how she's taking anything."

Seeing someone familiar, I guess I'd been hoping for

a real conversation. Jonesey, as usual, skipped over the ugly part.

"But you, you're okay. You. Are. A. Survivor. Say it with me."

I shook my head. "Little late for surviving, don't you think? I'd like to say it's good to see you, Jonesey, but the platitudes are making it tough. Can you cut the crap for old time's sake?"

He gave me a noncommittal shrug. The kisser had come up behind him, slow like a shadow, and started nibbling at his ear. Not in a cannibal way, more like she was sucking on a pacifier, which only made it creepier. Jonesey acted as if he hadn't noticed her. "What kind of information are you looking for?"

For half a second he looked like the down-and-out corpse I'd once used as an informant.

"For starters, how much of this Kyua bullshit is grounded in actual fact?"

He scowled. "All of it. All of it's real."

Finally noticing the kisser, he pushed her away like she was a big fly. It was gentle, as shoves go, but she stumbled back, sank to her knees, and took to sobbing like she'd been slapped by a lover. When the sobs didn't get an immediate reaction, she started wailing.

"Newcomer," Jonesey said, as if apologizing for her. He knelt and petted her, his hand a gray wallet against the dried grass of her hair.

"It's okay," he said. "Kyua loves you."

He kissed her on the forehead. She closed her eyes and quieted. Other than a freaky snog between myself and Nell Parker, it was the most affection I'd ever seen between two chakz.

When he rose, she stayed put, as if awaiting further orders.

"A lot of chakz had faith when they were alive," he said. "Sure, after they died, some stopped believing, but some didn't. Right now, here in the camp, we've got a Muslim who still does his five daily prayers, six practicing Christians, and a Buddhist. But most chakz feel abandoned, like belief is only for the livebloods, that by our nature we're damned, or somehow not part of God's world. It doesn't make them any less hungry for hope. So, Kyua. So, it's real."

I squirmed. "Let me rephrase the question. How much of this bullshit has some kind of objective basis? As in, do you know what kind of projects ChemBet is really working on?"

"Ah," Jonesey said, crooking a finger. "Let's talk."

Moving at a decent clip that left the other chakz behind, he led me to the rear of the hall. I hated to say it, but it was more than his voice that had improved. He looked . . . healthier.

As we maneuvered the chain-link maze, he pointed out a few security cameras I'd never have spotted. "Those are video only. They don't have the staff to monitor everyone round the clock, so they rely on audio sensors designed to detect moaners."

Suddenly he grinned and grabbed me around the shoulder. "Detective work! Ha! Been so long since the streets and all that badass stuff. Should I call you by some code name in case someone's listening?"

"The name on the card I used is Seabrook. But from what I've heard, the disguise isn't great. It's only a matter of time before a liveblood spots me."

"You have *got* to fix that attitude! You are a *master* of disguise! Stop being so negative." He moved his shoulders upward, giving me a glimpse of his old plaid shirt, still on under the jumpsuit. So maybe it had melded with his skin.

"I'm not negative. I'm positive. I'm positive you're crazy. This isn't about self-image, it's about a ticking clock. Nothing lasts forever, right? So whatever I do has to be sooner rather than later."

He opened his mouth in a way that made me terrified he'd launch into another motivational speech, but a mechanical trill from his pocket cut him off. I recognized the first few notes of Michael Jackson's "*Thriller*." Looking like the arrogant Yuppie he must have been in life, Jonesey held up a finger as he flipped open his cell.

"Martha! You did it! You *dialed* the phone and now you're *talking* to someone! You didn't think you could do that yesterday, did you? Now focus on remembering how I set it up for you—I'm four, like a *door*, your sister is five, 'cause she's still *alive*. Four door, five alive. Got it? You go, girl!"

He flipped it shut.

I stared at him. "You can program your cell?"

Proud as a puppy who'd learned to crap on the newspaper, he nodded. "Takes like an hour to get one number into the speed dial, but, well, I have a lot of time here."

Swapping the chain-link walls for corrugated steel, we reached an intersection between buildings. Jonesey pointed at one of the doors. "Mine, but we should probably talk out here."

"Afraid I'll contaminate the positive energy?"

"More like my work may have merited some extra

attention. I'm doing so much to keep spirits up here, they may never ship me to the testing labs." He got quiet for a bit, then noticed I was staring. "What? Do I have a piece of chak on me somewhere?"

"No, it's just . . . you look . . . *better*. I'm not saying you'll win any beauty contests, but your eyes are clearer, you're more reactive. You've even lost a bit of your slouch. If we ate, I'd wonder if they were slipping something into the food."

He looked around, at the walls and fences. "It's simpler than that. Losing your freedom is supposed to be terrible, but think about it. We're out of the elements, we have roofs, a slower pace, the bleach is free. The lack of stress really works for us. What was it, a month ago you said I went feral? Since I've been here, nothing."

"Next you'll tell me that no one ever goes feral here in Shangri-la."

"Fewer than you'd think," he said. He pointed to a chak lazing in a chair like he was sunning himself. "Hagado there used to be a concert pianist. When he arrived he was so out of it, even I thought he'd blow in a day. That was weeks ago. Now he's picking out "*Twinkle Twinkle Little Star*" with one finger. Sure, it's not *his* finger. I don't know where he found it, but still, failing that test on purpose was the smartest thing I've ever done."

"You failed *on purpose*?"

"Hey, hey, hey! You said yourself I look better . . ."

If there were any moisture in my mouth, I'd have spit on him. "This is a showplace for the press, so they can show the world how humanely we're treated. All your preaching helps them out! You're a patsy." I grabbed the cloth of his jumpsuit. "Do you have *any* idea what the other camps are like?"

He held my wrists and actually forced me to let go. I hadn't remembered him being that strong. A gravity crept across his face. "As a matter of fact, Hess, I do. The overflow camps where they take most of us are just walls, or fences. They don't even have buildings, let alone bleach. They're pens where you wait to rot or go feral. Close enough?"

I was still angry, but caution kicked in. I rubbed my wrists, checked for loose bones. "You're still connected. How?"

"The cell phones. Every chak has one, right? I've got eyes in the other camps, Fort Hammer, and more. The only place I don't hear from is the lab. They take the phones away after orientation. But it's a great network to spread the news when it happens."

"When what happens?"

"This is more than a showplace. This camp really does supply test subjects for ChemBet. One day soon, they'll find a way to bring us back to life. Real life."

"Bullshit. At best ChemBet's trying to figure out how to kill us. At worst, they're making new monsters."

He put a hand on my shoulder. "For an old friend, I'll put it another way, real obvious. If you had, like, terminal cancer, and there was the slightest chance of a cure, wouldn't you want to try it?"

I tried to steady my body. "Not if it was from the same freaks who gave me the cancer. Travis Maruta committed suicide because of what his work had done. Maybe Kyua knew something you don't?"

"His death doesn't matter. It's not his body. Forget

soul if you have to. It's his ideas, the ones that make their way out into the world and change it. It's his wife, his employees, even his notes. All that's alive. All that's hope. All that's Kyua."

"You're nuts, Jonesey."

He crossed his arms over his chest. "Okay, now tell me how that makes me different from you?"

He had me there.

"See? So tell me why you're here. What are you looking for? I know you're not just hiding out."

It was a mistake to answer. I knew what he'd think the blue stuff was, but with Misty gone, I didn't have anyone to bounce things off. Jonesey clearly knew the place, and his connections were usually real. So I told him the whole story, even the parts no one else would believe. As I spoke, he got excited, blasts of air flying from his nose like he'd discovered a new way of laughing.

"Hess, you beautiful bastard! Hess! That's it! You've got it! It's got to be the cure! And you don't even believe in fate."

That much I expected, now the trick was whether I could talk him down. "Easy on the Kool-Aid, Jim Jones. Maybe someday your Kyua will come, but think about the current situation. That arm didn't get divorced from its body due to irreconcilable differences. Saying something's fishy is an understatement."

But Jonesey wasn't about to let the facts ruin his fun. "I've got connections, we can get you out tomorrow. You go, you get it, and you bring it back to my people! We'll test it ourselves!"

I looked behind him. "You got a lab up your ass? Decontamination suits? You said yourself it takes you an hour to punch a number into a cell phone."

"So bring it back to ChemBet! I'll make the call. I'll get you immunity!"

When he flipped open the phone, I slapped it out of his hand.

"Stop it! Haven't you heard anything I've said? At least three groups are looking for this stuff? Don't be crazy."

He looked at the fallen cell. "They said Einstein was crazy."

"They also called a lot of crazy people crazy! Look what they did to Misty."

"But with Kyua it can all be fixed. All of it. Misty could even bring back Chest—"

Before he could finish the sentence, I slammed him into the wall.

"You *don't* know what that stuff is."

Jonesey moved his head back and forth, but didn't try to get away. "Forget I mentioned it. Forget I mentioned that *you* might have the power to save everyone. Don't even try, Hess. Just let us all . . . rot."

I hissed at him. "Sing 'Kyua-Kumbaya' all you want, but deep down, you try to remember how we all got here. Two steps. The first, Maruta and ChemBet. Remember who they are. The second step, *you*. Remember who *you* are."

"Oh? Who am I?"

I had to spell it out for him. "You, Jonesey, are the idiot who put together a chak rally that turned into a massacre. How many chakz burned that day? How many livebloods died? Got a rhyming game for that? A mousand, a louseand . . . a *thousand!* All the camps we've got now, full of rotting chakz? *Your* fault, Jonesey. Yours. Next time you make a speech about how we should dance into that testing facility, think about where you led us last time! Remember who you are."

Maybe I got through. He wasn't smiling anymore, at least.

"I will, Hess. Long as you remember who *you* are."

16

I thought I'd had it when they brought me in for my first physical, but Jonesey insisted it would be fine, that I just had to keep a good thought. He also told me he had a surprise for me later. I couldn't wait.

Half the walls were cinder block, half white cloth mounted on wheeled frames. The floor plan could be changed at will, like flats on a theater stage rearranged for different scenes. Yesterday, it could've been a supply space, today it was a medical exam room. The overall effect left me feeling like I was in a pretend-doctor's office.

My shirt was off. Some chubby guy in a lab coat, cigarette dangling from chicken lips, pressed a stethoscope into various parts of my body. If he'd actually been a doctor, he'd have spotted my fake scar, but I guess he was just playing one on TV. Then again, he did have the stethoscope on the right way. And a dead body, sans the élan, je ne sais quoi, or whatnot, looks fake to begin with. A mannequin might look natural to someone staring at torn, dried flesh and dangling limbs all day.

I acted my part, exaggerating my limp, twisting my body. Whenever he got near the fake hair, or the eye-glob, I shivered and winced as if it hurt like crazy. That was easy, since my eye did hurt, ever since the flame-throwers. I wondered if the scar-putty had welded onto my eyelid, the way Jonesey's plaid shirt was part of his skin. There was going to be hell to pay when I pulled it off.

If I ever pulled it off.

Dr. Death couldn't care less. When he wasn't prodding me or making notes on a tablet, he was flicking ashes on the floor. Despite his shape, or lack thereof, he was young, probably a low-level researcher, and just nerdy enough to wear a pocket protector with the ChemBet logo on it.

He took some time fingering the bullet hole, grunting what sounded like approval about the stitches. It was dry now, whatever wetness having seeped out long ago.

"You patch this yourself?"

"Yeah."

I got a big note for that. Maybe I'd be nominated for membership in the sewing circle. Past that, I wasn't sure what he was looking for, but I hoped he'd found it. If I was ever going to figure out what was going on with those vials, I'd have to get into the lab.

A new screen flashed on the tablet. He blinked, read the first line, then said in a cheery voice, "My name is Steven. How long have you been here, Mr. . . . . Seabrook?"

Was it two days or three? Not sure, I reached over to where my jacket hung on a hook and pulled out my recorder. With a prissy sort of disapproval, he took it away before I could press PLAY.

"Hey! That's mine, pal. Bought and paid for."

He didn't look at me, just made a note, then spoke again.

"My name is Steven. The point of this part of the exam is to test your memory. You'll get it back when we're done. What did I just ask you?"

"How long I've been here?"

"Great. And the answer is?"

I tried to sound certain. "Two days."

He made a note. "And what's my name?"

I knew Dr. Death was the wrong answer, but past that . . .

"Uh . . ."

He looked up at me and asked again. "What's my name?"

When livebloods talk about memory farts, they say things like I drew a blank, or it's on the tip of my tongue. This was more like you're walking along and the road, which was fine a second ago, disappears. There's a blank spot where the path was, and not so much as a detour sign.

I could tell from the look in Dr. Death's eyes that I'd failed. There was more, a light in my uncovered eye that I kept seeing long after he pulled it away, some raps on my knee with a little rubber hammer that made my hand twitch. We both thought that was pretty funny, actually.

Then he handed me my recorder and told me to put my shirt back on.

"That it?" I asked.

"Uh-huh."

"Do I get in?"

I guess I sounded eager, because his eyes narrowed. "Do you believe in Kyua?"

Should I lie? Was it part of the test or was he satisfying his own curiosity?

"I believe in better living through chemistry."

I didn't get a lollipop, but he gave me an admiring nod. "Good sense of humor."

I pointed at the tablet. "You want to make a note of that?"

He shrugged, making his cigarette bounce a little. "Maybe next month, if you're still funny."

"I don't, don't, don't want to! No way, no way!"

The commotion came from behind one of the screens. The hanging fluorescents didn't cast any shadows, but as the hubbub grew, someone staggered into the screen, pushing the cloth back and giving us a look. I didn't really have to see who it was. I'd recognized the voice, the way the pitch jangled what nerves I had. It was Hudson.

Two interns were trying to stuff him into a straitjacket. As one tightened the straps, the other pulled the privacy wall back into place. Hudson's voice grew muffled, like he'd been gagged.

I felt like I should try to get him out so he could spend his days happily twitching in a field on some farm, but there wasn't much I could do. Dr. Death had buried his head in the tablet as if he were trying to pretend nothing had happened.

"Hey," I said. "That's my roomie. His name is Hudson. I don't think he wants to go."

He kept looking down. "According to our tests, he

doesn't know what he wants. He's paranoid, delusional. Besides, legally he doesn't have a choice."

"Is it really paranoia when some people are out to shove you into a straitjacket and experiment on you?"

"That question is above my pay scale."

I was going to say flipping burgers was above his pay scale, but I asked, "Why take him and not me?"

"Dr. Maruta's doing a study on chakz with severe nerve damage."

"Maruta? I thought he was dead."

He eyed me like I was still failing his fucking test. "Dr. Rebecca Maruta. His wife. She's head of the department now."

I'd read that somewhere. "Right."

Once the muffled protests faded, Dr. Death sent me on my way. "See you again in about a month."

A month. I was afraid by then I'd forget why I was here, but I headed out like a good little corpse, following the exit arrows along the cinder block, glancing around to see if I could tell where they'd taken Hudson.

I was almost out of the building when I saw Jonesey coming in. I slowed as we neared each other. "Can some of those strings you pull get me into the lab?"

He stopped short and stared at me. "You failed? They don't want you?"

"Sue me." I needed him, so I tried to be conciliatory. "Look, if I get in and find out ChemBet's on the level, I'll give them the stuff, okay?"

The right side of his lips shot up in a wry half smile. "You're so convinced they're evil, it wouldn't matter what you found."

"Evil's a big word. Let's just say I think they're wildly incompetent."

He shook his head again. "I can't help you."

"Come on, Jonesey. For Misty."

"I didn't say wouldn't, I said I couldn't. I just pulled in every favor I had, and even then it wasn't easy to get them to let me go until I said I'd cancel the Kyua meetings. You may think you're powerless, Hess, but our chat had an effect on me. It made me decide to stop talking about faith and put my money where my mouth is. That was my surprise, but I thought you'd be coming with me."

It took me a second. "You're going to the lab? How soon?"

"Today. We load up behind the meeting hall at four p.m. It's a nice big bus, I've seen it, air-conditioning, cushioned seats, LCD screens, the works. They may even have a movie for the drive. I'm going to Kyua in style, Hess. And I have you to thank for it."

"They just dragged my roomie off in a straitjacket, kicking and screaming. He says it's like a torture chamber. Thank me if they don't cut you up into pieces."

"Hudson, right?" Jonesey tsked. "I think he'd be in pain no matter where he was. Just doesn't get it, just won't let go."

"Ah . . . I'm not even going to bother trying to talk you out of it. Is there any way you can sneak me onto the bus?"

He bobbed his head. "Residents are encouraged to say good-bye to friends, and a few always show up. It wouldn't be strange for you to be hanging around. You'd never make it onto the bus, that they're real careful about. Don't pay much attention to the baggage holds, though. I could pack a little something to put there, try to wedge a strap into the latch so it doesn't close all the way. The rest would be up to you, but I *know* you can do it."

He was wrong about "a few" chakz showing. Once word spread that their high priest was ascending, anyone who could walk, slouch, or crawl had to be there. They all said their good-byes, some to Jonesey, some to fellow chakz, others to fence posts.

The guard at COC usually looked pretty calm, but there were so many postmortem well-wishers, I could tell they were worried. They looked even more tense when they had to pry a few residents off of Jonesey. The ear-biter was back, and she was the toughest. When they pulled her away, she started in with the sobbing again.

Once he was a safe distance from her, Jonesey turned back. "It's okay! It's okay!" Thumb to his ear, his pinky to his mouth, he nodded and said, "You can still call me until after I'm in orientation, like I showed you. One for fun, two for you."

She reached into her pocket, pulled out a cell phone, and stared at it like she was going to eat it.

With that little kindness crossed off his to-do list, Jonesey, a rucksack over his shoulder, walked to the far side of the bus. He reappeared without it, waving to the crowd.

"You can *all* call. Kyua is coming!" he said before climbing into the bus.

With him no longer sucking up all the attention, I spotted someone else I knew among the boarders. Surprise, surprise, it was Bad Penny. I hadn't seen her since we arrived. They'd put her in some cheerier, more child-like clothing that didn't quite go with her skin or disposition. Looking miserable, she marched on in behind Jonesey. I hoped the hell I hadn't rescued her from the frying pan just to shove her into the fire.

The other passengers, hepped up on Kyua, all looked thrilled, all except Hudson, that is. Even in his straitjacket, he had to be forced on.

With Jonesey out of sight, the crowd didn't thin as much as dribble off. The last few chakz still boarding, I made like I was leaving, but headed to the far side of the bus. Like Jonesey said, it was a big sucker. The chak heads pressed against the tinted windows looked like senior citizens being taken to Atlantic City.

Eyes on the guards, I put my back to the aluminum side and felt along the lip of the first baggage compartment. Locked tight. I shifted to door number two. It looked just as closed, but when I pulled, it popped open into the back of my legs.

Good old Jonesey.

Speaking of mixed bags, I went to my knees, slipped in, moved the rucksack off the latch, and yanked the door shut. When nothing happened for a minute, I figured no one had spotted me.

It was cozy for a luggage hold, roomy, and not completely dark. The seams let in some light from outside. A tug at the lining gave me a view up into the seating area. I saw Jonesey in his comfy chair, head bopping to a tune only he could hear, pleased as could be. If the bright socks and buckled shoes were any indication, Penny sat next to him, looking like she was trying to ignore him.

He leaned forward, tapped on her little knee, and said with a smile, "We're going to Kyua."

I heard her voice answer: "Are you fucking nuts?"

If I ever had a daughter of my own, Penny would probably kick the shit out of her.

As the bus farted exhaust and rolled out of Camp Chambers, it finally came to me.

Steven. The doctor's name was Steven.

17

ChemBet was undead itself in a way. It started life as a pharmaceutical company in the early nineteenth century, back when folks like J. Marion Sims used a shoemaker's awl to move around the skull bones of enslaved babies. Now he's called the father of gynecology. Anyway, they expanded into things like medical devices and women's sanitary napkins. They were the world's third-largest drug company when the Marutas came to work for them.

Consistently named a great place for working mothers, they were trusted a bit more than their competitors. ChemBet was top-notch, as well liked as giant corporations get. That's one reason the RIP spread so quickly. Another was, of course, the whole bringing the dead back thing.

They were number one for a while there, but when people saw the results, fingers pointed, heads rolled, and a CEO or two resigned in disgrace. Ultimately, though, ChemBet was too big to fail, and went on its merry way.

Like me, it'd gotten this far. Must mean something, right? Then again, if you drive a car off a cliff, you can pretend you're flying right up until you hit bottom.

The wheels on the bus went round and round. It was warm on one side of me, cold on the other. I drifted off, but wouldn't call it peaceful. I dreamt I was alive. Dad was there, storming around the house, looking for his fingers, insisting I'd misplaced them.

"If your fucking head wasn't attached, you'd lose that, too!"

Even then, I couldn't do anything right. Where the hell had I left those fingers? Dad was so pissed, he forced me to chew on the neighbor's collie.

"Chewing dogs is all you're good for!"

It was weird, even for him.

When I woke up, my wig was off and half in my mouth, which explained the part about the dog. The real hairs on my head, exposed to the air for the first time in a long while, hurt. The engine thrumming was gone and it was dark even along the cracks.

Once I finished pulling synthetic strands from my teeth, I felt the wig. In the dark, I couldn't tell if there was enough left to bother trying to wear. For better or worse, I'd eaten my disguise.

Reluctantly, I tried to peel away the scar-putty. That didn't work, so I pulled, and then yanked. There was a disturbing tearing sound as a big blob of something came free. Harder bits seemed stuck in the gunk. It felt wet to the touch. I hoped I hadn't yanked out my eye. Pain is tricky with chakz. Sometimes we feel it, sometimes we don't.

Well, getting caught as Hessius Mann *might* be the better move. Legally, they'd have to turn me over to the police. Corporations always follow the law, don't they? And maybe pigs would fly out of my butt and give everyone in Fort Hammer a free e-reader.

At least knowing where their precious McGuffin was hidden gave me a bargaining chip.

All undressed with no place to go, I listened to the stillness, then pushed the door halfway open. A lack of wind coupled with the feeble glow of a distant emergency exit sign told me I was inside. I rolled out. My eyes, or maybe *eye*, as adjusted to the dark as it was going to get, I stood. My legs wobbled precariously, the muscles stiff from the trip.

The space was cool, tall and wide, the air mixed with the smell of concrete, gas, and oil. Calling it a garage would've been an insult. I was in a full-fledged vehicular depot. A huge vent system, for exhaust fumes, ran above three buses, four vans, two utility vehicles, and three golf carts.

Otherwise, it was empty as a tomb.

I made for the exit sign, eventually hearing a soft buzz. I thought it was the sign, but it came from behind the gray fire door below it. Either the door seam was completely sealed, or there was no light on the other side either.

I put my ear to the metal. The hum was louder, but I didn't hear anything else. Not seeing any alarms connected to the handle, I pushed. It opened into a cinderblock hall, dim, but not completely lightless. Stepping in, I lost any sense of the hum's direction. It was all around, like generators, or warp engines.

Twenty yards to the right, a set of double doors oozed bright light at the edges. Once I was in the lab, staying out of sight for long would be tough. But staying out here would be pretty useless.

The hall beyond the doors was wider and more finished, lined with two-tone drywall, lit by fluorescents. Faux wooden doors sat at regular intervals, each with a chart hung in the center. Wheeled metal carts sat near the doors, all with instruments like scalpels and probes. At the end of the hall stood a tall canvas laundry cart, a sign designating the contents as medical waste. But you could say that about any chak.

I crept to the closest door and had a look at the chart. The name at the top rang a bell. One of the chakz from the camp. Checking more charts, I found Jonesey's, but decided to keep moving. Bad Penny might be around, but I didn't know her real name. Hudson was here, and that was about it for names I knew.

I was almost at the end of the hall when the handle on the door to Hudson's room turned. I'd barely ducked behind the laundry bin when the end of a gurney emerged. Judging from the way the legs vibrated, Hudson was on it. He shook so much, the gurney slammed the sides of the doorway, making it tough for whoever was pushing to get it into the hall.

I heard tsks of disapproval, then male grunts. The gurney straightened and wobbled into the hall, revealing Hudson's struggling arms, one wrist sporting a thick plastic tag. His head appeared last. It looked like my former roomie had a lot to say, but the black strap holding the gag in his mouth made it tough to make out.

Two strong men, one pale white, the other African

American, but otherwise looking like a matching set, manned the gurney. Behind them, a troll-like figure emerged. It was my first glimpse of Maruta's widow, Rebecca, the dominatrix.

As her men straightened the dolly, she marched in front of them. Petite describes her size, but compact's a better word. She was compact with razor blue eyes, red hair coiffed with deadly seriousness and a nose so pointy you could impale fairies on it. Her thin arms elbow deep in black rubber gloves, her yellow lab coat flowed around her shapely figure like a gown. But even her curves looked like something you'd cut yourself on.

Once in the lead, she looked back. "Keep the gag on until he's in prep. Make sure the doors are sealed and the monitors off. I don't want any records of this."

Her tone had the even clarity of an instruction manual, but as that last bit sunk in, her lackeys eyed each other.

"Come now, it's the end of a long week. I'm allowed some fun, aren't I? I just want to see what exactly causes the dyssynchrony. It will be the only useful thing he's done since he died."

She passed me, then disappeared around the corner, allowing the men a moment alone. The white, sandy-haired one looked like he was about to puke. The other's expression said, *forget about it now, we'll talk later when she isn't here.*

They steered the gurney into the boss lady's invisible wake. A few more rattles from Hudson made them hit the bin I was hiding behind. It tilted right in front of me, but not enough to tip over.

I heard elevator doors open, the rubber wheels roll

inside. When the doors closed, I got up and followed. The light told me they'd stopped on the second of three floors. A sign next to the elevator said, IN CASE OF EMERGENCY USE STAIRS, so I did. All the stairwell doors had tall vertical windows, so I had a peek at the second floor. Beyond a high-ceilinged area was a set of thick, windowed specialty doors made of some sort of high-end plastic, or composite material. According to the sign next to them, they were sealing off something called the Sterile Zone.

From the looks of things, the Sterile Zone was having itself a hygienic hoedown. Figures with gloves and face masks kept moving past the windows. It didn't take a genius to guess Hudson was in there somewhere. Whatever Ms. Maruta had planned that she didn't want recorded, I doubted it was Jonesey's miracle cure. Granted I didn't like the guy, but I already liked her less.

Rescues have never been a specialty, but I knew if I waltzed in and tried to stop them with my clever banter, I'd likely wind up getting the same treatment. There were other possibilities, such as creating a distraction like they did in the movies. A red plastic button sat beside the mega-doors, marked IN CASE OF EMERGENCY. If I slapped the sucker, bet it'd make some noise. But what about after that? Where would I hide? Their safety protocol would send them all running into me. The building was big. There'd have to be more buttons. All I had to do was find one.

I headed up another flight, to a carpeted office suite full of plants and potted trees, like it was pretending it was outside. I was on tiptoes at the stairwell window, trying to see if there was another EMERGENCY button around

when a thirty-something female in a smart business outfit popped out of her office. I ducked as she passed. When
she got on the elevator, I slipped through the door she
left open and locked it behind me.

Most of the room was taken up by one of those glass
desks with a metal frame. I thought they were supposed
to make things look neater, but aside from the mess on
top, the glass provided a great view of the mess beneath.
Next to a coffee mug in a light brown pool, and a photo
of a chubby-faced eight-year-old, sat a laptop, which
meant I had a shot at actually finding out about the vials.

There were two open documents, one was Hudson's
file with notes from the boss lady. Mistress Maruta had
actually done some homework, she even had a theory
about why he was so irritating. Maybe she wasn't as second rate as her reputation indicated.

There were a lot of ten-dollar words describing how
Hudson's nervous system had the "peculiar ability to dis-
rupt interactional synchrony." I gave myself a pat on the
back for following as much as I did. Apparently, every
conversation has a rhythm that creates expectations.
Hudson was perpetually offbeat, disorienting and ultimately infuriating to anyone who talked to him for long.
His arrival in the Sterile Zone was listed, but the list
didn't give me any idea whether they'd be giving him a
CAT scan or yanking stuff out just to see what happened.

The second document was a quarterly overview of the
lab's various projects. There were enough incomplete
sentences to tell me it was a work in progress, but it
spelled out the boffins' best guesses on how chakz
worked. Since it was an internal ChemBet document, it

was the first thing I'd ever read about chakz I thought maybe I could trust. I was fascinated to say the least.

Before he tap-danced off the mortal coil, Travis Maruta theorized that we chakz had something in our brains, previously known only to exist in sharks, called the *ampulla of Lorenzini*. Sounds like a nice Italian beach, but it's actually a set of nerve clusters that detect living things through their electrical activity. Sharks use it to find prey. Travis was pretty sure it also existed in LBs, but geared toward sensing the presence of fellow humans, explaining the way people can often tell when someone's watching.

In chakz, the ampullae are overactive, something Rebecca had proven just last week. Not only that, she'd demonstrated that chakz give off less than half the electromagnetic field of a liveblood, making us tougher to sense, especially when we go motionless. We sense LBs easy, they can't sense us.

I wanted to say *cool*, but there wasn't anything about *how* she'd proven this stuff, an omission that irritated my *ampulla of There's Something Fucked Up About This Place*. Fun fact: Doctors still use the data Nazis collected by dunking people in freezing water to help treat hypothermia.

I felt dirty, but I kept reading, especially a section on the chak limbic system. That's part of the brain that controls behavior, emotion, and, you guessed it, long- and short-term memory. In chakz both were totally screwed. Our "myelin sheaths" were way thin and "exhibited extreme peculiarities" maybe explaining the distance we feel from our own bodies.

At the same time, in "emotionally charged situations"

those peculiar neurons go into overload, lighting up like a switchboard, explaining that electric syrup sensation I get. Continued sheath degradation could be what made chakz feral. A particularly long sentence suggested intensive amino acid therapy, but by then my attention span for the big words had been exhausted. Most of what I was learning only confirmed what I'd suspected all along—even ChemBet didn't know all that much about us for sure.

I rubbed my brows, looked away, and happened to catch my reflection in the window. Finally, a little good news. The lid looked droopy, like a pillowcase a size too large, but my eye was still there. Three cheers for depth perception.

But as long as I had the belly of the beast open in front of me, I had to focus on what I needed. Which was . . . what? An interoffice memo about a missing arm and a briefcase?

Finished with the open documents, I accessed the network, excited to find what looked like the late Travis Maruta's personal directory. At least it had his name on it. Unfortunately, the only file, called "StarStuff," was password protected. I tried "password" and "admin" but the boffins were smarter than that.

Another folder caught my eye. It was full of test subjects half a year or more old, predating the Chak Registration Act. They'd been poking chakz before Camp Kyua existed. No big surprise there. Getting volunteers is easy when a grunt can just as easily mean "yes" as "no."

The name on one of the files was familiar, though: Ashby Shinkle. Ashby was the reason I doubted even flames could destroy a chak. He was a juvie executed for killing a cop during a convenience store holdup. A security tape turned up, showing that the officer's gun discharged accidentally. The poor bastard shot himself. So Ashby was ripped. I met him in Bedland, one of the biggest zombie towns. He was hanging with another chak, Frank Boyle. They'd both still be around if it wasn't for me.

Long self-flagellation story short, Frank ended up D-capped and Ashby was dumped in a vat of acid by a certain psychopath hoping to destroy him permanently. It was one of those sure things that didn't work. Ashby's skeleton, no cartilage, limbic system, or ampulla of whatever, climbed out and wreaked some unintentional havoc. Jonesey and I tracked him to Collin Hills, where I had to beat his skull to powder with a baseball bat before he killed any innocents. Even the pieces looked like they were shivering.

Turns out Ashby was part of an early experiment that involved a second RIP. They were thinking it might repair some of the postmortem damage to our bodies. Made sense. Ashby was always drifting in and out of reality, so, Frank volunteered him. After that, ChemBet, like a child who didn't take care of its toys properly, lost track of him. Score one for my incompetence theory.

It seemed as if the Marutas were *trying* to fix us. But I also found some later abstracts chronicling efforts to discover a better way to terminate us. One, from the killing-two-birds-with-one-stone school of thought, proposed that with the right kind of pressure and instigating enzymes, chakz, like the dinosaurs, could be turned into crude oil.

There were thousands of files, most with coded names. I kept looking, thinking if I tapped into the right directory, I'd stumble onto all nine circles of hell. I was still searching when a high-pitched electronic whine put me out of my misery.

The lights in the office blinked on and off, on and off. Through a window, I saw all the lights in the building doing the same. I heard livebloods rushing along the hall. While I'd been sitting here reading, someone else had set off the alarm. Had they realized I was here? I didn't see any cameras.

I grabbed the laptop, crouched close to the door, and opened it a crack. Slivers of flapping jackets and lab coats were making for the stairs. Once the floor looked empty, I stepped out.

With the stairs busy, I hit the elevator button, hoping it hadn't automatically shut down. When it opened, empty, I got a weird tingle, a little thrill at the thought I might get out with the laptop. It vanished when I remembered Hudson was still in the Sterile Zone. Instead of heading for the basement, I groaned, sighed, and pressed two.

At the second floor, the car didn't just stop, it slammed to a halt. The doors opened with a dying sigh. The lights in the car went off. And there I was, facing the mega-door to the Sterile Zone.

Through its window, I saw Mistress Rebecca and a sizable entourage. They hadn't left yet, but were headed my way. I threw myself against the side of the elevator, my body concealed only by the two-foot bit of wall holding the floor buttons.

The fancy doors to the Sterile Zone opened with a haughty hiss. A gurney wheeled out onto the tile. Whatever was on it wasn't struggling anymore.

"Another day, another lockdown," Maruta said. She sounded cheerful. "I keep telling admissions they should either embed the tracking tags in the abdomen or stitch them on. Half the time the senseless things gnaw them off by accident."

The next voice didn't sound happy at all, more like sick. "Where should we leave . . . the subject?"

"Oh, out here in the holding area's fine. Hurry along. Good thing we had that espresso machine put in the safe room. Demitasse, anyone?"

They filed past me, pulling off their gloves, she discussing lattes and cappuccinos. When I stuck my head out, they'd reached the opposite end of the hall. The door there was held open for her. Beyond it, I caught snatches of rent-a-cops in black uniforms, on their way to handle whatever had caused the alarm. The doors closed and I was alone again.

Parked in an open space beyond a dividing wall, I could see the edge of Hudson's gurney, its silver flashing in the lights. When I heard a dry rasping, I couldn't pretend they'd left him watching TV.

Remembering his first name, I called, "Palmer?"

The rasping quickened as if in recognition. I stepped past the wall and realized I didn't need a computer to access the nine circles of hell. They were all here, right in front of me. I dropped the laptop. Its casing cracked against the tiles.

Hudson was beyond naked. He was laid out flat, every bit of his skin slit open and pinned to the side, exposing his innards. Most of the muscles had been severed from the bone, laid neatly to the side. His skullcap was open, too, sharp instruments still poking into the brain. His trachea was detached from the lungs, twisted up like a black rubber hose covered in goo. His lungs, still attached, puffed air through the hole that was left. That's where the rasping came from.

And the son of a bitch was still twitching.

All open like that, entrails out of place, he was still twitching.

This wasn't about interactional synchrony. Mistress Rebecca didn't like him. She'd cut him up for fun. If I was looking for new monsters, I'd found one.

18

The world's full of pain and body parts, but if I'd seen worse, I didn't remember it. I wanted to turn my head, but couldn't. Not that it would've mattered, the image had moved into my brain and kicked everything else out. My chest, arms, and hands tingled. All ten fingers straightened and swelled, like they'd been filled with toothpaste and were ready to burst.

Hudson had been disassembled. He was opened up, then whatever was inside him had been opened up, and so on, until there was nothing left. I wanted to put him out of his misery, but without a crematorium handy, all he could do was suffer, all I could do was watch.

I understood savagery, a primal instinct that could misfire. After all, I'd killed a guy with an axe. But it wasn't something bestial on display here. I'd seen the work of serial killers fulfilling a grotesque sense of art. But this had no aesthetic. It lacked any passion at all. These were mechanical cuts made by a seamstress with a razor. The opposite of Jonesey's wide-eyed idealism, the work said, in no uncertain terms, that all existence was pointless except for the shape it had.

The lights kept flashing, the alarm kept sounding, a high tone followed by a deeper one. True to form, Hudson's rasping was offbeat with both, a fingernail raking a blackboard. At first I thought that was all I was hearing, but there was something else.

Beep, flash, beep, rasping breath, flash, beep . . . and then a *shpp*.

The long wide space was orderly and lifeless. There were instruments, hampers and garbage, a row of steel cabinets, and other gurneys, whatever on them covered in sheets.

Beep, flash, *shppp* . . .

It wasn't footsteps. It wasn't mechanical. The area I was in ended in a half wall, but there looked to be about another ten feet between it and the exit. There was someone in there. Another subject, kept away from the rest?

Rasping breath, beep, flash, *shrppp* . . .

I stepped away from the gurney, far back enough to see a coffee table covered with magazines, and the edge of a lounge chair. A figure was sitting in it, reading, turning pages. That was the sound—*shrp*.

Struggling to control my vibrating arms I grabbed the biggest, sharpest scalpel I could find and headed toward the figure. I don't know if I actually would have killed someone, but I was so pissed, I wanted to. It didn't matter if it was a boffin, a lazy guard, or a bagel lady. They were all cogs in this madhouse. Someone should pay.

shrpp . . .

I picked up speed, jumped the last two feet and saw, in the middle of a pool of sun from a skylight... "Jonesey?"

It was John the Fact-less himself, the reverend Jim Jonesey, server of the Kool-Aid. Happy and about as self-aware as a clam, he was flipping through *The New Yorker,* yellow tag dangling from his wrist.

He picked his head up. "Hess, oh hey, hi. Glad you made it in. The room was a little cramped, so I thought I'd stretch the old legs. Spotted this cozy little corner, and said to myself when was the last time you took the time to sit down and read a magazine?"

I reared, flabbergasted. "Don't you hear the alarm? Don't you see the flashing lights?"

He looked around as if noticing for the first time. "Some kind of fire drill going on?"

I grabbed his arm and heaved him to standing. "I don't care if you're yanking my crank or rotting from the inside out. There's something you're going to see."

I took him back toward the gurney. As we got closer, he heard the rasping and got a puzzled look on his face. The expression was kind of boyish, like maybe the surprise that was waiting would be delightful. I pushed him at Palmer Hudson's remains. Knowing Jonesey saw it too somehow made it easier for me to look again.

"Meet Kyua. Here's the hope you've been preaching. *This* is what they do to chakz here."

The smile stayed, but I think that was shock, because his skin actually faded to a whiter shade of pale, like whatever there was of Jonesey had left the building. It wasn't satisfying, like I'd hoped, or an argument I'd really wanted to win. When he went down to his knees, I put my hand on his shoulder and squeezed, a vague effort at offering comfort.

Then he took out his cell phone and started snapping pictures. What the fuck?

While he talked, he kept clicking. "I want them all to see it. I want them all to know."

I pulled at his arm, but all of a sudden his strength was back. He didn't budge.

"What are you trying to do," I said, "start another riot? Any chak that sees this will go wild, and then what? They'll get cut down today instead of tomorrow."

He whirled at me, eyes wide. "They have a right to know!"

I rattled my brain for a comeback, but didn't have one. There wasn't time to debate it anyway. A dull, steady tromping rose above the alarm.

"Jonesey, someone's coming, we've got to get out of here."

He snapped another picture. Humans, alive or dead, suck at locating audio, but I knew the sound was coming from the stairs, and it was loud enough to mean lots of company.

I shoved him to get his attention. "Let's go. Now!"

He shook his head. "It doesn't make any difference. It doesn't make any goddamn difference." He folded the cell phone, then covered his face with his hands.

The footsteps were louder.

"Just leave me here . . . just leave me . . . maybe I can take more pictures . . . I've got to be more than this. I have to rise above."

He reminded me of Misty, in shock after seeing Chester.

"Nothing living or dead is going to rise above that so fast. . . ." I said.

"Then I can't be living or dead. I've got to be something else, something not real. A dragon. I've got to be a dragon. . . ."

He was babbling, which was only slightly better than moaning.

I tried to drag him along, but he shook me off. I didn't want to leave him, but I didn't want to stay just to hold his hand when the flamethrowers came.

Unlike me, Jonesey was a registered subject, allowed to be in the building. I doubted that would make much difference long term, given what he'd seen, but if I was ever going to figure out what was in the vials, I had to leave. Without that to keep me going, I might as well kneel next to him and babble myself.

I raced down the hall, calling for him to follow, but he ignored me, going on about being a dragon. I looked for another way out. There wasn't any. I'd have to risk using the same hall Mistress Maruta and her friends had. If I could just get past the double doors. No. Fuck. More footsteps. That left hiding.

I loped toward the other gurneys, hitting two as I fell behind them, mussing the symmetry. As I hit the ground, a gray hand tumbled from beneath a sheet. As if the day hadn't been bad enough, it was small, a child's hand, a raggedy. The skin above the wrist was peeled open. The exposed muscle shivered.

"Penny?"

Had those bastards done this to her, too? Maybe Jonesey was right, there wasn't any fucking point. . . .

"Over here."

A metal cabinet opened. In its darkness, Bad Penny's eyes glowed. I looked back at the hand, then at her again.

"Christ, I thought you were . . ."

"Please. I ditched my tag and got myself out of that room. I think that alarm's for me. Can you help me get out of here?"

Still not believing what I was seeing, I shook my head. "Not right now. They're coming from both sides."

The double doors at the end of the hall opened. I grabbed the metal cabinet door and tried to pull myself in next to Penny.

"Fuck off!" she squealed. "Find your own hiding space!"

"No time," I said. She kicked, but let me fold myself in.

"This is ridic—"

"Shhh!"

Four black-shoed figures marched by. One wore brown pants, but the other three were in uniform. Not the black the security guards wore, striped dark blue. Cops. I struggled against an old instinct to feel relief. I reminded myself I was a chak, and worse, wanted for killing one of their own.

When all four men froze, I thought they'd spotted me, but then they rushed farther down the hall. It was Jonesey they'd seen. He was still standing in front of Hudson's gurney, snapping pictures and raging.

"I'm a dragon, I'm a goddamn dragon." His dry voice quivered like Hudson's innards, not so the voice that interrupted. That one was wet, full of a more natural bile, and ridiculously familiar:

"Drop that fucking cell phone, before I shove it down your maggot-infested throat!"

The man in brown was Tom Booth. What the hell was he doing here? I hadn't seen where the bus took us. Could we be in Fort Hammer?

I didn't have time to wonder about Penny and Booth showing up at the same time, before a third coincidence happened. My cell phone rang. I'd forgotten I even had the damn thing.

Penny and I twisted round each other so I could get to it before it rang again. Booth was busy screaming at Jonesey, and the alarm was still on, but the phone was loud. It was in the middle of the second ring when I finally snagged it between two fingers and pulled it out.

Who the fuck? I looked at the CID.

Misty was calling.

Hail, hail, the gang's all here.

19

Frantic, Bad Penny jutted her chin at the phone. She wanted to know why I hadn't turned it off yet, why I hadn't stopped the ringing that put us both in danger. But Misty was calling.

Outside, Jonesey resisted the police as best he could, yammering about civil rights and dragons. "It's like you don't even get that your own rage is destroying the system you think you're protecting!"

Booth responded with increasingly colorful descriptions of what would happen to which of his orifices. "You don't lie *down* in two seconds, I'm going to shove your arm so far up your ass, you can grab your own tongue."

They were shouting loudly, they could miss the sound of a quiet conversation.

I looked at Penny and mouthed: *I've got to get this . . .*
Are you kidding? she mouthed back.

Realizing I wasn't, she gave me a swift kick that rattled the cabinet door, then stretched both hands to grab the phone. Her elbows pinned in the cramped space, she was at a disadvantage. I was able to keep her little fingers back with the flat of my arm. As the phone rang a third time, I flipped it open.

"Misty," I whispered.

Her words were mixed with digital gaps: "... sound ... away ... you ... out ... blue ... yet?"

I shifted, trying to improve the signal.

Jonesey was alternating quotes from the Bible with *The Lord of the Rings*, but Booth had gone quiet. Had he heard me?

"Mother of God."

No, he'd spotted Hudson. Processing that would distract anyone. I got another bar.

"Misty, you all right? Where are you?"

"It's damp, dark, and dirty and I'm sitting next to a stain that looks like two dancing rabbits. Well, one looks like it's dancing, the other looks like it's being dragged along. I nearly cracked the phone when I sat on it, pulled it out, saw your number, and thought it was one of those signs you don't believe in. Like fate."

She was talking fast, but the tone was dull. Her voice was hoarse. She was using.

"I thought you were with Mary."

"She's here. This was her idea."

"*Her* idea?"

"After she found out her cancer's stage four, she was dying for some cat's pee. So, I said, fuck it. Fate. Like Chester dying, like me dialing you with my butt crack. And, speaking of crack ..."

She made a sound she probably thought was laughter, but didn't play that way.

Even if Misty had given up on saving herself, Penny hadn't. When I'd shifted to improve the signal, I'd also given her some elbow room. She grabbed my wrist, brought her other hand up, and tried to take the phone. She was strong for a dead kid, or maybe I was weak for a dead man. Either way, I managed to bring the phone back to my ear.

"Misty, maybe you should turn yourself in."

Penny bared her teeth like she was going to bite if I didn't hang up.

"Ha! Do you have any idea how much more drugs cost in prison?"

Penny seethed. She pointed to her ears and mouthed, *Listen, you idiot . . .*

I thought she wanted me to listen to *her*, but she was pointing at the metal door in a deeply agitated way. It wasn't just Booth who'd gone quiet. I couldn't hear Jonesey either. What I did hear was the slap and thud of a body being punched and tossed around. Jonesey had lost the argument.

"Can't talk now, Misty."

She didn't take it well. "Oh, is this a bad time? I'll call back after I've OD'd. I have no idea what I expected from you. Do you even know what the blue shit is yet? The stuff that destroyed my life?"

Penny lunged for the phone again. I moved my foot to hold her in place.

"A little. It's from ChemBet. Jonesey thought it was some kind of snake oil that could bring chakz back to life, until . . . urgh!"

The kid had grabbed my bad ankle and twisted like

she meant to break it off. My back against the side of the cabinet, I pressed harder into the kid's chest.

"Is it something we could use on Chester?"

"Misty, don't even think that!"

"Shut up, asshole!" Penny said.

I didn't realize how loud I'd been until the cabinet door opened.

Booth watched as one man dragged me along the floor. It took two to get Penny out. She was like a cornered pit bull, still kicking even when they got her on her feet.

Her eyes brimmed over with hatred, not for the police, for me. "Idiot! Fucking idiot!"

She cursed me so long and so hard even Booth was impressed. He let her go on for a good minute before saying, "Enough. Shut her up."

A puffy-eyed rookie with straw-colored hair tried to shove a gag in her mouth. He nearly lost his finger. The poor guy's face blanched when he saw it was bleeding from the bite.

"Don't worry," I told him. "It's not *28 Weeks Later.* There's no infection that'll turn you into one of us. You might want to get a tetanus booster, though."

With a grunt from Booth, another man moved in and held her mouth open as the straw man reluctantly wedged the gag in place, then followed up with a set of handcuffs. When she kicked again, Booth pushed her to the ground.

As if it would do any good, I said, "Easy, she's just a kid."

"All done with the dead strippers, Mann?" Booth

said. He grabbed my phone. "Cradle-grave robbing now?"

As the alpha dog put the cell to his ear, I tried to look submissive. "It's Misty. She's all broken up about Chester. Maybe you could try to find out where she is, for his sake?"

Booth paused. His men looked at him expectantly. Chester was well liked, even if his taste in women made him suspect. With a grudging nod, Booth spoke in an ever-so-slightly softer tone.

"Hello?" He looked at the display. "She hung up."

"Call her back. You know people are after us because of that stupid briefcase. If they find her before you do . . ."

Wrong move. Not humble enough. "I'm your social secretary now?"

I lowered my head so much I wasn't sure I'd get it back up again.

He tossed the phone to the cop with the scarecrow hair. "Get the last number. See if it's got a GPS."

It was something at least. With the cops here, I thought all the running and hiding was over. As they cuffed me, a dozen questions came to mind, but I could ask only one at a time, and doubted I'd get answers for any.

"What brings you boys here? The lab next door complain about a noisy party?"

Booth's eyes fixed on me. "You shamble into the damndest places, don't you?" He waved a hand at Jonesey. Like Penny, he was bound and gagged on the floor. "And your coffin-buddy's a regular Weegee, taking photos of proprietary work."

"I didn't realize torture was considered intellectual property," I said.

He hesitated, unsure, then said, "You can't torture the dead."

"For pity's sake, Tom, you don't believe that." I aimed my cuffed hands at Hudson's body. "Hate me, hate chakz, but you can't tell me you're all right with *that*."

He didn't look, but when I did, I noticed something different about the gurney. "You had him covered with a sheet. What's that? Respect for the not-quite-dead?"

Booth hissed. "I didn't want anyone getting sick. You'll see how much respect I have for you once we book you on murder charges."

"You know I didn't kill Chester . . ."

"Get them all back to the van."

The scarecrow started dragging me away. "Booth, who's yanking your chain? The mayor's office? Some big donor? Don't tell me you're working for ChemBet, now?"

"You want a gag, too? Jensen . . ."

A new voice clipped his command. It was low for a woman's, sweet in a practiced way, but dripping with something darker.

"I'm afraid the situation's a little more complicated, Chief Detective. You and your men are trespassing. I happen to know you don't have a warrant."

Looking all comfy in the folds of her lab coat, Rebecca Maruta stood dead center in the open double doors. Have to hand it to her, her outfit coordinated nicely with the security guards behind her. Her rubber gloves matched their black, and the bit of yellow on their shirt epaulets was the same shade as her coat.

There were seven I could count, but there could have been more in the hall behind them, all hired, no doubt, based on their resemblance to professional linebackers. They also all carried MP5s. They're 9mm submachine guns, German design, most widely used machine pistol in the world. Funny what I remember sometimes.

Despite the sudden show of firepower, Booth stayed calm. He probably couldn't believe they'd actually threaten police officers. Still, rather than take his customary Neanderthal tone, he answered evenly, "Probable cause. What with all the alarms, we naturally assumed there was a crime in progress."

Her lips briefly curled into an arrogant half smile, but she quickly dropped it for a fake look of sympathy. "No crime. One of our subjects got loose. Putting aside the fact that you're out of your jurisdiction, it's half a mile from the grounds entrance to the building. What were you doing here in the first place?"

He shrugged. "I had a few questions about some DNA samples I thought you or someone from your staff might help with."

"I'd be delighted. But some other time perhaps? You can call my assistant for an appointment."

Booth nodded. "Okay. We'll take our perps and go, then."

The second he moved, she inhaled sharply. "Oh, that is a problem. These are all volunteer subjects, under our auspices. What are the charges?"

"Resisting arrest."

Funny how he didn't mention I was wanted for murder. Was he hoping she didn't realize who I was? Freaky to think it, but was Booth trying to *save* us?

If he was, the frigid glare that took Maruta's face told me it wouldn't be easy.

"Yes, yes, yes. Much as I enjoy the delightful tension that comes from suppressing resistance, as you said yourself a moment ago, our work is proprietary. I can't allow anyone who's seen the lab to simply leave. Especially Hessius Mann."

I gave her a look.

"Don't bother pretending to be shocked. It's boring. I discovered him when he requested a transfer to the Chambers facility. Given the ridiculous disguise he wore until recently, I'm surprised you didn't pick him up sooner for being an eyesore. Who knows what he's discovered while he was wandering about?"

"Then why'd you let me in?" I said.

"Shut up, Mann," Booth said.

It may have been a reflex, but I think he was warning me.

Regardless, Maruta talked to me directly, her tone like a mother admonishing her bad boy. "I think you know. You have something of mine. Something old, something new, something stolen, something blue. Maybe you don't recall it, poor thing, and here I am being rude. A briefcase? A little beat up perhaps?" She made a rectangular shape in the air with her hands. "About yay by yo?"

Booth seemed fascinated by the exchange, but finally remembered he was there. "Mann's wanted in a cop killing. The only place he's headed is back to the station."

I was starting to think that was the best place to be.

Like a lizard-man peeling away a human mask, Maruta's sympathy vanished into that half smile. "You continue to misunderstand, Chief Detective. I can't allow *anyone* who has seen our work here to simply leave. You really should have knocked before you came in."

And then her guards opened fire.

20

Don't let anyone ever tell you otherwise, surprise works great. The flying bullets took up most of the hall before any of us could think about moving out of their way. That was a given for me, with chak reflexes. It was also understandable that the liveblood cops, even with their training, would be taken off guard. I did expect more from Booth. I'd seen him duck and fire in less than half a second, even with his holster clipped. Not this time.

I didn't do any better. Unable to decide whether to run or drop, I spun and sank. The last thing I saw while on my feet was the straw-haired cop falling backward, hand clamped to throat.

I wasn't exactly unscathed, but I was on the ground before I saw the hole in my sweater. Shoulder wound. No biggie. Not that I enjoyed it. At least now, I was in the best position to avoid being riddled, facedown on the ground, like Penny and Jonesey.

Seconds later, the three cops were dead or wounded

and Booth hadn't even drawn his gun. When at last his hand did move for his piece, there were ten weapons trained on him. Robbed of other options, he screamed. It was the same sound he made when he found me standing in Lenore's blood.

At least this time, the rage wasn't directed my way. "You crazy fucking bitch!"

In a lazy display of contempt, Maruta tsked. "You've a gift for the obvious."

One of the officers, wounded, tried to stand, blood streaming from his hip, right along the dark ribbon of his uniform pants. Maruta, vaguely bothered by the interruption, nodded at one of her NFL-sized grunts. He walked over, drew his sidearm, and aimed it at the man's forehead.

Booth gave off a pitiful wail, and lunged. A gun butt whacked across the back of his skull put him out of his misery. Not particularly caring that he was unconscious, Maruta continued talking to him.

"Impatient, just like my husband. Little man, I used to call him. Be patient, little man, I used to say. I wasn't going to kill your cub, Chief Detective. He's going to be one of our exam subjects. Living volunteers are hard to find. Be patient, little man."

An exam. Like Hudson. Hearing that, I got up and threw myself at the grunt. Wish I could say I was more successful than Booth. I got within a foot, but he didn't bother raising a hand. He stepped aside and I sailed past him. I felt his boot heel in the small of my back, then ate tile.

I heard footsteps, saw Maruta's flats stop in front of me. When her grunt flipped me over, I found myself looking up her lab coat and getting too much information. Her lingerie was made of a kind of rubber, like the gloves. Maybe they were easier to swab clean.

She went to her knees and poked a finger into my shoulder wound. Aside from disgust, I felt the pressure. One or both made me queasy, but there was no pain. Her finger dug in like a little snake and prodded my insides.

She kept yapping, reminding me of a doctor who liked to chat during proctology exams. "Clean shot. No harm. You're remarkably lucky considering what you've been through. But trust me, it's nothing compared to what's coming unless you tell me where those vials are."

"You think I'm going to tell you anything?" I said.

She withdrew her finger. The top third was marred with some grayish goo. It was thicker than the stuff that came out of my abdomen.

"Yes, I do," she said.

She licked the tip, a pinprick of gray smearing her straight white teeth. When the nearest grunt gagged, she looked at him. "Come now, there's no rot, so it's perfectly sterile." She held her finger out to the pasty-faced grunt. "Tastes a bit like haggis."

That did it. His cheeks puffed. He stumbled out of the room. Wished I could join him. Maruta glowered at the others, daring anyone else to leave. There was a glint in her eyes, like she was thinking of forcing everyone to have a taste of me.

Had Rebecca always been this psycho, or did she dive off the deep end when Travis called it quits? I wondered if the shareholders knew about this. Ha. Maybe I could file a consumer complaint.

Fortunately, a muffled groan from the back of the room broke her focus.

It wasn't one of the wounded. It was Jonesey, loud and getting louder despite the gag. Penny had been next to him, but she was gone. Took me a second to see she'd crawled under a gurney and was half covered by its sheet. Did she think she was hidden?

Jonesey let rip with a pained lowing. I listened to two more of his long, deep wails, before I admitted to myself he was going feral. Back when he'd attacked me in an alley, I thought it was just a matter of time. Seeing Hudson was the straw that broke his myelin sheaths. Horrifying as that was for me, it must've been worse for a true believer, like watching your god eat your children. And I was the one who forced his face in it, the one who thought he deserved it. Funny how much damage I cause when I'm trying to do the right thing.

From the looks of things, the lizard-brain steering his body couldn't do much with it. Its struggles against the bonds became more rhythmic. Its back spasmed in tune with the alarm and the flashing, as if the lights were electrocuting it. How long before that was me?

I couldn't afford to let go. I had to keep it together long enough to take this place down, long enough to try, anyway. Not that I had a plan.

I heard Maruta say, "What a pity. I so wanted to get to him while he was stable, poke my finger into that delightful mind of his. I may well have discovered exactly which part of the brain was responsible for his self-delusion." She rose and rubbed her hands. "Oh, well. Time to clean up, my little men. Quality, service, cleanliness, and value!"

She marched through the double doors, leaving the

work to her grunts. Booth was carried out. Penny, once she was dragged from under the gurney, was shoved next to me, and we were both forced to march out. I never saw what they did with Jonesey, but I doubt it was pretty. I hoped he was with Kyua, real or not.

We were taken to a windowless room, where Booth's motionless form was already waiting. All three of us were chained at the ankles and left there.

For the longest time, Penny and I sat there, watching Booth breathe.

"You know him?" she asked.

I nodded. "My boss. When I was alive."

"Doesn't like chakz much, does he?"

"Least of all me."

"So he's probably not going to like it much when he wakes up and finds out he's chained to two of them, is he?"

"No, he's not."

She shrugged her good shoulder. "Should we kill him?"

I made a face at her. "No! Jesus, who raised you, alligators? We're trapped by a psychotic sadist with armed guards and you want to kill someone just to buy a few more minutes?"

"Yeah. Pretty much. A few minutes can be a long time."

She was right about the last part. "Penny, I'm sorry you got dragged into all this."

She sneered. "That and a dollar . . . crap, he's moving."

We pulled away, but the three-foot chains didn't let us get very far.

Booth sat up and rubbed the back of his head.

"Shit," he said, looking at the ground.

He looked at the ceiling and said, "Shit."

He looked at the walls and the locked door and said, "Shit."

He looked at me and Penny and said, "Shit."

Then he saw the chain and said, "Shit."

Each time he said it louder.

When he looked back at me, every muscle in his face tight and bulging with rage, I said, "Well, don't expect me to disagree."

I knew whatever happened next wasn't going to be pleasant. He grabbed the chain and yanked. I fell to the side, my leg jutting in his direction. He kept tugging, like he could pull the metal clear through my ankle. Maybe he could. Alive, I might've been able to stop him. Now? A better bet would be to offer to snap off my foot to save him the trouble.

Penny had different ideas. She jumped on his back and clawed at his eyes, yelling, "Let go of him!"

I didn't get the sense it was out of loyalty. I think I blew any affection she might have had for me after my cell phone chat with Misty. She probably figured she had a better chance of not being mangled while I was still around.

Booth bellowed, rose, and slammed her backward into the wall, dragging me along the floor in the process.

"Take it easy! You could crack her fucking spine! I'll try to help you get the chain off," I said. Ignoring me, he moved to slam her into the wall again.

Penny screamed, opened wide, and bit into his ear.

If I was the biggest pacifist in the room we were in trouble, but I couldn't let him hurt her any more than I could let Penny hurt him. I waited until he had one foot off the ground then pulled the chain hard. His leg flew out from under him. His ass hit the floor.

I hoped that would give me a second to reason with him, but the kid didn't know when to quit. Penny's feet near his head, she whipped some chain around his neck and pulled until he couldn't breathe.

I pushed forward along the floor, grabbed her hand, and pried her fingers off the chain one by one. "Let him go!"

She chittered like a rabid squirrel, then squealed, "He's crazy! He'll snap our feet off to get free!"

I didn't have a good comeback, especially since she was right, but I wasn't her only problem. Booth had wedged his hand between Penny's chain and his neck. Now he moved up and forward, taking her off the ground, ankle first.

It was like that for a while, me dragging Booth off Penny, then Penny off Booth, getting twisted, scratched, and punched along the way. Like I said, it would've been easier to lose the foot.

I tried to appeal to their egos. "You idiots! Don't we have enough to worry about, like vivisection? Tom, you heard her, Maruta's planning the same for your man that she gave Hudson."

He hesitated. Penny used the pause to punch him hard in the jaw.

"Stop!" I growled.

"I will if he will!"

To his credit, Booth didn't counter. The thought of what might already be happening to the wounded officer sobered him. He sat on his haunches, rubbing his jaw.

Penny squirmed away the three feet that the chain allowed, huffing and puffing as she went, out of breath.

And I finally noticed something I should've spotted a long time ago. If I hadn't caught it while I was worried about my own disguise, I should have while we were hiding in the cabinets.

"Fucking chakz!"

"Tom, look . . ."

"Fucking, goddamn, shit-ass chakz!"

"Look at her! She's panting. *Breathing*. She's not a chak. She's a liveblood. I think there's a bruise swelling on her cheek."

Penny laughed hard, but with all that skin missing from her face, it came out more like a rush of air.

Booth stared at her. "But her face, her shoulder . . ."

"Chemical accident," she explained, a half smile on her half face. It wasn't like Maruta's. A half smile was the only kind the kid could manage.

I stood up. "Who the hell are you?"

"Like I'm going to tell you?" She laughed again, then used a piece of her sleeve to wipe off some of the makeup that kept her face white. I'd met a chak who'd made himself up as a liveblood, but never the other way around.

Booth was so shocked, he actually talked to me. "Where do you know her from?"

"She was at the site where Chester died, at the motel Misty and I were hiding in, then at the exam center, and in the camps," I said. "Christ, I'm a complete fool. She's been following me. She's after the briefcase, too."

She tapped her temple. "Now there's the brains that got you here."

"Then you killed Chester on purpose."

"No," she said, her young voice full of aged contempt. "Haven't you been paying attention? I thought the briefcase was in that car. You, of all people, should know what a fucking *accident* is."

"But you're working for the same people who chased us?"

"Please."

"Who were they?"

"I don't know. I'd say military if they weren't so stupid, shooting at the car carrying the only sample of Travis Maruta's final project."

"Maruta's final project," I repeated. If those were the only samples, maybe they couldn't replicate it. No wonder everyone wanted it, whatever it was. I looked at my old boss. "That news to you, Tom?"

He shook his head, no. "I'm hoping it's a way to send you all back to the grave."

"Most of us probably wouldn't mind. Penny, do you know what it is?"

Her eyes twinkled. "Sure, and I'll tell you if you tell me where it is. Doesn't matter much with us all stuck here."

"You've got a point. Okay, deal. I put it in a locker at the Fort Hammer Plaza Station. The key's back in my office."

"Great. My turn. The vials contain a new natural flavor of Kool-Aid, no HFC, no unhealthy additives, no calories, and it even cures diabetes."

We looked at each other a while. She spoke first. "Is it safe at least?"

I shrugged. "Safe as things get."

She scanned my eyes, like they were going to tell her something, then gave up. Something sharp and silver slipped into her hand, from where I couldn't tell. As she used it to work on the lock that held her ankle, I got a closer look. It looked like it was made out of cheap cafeteria silverware, sharpened and welded together.

"We've all shared beautifully, but, seeing as how Rebecca also has no idea where the briefcase is, the only things I'll get from sitting around here are bored, dissected or both."

The ankle brace dropped away.

"Why didn't you do that while we were fighting?" Booth asked.

"Didn't want you to know I could. Could've killed you anytime, by the way, but I wanted the decaying dick here to like me a little longer."

She walked to the door and worked the makeshift tool into the lock. Once the door was open, she peered outside. "Now *that's* interesting. Come look."

As she held the door a little wider, Booth and I got to our feet and approached. The long hall was white and sterile as a brand-new Apple gizmo, except for one thing: there were corpses in the distance. Like living stains on a clean kitchen floor, chakz wobbled and moaned. Between the white of the walls and their gray, the yellow tags on their wrists stuck out like traffic lights.

"Ferals," Booth said. His hand reached for his holster, but they'd taken the gun while he was out.

A series of sharp snaps and crackles told me there were more than we could see, and that Maruta's little men were using their MP5s on them. The ferals rocked and turned in the direction of the sound.

"Jonesey's cell phone network," I said. "The pictures must've gotten around. The ones still in orientation probably freed the others. It's what I would do. Anyone have any idea how many chakz they keep here at a time?"

"Two hundred and thirty-seven," Penny said matter-of-factly. "A nice cover for my escape."

When she moved to exit, I grabbed at her, forgot the missing shoulder and wound up holding the cloth of her coat. "Aren't you forgetting something?"

She shook her head. "No."

I pointed at the chains still on our ankles. "You're going to leave us like this?"

"Why not?" she said, sliding her tool up her sleeve. "Consider it payback for using your cell phone in a public place. There was a file I wanted to find before I broke you out, but you screwed all that up, didn't you? Besides, the more noise you two make, the easier for me to get away. You survived this far, I'm sure you'll make it."

"Unchain me!" Booth screamed. He jumped at her. She leapt back easily and blew him a kiss.

"Aw. You missed! So long, handsome." Still looking at Booth, she bobbed her head toward me. "And try to be nice to stupid over here. He saved your life."

She flew down the hall, away from the ferals, moving faster than any chak or liveblood had a right to. As soon as she vanished from sight, I realized who she was. She'd been holding back the two times I grappled with her.

"That," I said, more to myself than Booth, "was a Red Riding Ninja."

21

Jonesey used to say that if you truly wanted something, all you had to do was act "as if" it was already true. That's what Tom Booth did. Acting as if I weren't chained to his ankle, he headed after Bad Penny, almost pulling me off my feet with his first step. Forget about keeping up with him. Even free I had a limp. As he pounded after her dust, I focused on remaining upright, but it didn't go well.

He turned a corner hard and stopped. Scattered in the open cafeteria space ahead of us were about twenty ferals. They were tearing at the walls and serving counters, attacking chairs and tables. A soda machine got the worst of it. The only sign of Penny was a door clicking shut at the far end of the space.

I was trying to see if there was anything resembling a path through them, when Booth headed for the door and this time did pull me off my feet. Next thing I knew, I was sliding across the floor, looking up at ceiling tiles and the crotches of the living dead. The extra weight didn't seem to slow him. The stairs beyond the exit door would hurt, but we never got there. Penny had somehow managed to lock the door.

Booth pounded at it and growled with his nice, wet, liveblood voice.

"Quiet! They'll hear you!" I said.

"So what? They already see me."

"Liveblood screams attract them. At least let me up," I said. "No way you'll get past them dragging me."

That didn't stop him from trying. Using a plastic chair as a shield, he shoved his way into the throbbing cluster of dead flesh, trying to go out the way we came in. He clonked a head here, smashed a chest there, and screamed every time he swung.

Whenever he howled, a few snatched at the air like they could grab the tasty sound and pop it, dripping, into their mouths.

I didn't consider things completely desperate until a few more staggered in from the hall we'd just left. Now we were cut off, and unless Booth had it in him to cripple them all with that chair, our options were limited.

I grabbed the side of a water cooler to slow us, then tugged the chain to get his attention. Booth swung the chair my way, looking like he was going to crush my head with it.

I covered my face with my hands. "Don't they teach you anything? *Stop* screaming! You're bringing them from all over."

Instead of barking some clever response, he looked at the newcomers and brought the chair around in a wide arc. His swing threw a blond chak in a nurse's outfit into what looked like a dead tree trunk wearing a business suit and tie. They both went down, and this time, Booth didn't scream.

We still made great targets. Booth did anyway. All I had to do was moan and groan and they'd take me for one of them. Dodge as he might, a few got close enough to rake their nails, in some cases their bones, through his clothes. Drops of his blood hit the tiles. My back smeared them as we went.

We were heading for the open hall, but that wasn't a good thing. Booth, wounded, was slowing down and the crowd ahead of us was getting thicker. I looked around, then back at the far end. Crap. We'd missed it at first, because we were kind of busy, but next to the door Penny disappeared behind, was a cabinet with a hose, a fire extinguisher, and an axe.

I shouted "Tom, there!" about five times before he decided to pay attention. Hearing me, the dead looked around, but never thought to look down.

"Even an axe won't kill them all," Booth said.

"Not for the ferals, for the door!"

Moving with the crowd, we went a little faster, but his bravado and adrenaline were waning, and now I was slowing him down. Worse, every yank of the chain sent a bone-deep throbbing through my ankle. But, back to the wall, chair holding the dead at bay, Booth made it to the cabinet. And I'd been stepped on only ten or twelve times.

"You going to let me up now?"

"No!" he said loudly. They all moaned in unison at the sound. He shoved the chair's four legs into the nearest one, whose overalls made him look like a plumber. But there was something else about that one. As Joe the plumber tumbled over me, I noticed his skin was plump, thick with a puddinglike sheen that was very different from the typical desiccated chak look. It made me think he might be one of ChemBet's latest experiments. When the big son of a bitch fell on me, I found out the hard way that he was heavier than most chakz, too.

Crunched by his squirming chest, I called to Booth. "Don't *say* anything, okay? Just think. By the time you drop the chair, open the cabinet and grab the axe, it'll be over. You can't make it without me."

His face shivered, like he'd been electrocuted. I thought he'd been bitten deeply, but somehow I knew he was wrestling with the idea of dealing with me.

"I know you still think I killed Lenore. But as much as I swear I would have died for her, that I'd still die for her, I can't anymore. Neither can you."

He tried to swallow his next scream before it got too loud, then shoved Joe the plumber off me.

"Get up," he said. "Fast." He looked tired, as if he were about to drop the chair.

I bolted onto my good foot, opened the cabinet, and grabbed the axe. With whatever he had left, Booth cleared enough of a space for me to take a swing at the door handle. Unlike what I did to Flat-face in one swing, this time my first shot barely made a dent. The second knocked the handle off and set the door swinging inward.

Dropping the chair, Booth collapsed into the stairwell beyond. When the chair landed upright in the cafeteria, the feral in the business suit fell into it. Crazy in that special feral way, he looked around like he was wondering where the hell his desk was. I leaped over Booth, pushed the door shut and braced it with the axe.

Through a little window in the door, I saw the other

ferals push against the guy in the chair, trying to get to the door. I kicked the axe in tighter, the blade against the handle, the bottom against the floor. It held.

"I was going to use that to cut your foot off," Booth said, nodding at the axe.

Our positions had suddenly reversed. He lay at my feet, panting, his blood staining the floor.

"Gee, sorry. If I'd known I'd have tried to use the chair."

A quick blast came out of his nostrils. A laugh, or close to it.

Tom Booth and I were never friends, but when I was alive, we'd respected each other. My memory used to be photographic, and my instincts weren't half bad. He trusted both. Ridiculous as it was, even though he'd slept with Lenore, part of me wanted him to look at me like I was a still a cop.

"How's the bleeding?" I asked.

He looked at his arm, then tore some of the sleeve away. There were scratches on his skin, some deep, but most weren't seeping anymore.

I held my hand out to help him up, but he huffed and puffed his way to his feet on his own.

"Do exactly what I say until we're out of here and I won't crush your fucking head in," he said.

Below, we heard moaning. Above, moaning mixed with gunshots.

"Fine," I said. "But you do realize we're not getting out of here, right?"

Booth nodded. "Yeah."

A tall window in the stairwell gave us a view of the world outside. Below, two squad cars were parked in front of a marble version of the ChemBet logo, their motto carved beneath: QUALITY, SERVICE, CLEANLINESS, AND VALUE! Beyond a parking lot was a half acre of manicured green, a few abstract statues that looked like a bronze giant had taken a dump, then hills covered with junk pines. There were no other buildings in sight.

I pressed my hands into the glass. "Too thick to break. Gunfire's upstairs, so that's where Maruta's security men are. The chak dorms are in the basement. Assuming everyone got a gander at Jonesey's pictures by now, it's full of ferals. Which way do you want to go?"

"Wherever there's a phone," he said.

I felt in my pocket for mine, then remembered he'd tossed it to the rookie.

Booth headed down, slow enough for me to follow. Our chain sounded like a Slinky as it tumbled on the steps. The office space on the floor directly below looked vacant, so we stepped out. We heard moans, but they were distant, rooms away.

"Where are we?" I asked. "What city?"

Booth thought a second before deciding to answer. "We're about ten miles north of Chambers."

"What brought you?"

"I said I wouldn't crush your skull. I never said we'd swap tips."

A few seconds later, in a particularly plush office, on a desk full of flowers and cards, we saw a landline.

"Somebody had a birthday," I said.

"Shut up," Booth answered.

As he grabbed the receiver, I picked up one of the cards. Dated November twelfth, it was addressed to Rebecca Maruta, best boss in the world.

Before Booth got the receiver all the way to his ear,
he chucked it onto the desk.

"Dead."

Like a bad horror movie cue, the moaning got louder,
as if a wall between us and the ferals had suddenly crum-
bled. They were nearby.

"It's not the only thing."

Exiting the office, we saw how bad it was. Out of
nowhere, scores of dead, maybe fifty, came from both
directions, filling the space. We barely made it back to
the stairwell. When we closed the door, instead of being muffled, the sound echoed louder. They were coming up from below, too, fast.

I shook my head. "It's like they're coordinated."

"Up," Booth said, like there was a choice.

We picked up our pace. By the time we passed the
door held by the axe, we were taking two steps at once.
On the next floor up, there were more shots than moans,
so we stopped for a look.

In the center of a mezzanine, the best boss in the
world was standing on a table, looking down at the terrified group of boffins beneath her, clearly annoyed by
their weakness. Her NFL-grunts stood in a semicircle
around them, shooting anything that moved.

And there was plenty moving. Shredded body parts
lay all over. Legless ferals pulled themselves along by
their hands as their fellows clambered over them,
straight into the gunfire.

The ferals looked like they were trying to get to
Maruta and the boffins, as if they knew who was responsible. It was a plan. Not a very good one, but a plan.

How many chakz did Penny say they kept here? Two

hundred thirty-something? The livebloods would win easy, if their ammunition held out.

I heard a rush of air next to my ear, then saw the neat hole the bullet had left in the glass. Booth and I jumped back at the same time. We kept climbing. The last door locked, we both threw our shoulders into it until the latch broke, then fell onto a wide plain of black tar, feet tangled up in chain.

"Fuck," Booth said.

There were chakz on the roof. Maybe twenty. But they weren't moaning. They'd been talking. Seeing us, they looked up, as if we were interrupting a secret meeting.

Booth tensed, ready to run back. I put my hand on his shoulder, which only made him tense more. "Hold it. They're not feral."

When a few shambled toward us, their formation broke, revealing someone at the center.

"Jonesey!" I shouted, "You damn son of a . . ."

He held up a finger, handcuff dangling from one wrist. His other hand held a phone.

"No, I don't have the photo anymore. I already told you, this isn't my cell. They took that. I had to grab whatever I could."

Booth rushed toward him. "Give me that fucking phone!"

Ten chakz blocked our path.

Jonesey flipped it shut and eyed Booth. "I don't think so."

Booth reared. "You're not feral, listen to this. Give me that phone or I'll have you all arrested. I'll cremate you myself."

An airy rush came from their all their mouths.

Booth made a face. "What the hell is that supposed to be? Are you deflating?"

"No," I said. "They're laughing."

Booth moved for Jonesey again, but this time four chakz grabbed his arms and held him. He was too tired to put up much of a fight.

I looked at my resurrected friend. "Jonesey, what the fuck is going on? You faked the feral?"

"Worked, didn't it?" he said. "Look, a lot *did* go feral when they saw that photo. About half. That's real. This is sort of the command center for the rest of us. I've got some of the others trying to secure the perimeter."

"Secure the what?" Booth said.

Jonesey ignored him. "It's a revolution, Hess. The dead aren't lying down anymore."

I shuddered in disbelief. "You're going to take over the country with a hundred chakz? You'll be sliced into pieces by Maruta's men, or wind up gnawing on each other."

Jonesey lowered his voice. "It's not just here, I got word back to the Bones, to Bedland, to at least four of the camps. Not everyone's great at working the phones, but it's spreading. Organizing is keeping some of them from going feral."

"They'll cut every last one of us down!" I said.

He put his hand on my shoulder and squeezed. "They're already cutting us down, and worse. But there's always other possibilities, right? We've all got parts to play, especially you." He smiled and pointed toward another stairwell entrance on the opposite side of the roof. "Follow that down to the bottom, and it opens up out back. You can take one of those squad cars. Oh, wait a minute."

He thought a moment, mumbled a mnemonic and pressed redial on the cell.

"Bill? Remember those cars I asked you to put out of commission? Can we belay that order? Belay? It means stop, don't do it. Yes, that's right, don't destroy the cars. Got it? What? Oh . . ."

He walked to the edge of the roof and looked down. I followed. An angry Booth was dragged along beside me. Below, I saw the cars, hoods open, chakz ripping whatever they could from the engines.

"Never mind then. No. You're doing great. Thanks."

Jonesey hung up and walked us to the stairwell. "Well, you'll have to hoof it."

"Hoof it where? Where do you think I'm going?"

"To get Kyua," he said. "You've got to. The cure is our only chance."

Booth smirked.

"Kyua? Jonesey, you can't still think . . . even after seeing what they did to Hudson . . . ?"

He shrugged. "Satan is often God's companion. It was *his* project, right? Not hers. Of course I still believe."

I was speechless. Booth couldn't care less. He tried to look sincere as he asked, "How about helping us get these chains off and we'll do whatever you like?"

Jonesey gave him a benign smile. "You're lying. It doesn't matter. Can't help. No keys, no tools, just good thoughts." He held the door open for us. "Now, I've got a lot to do, you've got a lot to do, so . . . go!"

22

If we'd been outside, or riding in a car, say, Tom Booth's agitated muttering might've been quiet. In the high-ceilinged stairwell, his voice echoed louder than a shock jock.

"Revolution? *I'll* give them a fucking revolution."

His feet hit each step with increasing speed and fury, making it hard to keep standing again.

"Whatever happens to the LBs, it'll be worse for the chakz," I said.

"Poor babies. You already had your chance when you were alive. Screw this 'lab' and everyone in it, but in the cities? Those're *real* people your compañeros will be hurting, like the ones who died back in the plaza."

He hit the landing and spun for the next set of stairs. The chain taut, I had to grab the banister for balance. "What do you expect us to do?"

"I expect you to stay dead!"

I kept hold of the banister. The sudden halt didn't make him fall, but it stopped him.

I stared into his steely blues. "So did we! How many times do I have to spell it out? You want to get out of here, shove your fist in your piehole and slow the fuck down! The building's full of ferals and people, *real* people, as you like to say, who'll *really* shoot us. Jonesey's corpse commandos couldn't protect us from a girl scout with a slingshot. They're not going to last long. Neither will his revolution."

"Soon as the chain's off," he said, "neither will you."

"Christ, Tom, were you *this* much of an idiot when I was alive? What happened to you?"

He went back to the stairs, moving slower and without a word.

Jonesey hadn't lied. At the bottom, the fire door opened easily onto the back of the building. The day slapped us with one of its better versions of fresh, cold air. Past the parking lot was the pine forest I'd seen from the window.

"Road or woods?" I asked.

Booth felt in his inside jacket pocket. "Still got my badge, I can flag a car down."

"I call shotgun."

He looked at me. "A joke," I told him. "To lighten the sexual tension?"

Out of the lot, we followed a road that curved past the front of the building. We'd nearly reached the main road when the sound of speeding cars had us diving behind the hedges. When we heard sirens, my dance partner looked relieved.

"Police," he said, rising.

I tried to pull him down. "Yeah? Who called them? Maruta?"

No sooner did he grudgingly crouch than three un-marked SUVs sped by. Top of the line and recently waxed, they made Fort Hammer's squad cars look like go-karts. Keeping formation, they squealed to a halt in front of the building. When the doors popped open, ten more ChemBet linebackers leaped out. They carried machine pistols like the others, but they also wore body armor and carried shields.

"So much for coming back with just the cops," I said. "Your men are still stuck with peashooters, aren't they? Last I remember, we only had six sets of body armor, too. You're going to need the guard or the army."

When he looked at me again some of the anger was gone, but only because he was using part of his brain to think.

"There may be more coming. Woods, then," he said. "At least until we're a mile away."

We left the road for the pines. I hate undergrowth, and there was plenty. The live branches, too stupid to realize winter was coming, caught at my face and sweater. The dead ones grabbed at my pants. Booth, his scratches no longer bleeding, had gotten a second wind. He pushed through like one of those big machines they use to gobble the rain forest. I kept expecting him to run into a tree trunk and try to knock it over.

When he kicked a grapefruit-sized stone, he didn't even wince, he just bent over, picked it up, and carried it with us.

"What's that for?"

"What do you think, asshole?"

I decided not to guess.

Eventually we hit an open spot. I wouldn't exactly call it a clearing, more like the overgrown remains of a farm-stead and the fieldstone foundation of the main house. All that remained of one corner of the house was a single boulder with a tree growing from under it, snaking around before heading skyward. The tree left a little cranny at the base of the stone, just big enough for a small mammal to nest in.

Booth put his foot on the boulder, tugged the chain up and started slamming it with the rock he'd been car-rying. His blows were slow, powerful, reminding me how easily he could crush my skull. Not the chain, though. Six or seven strikes later, he was getting winded, the rock had impact streaks, and the chain stayed shiny and new.

I sat on the other side of the boulder and watched. He kept at it, growling, screaming, slamming, a King Canute commanding the ocean to recede. His sweaty grunts were no longer a danger, and kind of small compared to the woods. The absurdity of it was peaceful in a way. A couple of squirrels watched, too, taking us for nuts, won-dering if we were too big to stuff into their nests for the winter.

Bored after a while, I picked at my cracked, yellowed nails, hoping I wouldn't accidentally tug one off. After a longer while, Booth, red-faced and sweating, looked like his heart would burst. The sky was still glowing but our surroundings were dimmer.

"Had enough yet?"

He tightened his grip, pulled the stone halfway back, then dropped it. Arms hanging, he slumped to the ground, panting. I didn't tell him, didn't dare, but he reminded me of me.

"I liked it better when people just died," he said.

"You and me both."

Before he caught his breath would probably be a good time to try to talk to him. "Whether or not you want to tell me what you know, you might want to listen to what I do."

"Go on," he said, sounding kind of defeated.

I walked him through my last few days. I didn't look at him as I spoke, just rubbed my nails against the rock like it was an emery board. Nails and hair keep growing even after you die. Yeah, in a normal body they stop after a while, but it's just another way chakz are lucky, I guess.

I was surprised how much I remembered without my recorder. Poor Misty's lessons were more useful than I thought. I was also pretty surprised that he didn't flinch when I brought up the arm.

How much *did* he know?

When I finished, I hoped I could get him to fill in some blanks. "I know you don't think me or Misty had anything to do with Chester's death. Half the force *saw* us being chased. Calling us suspects, putting us on the run, was too insane even for you. So, someone high up had to yank your chain for you to fuck with an investigation into the death of an officer, right?"

No answer. I rattled off the few possibilities.

"Our beloved police commissioner McLaurin is a stooge. Mayor Kagan's in the governor's pocket, so it's all six of one, there. Even that slimy crew would be hard-pressed to mess with things this much. If it ever came out, it'd be worse than photos of them chakking up. But someone big wanted a cover story for all the noise, didn't want anyone else knowing that briefcase was out there before they could get to it. That leaves Rebecca Maruta and the toad. One or another twisted Kagan's arm, he twisted yours. That explains the cover story and why you weren't too eager to catch us, otherwise you could have gotten the guard to track my phone. Did you investigate the real culprits or did Kagan make you stop that, too?"

Booth's breathing had steadied. I vaguely remembered what it felt like to take long, steady breaths. "Not at first," he said.

I leaned back, almost feeling like a detective. "So he did. And here you are, out of your jurisdiction, storming into ChemBet, disobeying orders. Bad career move, Tom."

He looked down, defeated. "Worse for the men who came with me."

I tried to sound comforting. "You wouldn't have risked something like that without a good reason. You found something. That's what made Kagan put the brakes on you. What was it?"

He said nothing for a real long time.

"Come on, you bastard! We're probably the only two on the whole fucking planet who can piece this together. You went this far. Tell me, when did they stop you?"

"After the tests came back on the arm."

The arm. Pieces clicked together in my head, then they fell apart. One minute it started to make sense, the next it felt like a crappy episode of *Lost*.

"Okay, so you *found* the arm? You know it was moving?"

"Yeah, we found it and that scrawl, just like you said, in the Dumpster. A review of the security cameras caught it as far away as Main Street. At first we thought somebody's pet python had gotten loose and swallowed some luggage."

"Do you know what the fuck it was?"

He lifted his head and knocked it gently back against the boulder a few times.

"If I tell you, you'll go feral."

"I haven't yet, Tom, and believe me, I've had reason."

"Not like this."

"Fuck. What is this, the old joke about how do you drive an idiot crazy?"

He laughed. "You put him in a garbage can and tell him to piss in a corner. No, it's not that." He looked at me. "Sure be a hell of a way to get rid of you, though. Couple of words and you snap like a twig. Problem is, we still have this chain between us."

He was serious. What did he know? I kneeled down and looked at him. "If I go, snap my neck, smartass, tear the head off, break my ankle, and you're free."

He exhaled and looked around like he was hoping to spot an idea. His eyes settled on the hollow beneath the boulder.

"Okay, I'll tell you, but first you wedge your head in there."

I looked at him, then at the hollow. "What the fuck?"

"That way, if you do go, I can cripple you easy."

"If I didn't snap when I saw what Maruta did to Hudson, nothing you tell me could make me go, Tom."

"Then, you've got nothing to lose. Stick your head in," he said. He patted the rock he'd used to try to break the chain. "Go on. I could've smashed you a dozen times by now if I'd wanted to."

"Shit," I said. "There better not be a squirrel in there."

If it was some kind of trick, I didn't see what it could be. He was underestimating me, as usual. At least I hoped he was.

I got down onto my chest and wriggled my head against the cold dirt and hard stone until I'd gone in as far as I could go. I felt Booth lift my leg, pull my arms behind me and wrap half the chain around my wrists. There was no way I'd be getting out unless he let me.

"Do I get a safe word?" I asked.

"Who do I look like, Maruta?" he answered. "Mann, you know I can't stand you, so you know I've got a good reason when I ask you if you're sure you want to hear this."

"You asshole, I'm up to my neck in this. I'm the only one who knows where the case is, and everyone knows it. It's not like I have a choice. Tell me already. What the fuck was that arm?"

"I don't know *what* it was."

I tensed. I pulled at the chains, tried to kick him with my free leg. "You don't know? *You don't know?* How the fuck did a piece of work like you ever get to be chief detective?"

"Because the only other guy up for the job had a temper."

"Compared to you? That must have been one sorry SOB."

"It was you, you idiot. You didn't know?"

"Me?"

"You were the one with the fucking photographic

memory and the track record of breaking cases. But you were always blowing up. The men weren't afraid of you, but they weren't going to follow you, either."

Chief Detective. Shit. I could have been *his* boss. The real troubles with Lenore started over money. Chief Detective would have solved that in a flash. Everything would have been . . .

I thought of Vishnu and Arjuna. I thought of Pandora. I groaned, struggled, pulled the chains tight . . . and then let it go.

"If you're testing me, it won't work, Tom. I'm not going to lose it over some embalming fluid under the bridge. You were more of a leader, anyway, until you started porking a subordinate's spouse. Did you shove me under here just to let me know how close I was to not being as completely fucked up as you or are you working out your guilt with sadism?"

"I said I didn't know *what* the arm was. I didn't say I didn't know *who* it was."

"I'm listening."

I couldn't see him, but I imagined him shrugging. "The DNA tests showed . . . I don't remember the exact words."

"You got DNA samples? Tough to do with a chak."

"That's just it. Forensics said it *wasn't* a chak."

"Okay. Kind of figured it was some new ChemBet monster."

"That's what I thought, but they said no, the tests showed that it was *alive*, same as you and . . . well, same as me, anyway. It'd died twelve hours before we found it, they weren't sure from what, and the DNA was normal enough for us to try to track it."

"So I'm under here because you figured out who it was. What? Did I have a kid I didn't know about?"

He gave off a little laugh. "That's a closer guess than you think. You know how the database works, covers known criminals, city and state employees. The preliminary search came up with *your* name."

"It was *my* arm? Like they cloned me?"

"It was only a partial match, more likely a relative. When we went wider, we found a military file buried in the system. That's when it came up with an exact match. Lawrence Mann, dishonorably discharged."

I furrowed my brow so tightly, the skin clenched the dirt I was facing.

"My father's fingers were missing. He lost them in a drunken disagreement with a table saw."

"Well, now he's got a whole arm missing. We double-checked, triple-checked. That arm belonged to Lawrence Mann."

The darkness under the boulder swayed. My body filled with searing, electric syrup. My stomach and intestines roiled in agony. The rest of my body started to vibrate.

"What's this?" Booth said. "You going feral?"

"This . . ." I said between dry heaves, "is how chakz process emotion."

23

I couldn't move or see, which made it easier for the memories to yank me out of my body. They came in flashes, bite-sized bits, with sharp teeth. The only thing missing was the melancholic sax music. All at once my father felt so real and near I couldn't remember where I'd left the difference between us.

I saw Larry smiling in a photo, rubbing the hairs on his belly, a beardless Santa.

I saw him kicking our Labrador, Sheba. The dog whimpering, skittering into a run, vanishing, golden tail between her legs.

Larry ducking a thermos hurled by my sobbing mother.

The thermos shattering against the wall. I'd had no idea a thermos had glass in it.

Myself, twelve, holding a crowbar tight enough to make my fingers bleed, swearing I'd swing if he took another step toward my mother.

He laughed in a way that reminded me of the Santa photo, said he'd never hit her and that I was really still mad about the stupid dog running away.

Years later, he was sitting in our small kitchen, thin glass in front of him, quarter full, no water, no ice. He was hunched like an old man, rubbing his bad hand with his good one, petting it like it was the dog he'd hurt and he was sorry.

"Don't look at it, please," he said.

It's the only time I remember him saying please.

I saw the hand in all its glory, the one I wasn't aware I'd been staring at, with its half-missing fingers, three sealed at the top with little prunelike wounds, a pearl of white bone poking from the fourth.

I saw him leaving us for the last time, like the dog.

"I'll get you something," he said. Not even good-bye, just "I'll get you something."

The flashes came so fast and furious, they were bound to stop. Yellow teeth clenched, I waited them out, waited for their effect on my ChemBet-crippled limbic system to pass, waited until the present finally slouched back into view.

I saw the hard, dead ground beneath my dead face, the stony hollow filled with dark, felt the chain against my wrists and ankle, and I was glad to be here, in the lousy stinking present.

Lawrence Mann wasn't the worst thing to walk the earth on two legs. He was a bully, but not a sadist, violent, but not a killer, a drunk who fought the bottle as best he could, a deserter who stayed with his family until he couldn't. Like a lot of us, he was just really fucked up.

Cagey bastard, though. All those years, and here he was, back in my . . . well, back in whatever this was.

Booth was still holding the chain tight, waiting to hear a moan.

"Let me out," I told him. "I'm not going anywhere."

The tension on the chains released. I felt him grab my ankles. He pulled me out. Still nauseous, I shifted into a seated position.

"When he left, my mother told me he'd joined Special Ops, but I didn't believe her. She was always lying for him. So, when I got on the force, I checked and found his dishonorable discharge. That's why his file was in the system. I always figured he was dead or on the street somewhere, drunk and homeless."

I didn't say it, but I was also wondering if maybe that was why I wound up taking care of Misty. Because I couldn't do a thing for Larry. Not that I'd saved Misty either.

"So how'd he wind up with Travis Maruta's last project, and why bring it to you?" Booth said.

I shook my head. "No idea. I heard the crazy lady say live test subjects were hard to come by. Maybe they pulled a few off the streets. Or maybe he *was* Special Ops and he volunteered to become Captain America. Why me? A familiar face, if he was in his right mind, or any mind. I mean, the arm . . . could it think?"

Booth rubbed his temples. "Fuck do I know? I still don't believe *you* think. Christ, if O'Donnell hadn't been sticking his dick in that stupid nothing friend of yours . . ."

Before I knew what I was doing, I'd punched Tom Booth square in the jaw. The blow was so fast, it caught us both by surprise. He took the worst of it. His head twisted sideways long enough for me to punch him again.

"Don't talk about her like that!"

Next thing, Booth was on the ground, glaring at me with blue fire in his eyes. I kicked him in the side, sent his right shoulder into the little hollow, then, before he could rise, crashed down into him, knees first. I put one knee on his shoulder to keep it stuck under the boulder and the other on his upper left arm. All the while, I kept punching.

A thousand years ago, I knew how to fight. Since coming back, I'd avoided it like the plague. Chak bruises don't heal, our broken bones don't mend. A fistfight had higher stakes than a gun battle.

But I wasn't exactly thinking things through, and the next blow split his upper lip.

"She is not nothing! I am not nothing!"

The next shot turned his head sideways, leaving my hand to rake his incisors. When I pulled back, a flap of dry skin hung from my knuckles like beef jerky. When I punched him again, I left bits of my flesh on his teeth.

Repulsed, his free hand stopped trying to push my knee away and reached for his mouth. "Jesus, stop it! Get off of me! What are you, shedding?"

He tried spitting. Drops of blood from his lips landed on my shirt.

"Go ahead. Try to kill me," he said. "Give it your best shot. You think I'm Lenore?"

"I didn't kill her, you fuck!"

"Bullshit. I saw that look in your eyes before you raced out of the office."

I pulled back to punch him again, but stopped. I hated

him, I was furious with him. He'd slept with my wife, blamed me for her murder, treated me like I was nothing, but . . .

"I don't want to kill you, asshole. I never wanted to kill her, either."

His eyes narrowed. "But you did, didn't you? This a confession?"

My shoulders slumped. I pinched Booth's cheek. "No, like I've been telling you, Lenore was dead when I showed up. It was Lamar Derby, that lead you refused to follow. And I . . . well, geez, I've been thinking I *would've* killed her, if I'd gotten there first. I don't remember much, but I remember how those photos of you and her made me feel. It was like my insides were falling out, back when they were wet and I needed them for something. I thought I was just about fucked up enough for it. But, I didn't kill her, I wasn't going to hit Larry with my crowbar, Flat-face was an accident, and I'm not about to kill you, so . . ."

I got off him. He huffed, spraying more blood. "She said you hit her."

"Once. She hit back. I had a welt the size of a grapefruit. We both went to counseling. Never happened again."

He blinked and nodded. "That's what she said."

"Was she . . . still afraid of me?"

He shook his head. "Not that I could tell. Afraid of having kids, not with you, just afraid of having kids. I was a way out, big-time."

"Tom, you never had a relationship that lasted more than a month. Did you love her?" I asked.

For a second he looked like a boy who'd been caught stealing, or my father rubbing his half a hand. "I . . . don't know. Sometimes I think I should have. If we'd run off, she'd still be alive."

"Easier to blame me than yourself?"

"Oh, I blame myself. I blame myself a whole lot. I just blamed *you* more."

He twisted his arm out from under the rock, rubbed his teeth with his fingers and kept spitting until he was sure the dead flesh was gone.

"Who's Flat-face?"

"Never mind. I'll tell you later and you can decide whether the DA will want to press charges." I looked around at the dark. "So now what do we do?"

"We?"

"Fine. What do *you* want to do?"

He eyed me cautiously. "You're really not going feral?"

I shook my head. "You hate chakz so much you think you'd take the time to study them a little. We go feral when we feel hopeless, not when we're pissed. Truth to tell, I'm not even pissed anymore. I feel kind of relieved, like I should take myself out to dinner and a nice zombie movie or something." I looked at Booth. "You done with your bullshit, yet? Ready to tell me how you wound up at ChemBet?"

He wiped the blood off his face, then the dirt off his clothes. "Like you said, I thought the arm was the result of one of their experiments, so it was a lead. When we got there, that alarm was already going off. We let ourselves in, poked around, and I saw a few things I wasn't supposed to, like the fact they had no idea how to duplicate Travis Maruta's last project, code-named Birthday. He destroyed his records. Those two vials are it. And you'll never guess who hired the fake cop that went to your office."

"ChemBet."

He shook his head. "I'm not clear if the board of directors is in on it. He was a merc, Blackwater style. The paperwork was on Rebecca's desk. She paid for him with her damn personal credit card, so it wouldn't be on any corporate account."

I smiled in disbelief. "And you were going to arrest her?"

"Once I got the warrant. Being head of homicide has to count for something. With O'Donnell dead, I figured there wouldn't be a man on the force who wouldn't back me, or look at me again if I didn't. If the press found out before the governor, his hands would be tied. If not, fuck the pension."

"Okay, are you sure ChemBet's the one pulling Kagan and the governor's strings?" I asked.

"Who else?"

I help up a dried finger. "There are two possibilities. Whoever chased us and took Misty were shooting like they didn't care if they hit the case. If those were the only samples, Maruta's little men would've been more careful."

When I held up the second finger, I remembered a liquid shadow on a computer screen, too heavy for the air to hold, too fast for it to let go. "Then there's Bad Penny. That kind of ninja training can't come cheap. Think she could be military? Or from Krypton?"

Booth shrugged.

I wouldn't say we were buddies after that, but when we hit the woods again, we found a pace that worked.

It'd grown dark, but some roofs soon poked through the tree-blanket. A short time later, we stumbled into a backyard with rusty swings, weeds, and a house that should've fallen down ages ago. It was likely owned by one of many families barely holding on due to the economy. There were lights inside.

I stood behind Booth as he rang the doorbell. Even if Jonesey's revolution hadn't made the evening news, the last thing you want to see at your door after sunset is a chak.

An eyeball came to the peephole. Booth held up his badge.

"Police. I need to borrow your phone."

The eyeball went away, and then . . . nothing.

He rang again, waited, then held the button down, like a man thinking he'd make the elevator come faster through thumb-power. Inside, there was shuffling, doors locking, metal clicking. Booth gave up on the buzzer and banged with his fist.

A terrified male voice answered. "Go away! I've got children here!"

Tom rolled his eyes. "For pity's sake, I'm a police detective! I just need the damn phone!"

"I'm not trusting anyone. I've got a gun! I'll use it."

Booth took a step back. "Jesus, I told you I'm a . . ."

I don't know if the gun went off accidentally or not but along with the firecracker pop, a hole appeared in the surface of the door and a bloody scratch formed in the hair on the side of Tom's head. We ran.

"What?" Tom said. "We picked the only house on the block with a fucking meth lab?"

"That's no meth lab. That guy thought he was defending his family. Something's going on," I said. "Maybe Jonesey's doing better than we thought. Damn."

Two houses down, an SUV sat in the driveway, keys on the passenger seat.

"Well, that's a gimme," I said.

When I opened the door, Booth hesitated. I guess he hadn't stolen many cars lately.

"If you stop and ask, you could wind up with a hole in your chest."

He grabbed the keys and took the driver's seat.

As we pulled out, I flipped on the radio. The station was airing the audio portion of Nell Parker's show. It was not business as usual. Rather than chatting up a reassuring guest, she was appealing for calm.

"I repeat, the photos circulating on your cell phones are a hoax," she said, but she didn't sound like she meant it. Knowing she wouldn't be allowed to say anything important, I scanned for a liveblood news station and got some details.

There were riots going on at five local camps. Smaller scuffles had broken out in and around the city, all blamed on that "fake" photograph.

"At present, we have no idea if this was someone's sick idea of a joke, or the intent was to cause a panic, but the authorities assure us they will find the perpetrator. Our other big story, possibly related, is that homicide detective Thomas Booth, now wanted by the police, is still at large, considered armed and dangerous after having apparently turned his gun on his own men during a routine investigation at a ChemBet facility in . . ."

I turned off the radio. "Well, that's not good."

"Shit, I don't see how to win this," Booth said.

I closed my eyes, but the world didn't go away. "At this point," I said, "I'd settle for losing more slowly. Tom, the case, you want it?"

He looked at me like I was crazy. It was a step up, like he'd forgotten I was a chak. "The briefcase?"

"When I didn't know whose it was, I didn't give a rat's ass who got it. Now that I know it belongs to psycho-bitch, I'm fine with giving it to anyone but her. Got a vat of acid you can dump it into?"

"What if it's like your idiot friend thinks, some kind of cure? It's called *birthday* isn't it?"

"You don't believe that horseshit, do you?"

"No, but what do I know? I didn't think they could bring the dead back to life, or that an arm could move by itself."

"And you *want* more of the same?"

He shook his head. "Even if I still had a job, this would be way above my fucking pay scale." He blew some air between his cracked lips. "I've got a friend at a university lab in Boston. I could bring it there, see if he can figure out what it is."

Whether the zombie scuffles were getting bigger or smaller, we didn't see any. The trip to the warehouse was uneventful. I pulled open the big, squeaky metal door and let the headlights illuminate the oil stains, old crates, and other ghosts of commerce past.

"If I'd known you were coming, I'd have cleaned up a little."

I walked over to the vat where I'd sunk the case, and pulled it out by the rope. As I did, I spotted something lying in the gloom. On the floor, lying across a crowbar, was a set of bolt cutters.

I put the bagged briefcase, dripping gunk, on the floor. I headed for the cutters, pulling the chain between us taut. As soon as he felt the tug, Booth saw where I was headed and nearly got there before I did.

I slipped the chain between the blades and tried to squeeze the handles. Bolt cutters go through chain link like butter. The links in our chain weren't much thicker than that, but were made of sterner stuff. I put one handle down on the ground and leaned my weight into the other. Booth had to join in, both of us pushing, until the chain finally broke.

We were free, of each other at least.

"Going to crush my head now?"

"Not just yet," he said.

"Tom, I'm touched."

He went back to the briefcase and started pulling off the garbage bags and duct tape. The cuff was tight on my bad ankle. With the bolt cutters in my hands, I might as well take care of that, too. I shoved a blade between my pants cuff and the metal and squeezed. This time it sliced through easily.

"Should've started with the cuffs," I said aloud, but he was too busy arguing with the duct tape to pay me any mind. Two more snips and I was able to bend the bracelet enough to pull it off.

That's when I noticed a blinking red light inside, sitting on a little bit of circuitry. Crap.

"Tom," I shouted. "They've been tracking us!"

He was already ducking when a bullet sliced the skin on top of his hand. He was lucky it didn't hit bone. When it hit a metal post instead, it exploded into a little red and yellow flower that lasted half a second. It was the third time we'd been shot at today, but this time was the prettiest.

The SUV's headlights made us sitting ducks. I rolled into one side of the darkness, Tom into the other, leaving the briefcase behind. Coming into a wobbly crouch, I tried to figure out what direction the bullet came from, then crept out of what I imagined was the shooter's line of sight.

Booth and I knew enough not to speak and give away our position. The sniper knew enough not to fire and give away his. We were all very clever. I spotted him anyway. He was across the narrow street, an ape-shape in a bulky suit. His hooded head was misshapen, just like it would be if he were wearing night-vision goggles.

Keeping ape-man in view, I backed up slowly, staying low so I didn't trip over something. I had no idea where Booth was, I just hoped we didn't bump into each other.

The shooter crossed the street with the kind of easy precision you get from regular drilling. Even if he wasn't military, his training was. He was cautious, but not overtly so, as if he doubted one chak and a homicide detective could give him much trouble. His problem would be entering the light to grab the case. If he took the goggles off, he wouldn't be able to see us coming from the shadows. If he kept them on, close-up, the glare from the headlights would be blinding.

I thought that might give us a small advantage, but once he reached the SUV, he turned off the lights. Problem solved. His, anyway.

My back found the wall. I thought about doing the

dead thing, acting like I was nothing until they all went away, but Booth was out there, and I knew, with the briefcase at stake, he was planning something stupid.

So I headed for the SUV. It was easy enough. Booth had left the engine idling and the sniper didn't think to turn it off. The trick was to get there fast enough to make a difference, but carefully enough to avoid being seen.

I was maybe a foot away when I heard a familiar grunt and the sounds of a scuffle. The dark echoed with the slap of heavy punches, probably from Booth, mixed with quicker, heavier thuds, I assumed from the sniper's counterstrikes.

Hoping Booth might last two seconds, I hopped in the SUV and flipped on the headlights. Good thing, too. Tom was fighting two men, not one. The second entered while the lights were out, came up from behind and wrapped his arm around Booth's neck. Now, he'd pulled Tom back and up, took him off his feet. The other had a combat knife and was about to gut the head of Fort Hammer's Homicide Division.

The light surprised them, though.

In pain, each twisted their heads and reached for the goggles. Free, Booth landed a series of elbow jabs in the abdomen of the guy behind him, but the other one whipped his goggles off, took in the situation and regripped his knife.

I honked. All three of them turned toward the SUV. The hooded apes nodded at each other. One clocked Booth in the jaw, the one with the knife came for me.

Chakz aren't very fast, but SUVs are, and all you have to do is put them in gear and step on the gas pedal. The ape with the knife jumped, but the bumper caught him in midleap. He rolled around before grabbing hold of the hood, then, like a panther, he jumped for the windshield.

While he was doing that, I steered into his buddy. The car hit him head-on. Unfortunately, Booth didn't get out of the way in time and wound up sideswiped. One sniper down, I spun the wheel and slammed into a concrete support post. Momentum should've thrown number two off the hood, but either the SUV wasn't going fast enough, or he was real strong.

Either way, the car wasn't moving anymore, which made things easy for him. Rather than beat his way through the windshield, he jumped off and came for the door. Close-up, I could see his face was covered in black greasepaint, the whites of his eyes glowing like small versions of the headlights.

He pulled out a sidearm, fired into the door lock, then stopped moving.

What the fuck?

It took me a second to notice there'd been a slight change in his outfit. There was a new flap in the cloth under his chin, revealing skin. A fish line across his neck seeped, then gushed blood. As he fell, the expression in his eyes didn't change, like he'd never had a chance to realize he was dead.

The other attacker was on the ground. His leg was broken, but he was trying to rise. He never did. A shadowy form flew across him. In the second it took to pass over him, a figure drove the man's combat knife into the center of his chest.

The briefcase vanished next. It looked like it was flying through the air before I made out the figure carrying it, the same figure that had killed Happy Jack in my office what seemed ages ago.

Bad Penny.

I watched her go, leaping from shadow to shadow like a devil in black. The only clear shape visible was the rectangle of the briefcase.

Good thing it was empty.

24

There was barely time to enjoy the emptiness Bad Penny left behind, when a blast of blue and white assaulted the avenue between warehouses. The police. Made sense, I guess. ChemBet was monitoring us. Maybe the cops were monitoring ChemBet. More cars came from the other direction. I wasn't sure if they were police or what. To be completely honest, I'd lost track of who was tracking whom, but it was a party, a big one.

Booth was out cold. I probably should have told him the vials weren't in the briefcase, but I hadn't remembered myself until I saw Penny rush off with the case. There was no time to grab the vials now. Besides, having them on me in case we got caught was a bad idea anyway.

I hooked Tom under the armpits and dragged him to the SUV. We couldn't head out the way we came in, but the walls were cheap, thin corrugated metal. If I got up some speed, I'd be able to slam the SUV through the rear of the warehouse and make a break for it.

No such luck. The engine wouldn't start. The V-shaped cavity in the hood where the car had hit the support beam had done more than ruin the finish.

I jumped from the driver's seat as the first squad cars crunched to a halt. Car doors opened, feet hit asphalt. I'd never get Booth out of here before they spotted us. But these were Fort Hammer police, not mercs or rentals, men who knew and worked with him, bullshit charges or not. They may not have much love for me, but they wouldn't hurt their head of homicide without hearing him out first. He'd be arrested, but they wouldn't shoot him.

Leaving Booth in the passenger seat, I scuttled into the dark, nearly tripping over one of the fallen snipers. That, it turned out, was a lucky break. With his night-vision goggles and headset staring me in the face, I realized how handy they might be. Yanking them off his head, I hustled out through an open space in the wall that used to be a window.

Outside, it was pitch-dark and I was dead, so I managed to put six or seven warehouses between myself and the police without much trouble. I looked back every few seconds to make sure I wasn't being followed. I had no idea how many groups were after me now. The shadows could be filled with everything from balding pederasts to Mouseketeers, all eager for the secrets of Travis Maruta's final project.

Satisfied as I could get that I was alone, I plopped myself on the ground by a sputtering streetlamp to have a look at my new toy. The easy part was figuring out what the headpiece was for. I slipped it on and lowered the goggles over my eyes. After poking the sides in search of a button, I found one, pressed it, and heard the high-pitched whine of powering electronics. The unseen world lay revealed before me, etched in gross browns and sickly greens.

There were readings alongside the image, numbers and abbreviations, a menu. A spot right under the button near my right temple, moved a highlight around. Hoping it worked like a mouse, I put the bright green box on the word "COM" and double-clicked. What do you know? Maybe some things really are idiot-proof.

A voice came through the headset, electronically altered just like my old buddy the toad. "Have you secured the goods?" it said.

"You bet. Project Birthday is all wrapped up with a ribbon and a nice card. What name should I put on it?"

"Hessius Mann. You have quite a knack for survival."

It *was* the toad. "Yeah, wish I'd had it before the execution."

"I assume this means more of my men are dead. Pity. I paid a great deal for them."

"Really? I figured they were ChemBet."

"They were. That's why I had to pay extra. Did they put up a good fight?"

"The best. Technically, second best, otherwise they'd still be alive. You're probably not going to believe this, but the ninja got them."

The air had been quiet, but at that moment an icy breeze swept along the sidewalk. It made me wonder if Penny had already realized the case was empty, and had doubled back.

"Oddly, I am inclined to believe you," the toad said. "I've seen the footage from your office."

"That on YouTube already?" I looked up and down the street. A targeting cursor in the goggles zeroed in on some movement—a rat meandering around a trash can. Pretty cool.

"You still don't know who I am, do you?"

I kept looking. "I've narrowed it down. You're not Santa Claus or the Easter Bunny. But if you want to just tell me, don't let me stop you."

"Who has the briefcase?"

No need to lie about that at least. "The ninja."

"Pity. He's the only one in this whole situation I've been unable to track."

He. So he didn't know who Penny was. Hell, I didn't know who she was.

"Must be frustrating."

"Oh, there's more than enough data coming in to keep me busy. For instance, right now, I see that you're sitting behind warehouse G3."

I snapped my head left and right. How the fuck could he see me? They didn't bother putting security cameras down here. I looked up and saw the source of the breeze, a small plane, mixing with the clouds. Apparently they'd added a few pages to the army surplus catalog since last I checked.

"It's an older-model military drone, an MQ-1, if you're curious. With the press of a button, I could patch the video feed to the police, or ChemBet security. They have two . . . no, three cars in the area. With the press of another button, I could have it fire a Hellfire missile at you."

"Button, button, who's got the button?" I stood, planning to bolt. A dot appeared on my chest, rendered green by the goggles, but I had to figure it was red—a laser site from the drone. Acid, fire, and D-cap I had figured. What would be left of me after a missile strike? The temperature of the blast might take care of me, and even if it didn't there was a good bet that whatever remained wouldn't be talking much.

"I doubt you'd tell ChemBet, especially after you stole their men. The police, maybe, if you're the guy who has Kagan in his pocket. Then again I got away from them once. I really wouldn't use the missile, though."

"Why not?"

"Same reason your boys shouldn't have been shooting at us back on Essex Street."

"You said the ninja had the vials."

"I said the ninja had the briefcase. Seems they got separated."

The little light on my chest disappeared. "So you either have them, or you're smart enough to lie about it. You fascinate me. You always have. If you're telling the truth, I want you to bring the vials to me."

I laughed, nice and clear so he'd understand. "After what your dogs did to Chester and Misty? No way in fucking hell."

"I'm truly sorry about what happened to Officer O'Donnell and your assistant. But, to be fair, every man I've sent after you is dead. And from all appearances, you killed one with an axe."

"I slipped. Besides, I'm not seeing the moral equivalent between slaughtering innocents and protecting them. Then again, I'm a little slow these days."

"Protecting. Interesting that people can still be so special to you. I could help you find your assistant, get her into the best treatment program in the country."

"If you didn't shoot her first."

The toad sounded offended. "I'm not Rebecca Maruta."

"That makes three people you're not. Want to tell me why you want this crap so badly? You one of the assholes who think it's Kyua?"

Silence. I looked over my shoulder, trying to see if there was a quick way to get into the building behind me. Even if the drone had infrared that could detect a warm liveblood inside, it wouldn't see me once I was out of sight.

I was going to make a move when the toad said, "There's someone here I'd like you to speak with. Someone else I believe is special to you."

Did they bring my dog back, too?

There was a slight crackle as the voice filter came off.

A low, diffident voice said only, "Hello."

I recognized her immediately. "Nell?"

"Yeah. He . . . no . . . *we* want to invite you to dinner to talk things over. And yeah, he knows you don't eat, so I guess it's some kind of metaphor."

Despite playing word games with him, halfway through the conversation I was pretty sure who the toad was. Now it was an existential certainty, cold and absolute as an uncaring god. It was Nell Parker's owner, Colby Green. That's why Penny's description of the shooters sounded so familiar. Green's men dressed like the crooks from *Reservoir Dogs*. I'd even been calling them dogs again without making the connection.

"Has Green got a gun on you? A chain saw?"

"Not exactly, but I can't get away right now. It'd be nice to talk to you. I haven't seen you for a while."

"Not since you got me out of jail by selling yourself back to Caligula."

"I thought I was doing you a favor. Don't ask me why."

"Nell, I . . ."

She cut me off. "You've got two choices, come have dinner, or run as fast and far as you fucking can and get out of the country. Up to you."

She handed the phone back to Green. He didn't bother putting the voice filter back on. "Well?" he said.

"What's to keep you from cutting me up to get me to talk?"

He laughed. "You'd go feral. I'm surprised you haven't already."

"Okay, I'll be there," I told him.

"I'll send a car to Lydig and Brenner. Should take you half an hour to walk there. I'll let you know if you're being followed. If you need directions, follow the drone."

I slapped the side of my head, severing the connection.

25

Nell Parker. For weeks I'd been staring at her on the tube, pretending I wasn't feeling anything for her. The vibrations rattling my chest told me otherwise.

Damn.

I think I'd gotten over the fact that she went back to Green. What I hadn't gotten over was the fact that with a bomb about to bring an abandoned hospital down around us, I'd pressed my lips against hers. She thought I was nuts. So did I. Chakz are supposed to be in a state of perpetual sexual neutrality. There were plenty of chakz backing that up, selling their bodies to livebloods without so much as a shrug. But "supposed to" is a funny phrase. A D-cap is *supposed to* kill us. Arms aren't *supposed to* wander on their own.

The drone came out of its holding pattern and headed east. I followed below, my body listing on my Frankenstein ankle. It was hurting again. A glance at my hand showed some exposed knuckle bone from the beating

I'd given Booth. I'd lost count of how many bullet holes I had in me.

Bad as my body was, the real pain was that I hadn't realized the toad was Colby Green in the first place. Who else had the power or the perverted fascination? Everything about chakz fascinated him. Were we really alive? Did we have a soul? What happens if you tug on that piece over there? Not in a Lady Maruta sense. He was more into stroking than cutting.

I used to think ChemBet at least knew what we were, that they fed the world a line of BS to keep the rubes from panicking. Having seen their files, I now knew they didn't. No one did, not really. That's why Colby liked us. To him, we were the last challenge in a world that had otherwise grown boring.

A man's reach-around should exceed his grasp, right? And his fingers were in every orifice Fort Hammer had to offer, real and metaphorical. He had as much influence with the governor as ChemBet did, maybe more, given the chak pleasure palace he ran and the photos he kept of his guests.

The streetlamp at the corner of Lydig and Brenner was working well enough, and Green's limo driver was smart enough to park out of its light. When I came up and rapped on the window, he had an e-reader balanced in front of him showing some local news. A bloated guy with a beard, he was the sort who had trouble squeezing his gut under the steering wheel, even with the seat all the way back. If I startled him, he didn't move very fast. More like I was interrupting his break.

When he opened the door, the smell of flatulence wafted out. It was maybe forty outside, but he had the air-conditioning turned up full to hide it. Good thing I didn't have to breathe. I slid in, bones cracking as I settled into the deep upholstery.

When the driver was back at the wheel, I asked, "Anything on the chak rebellion?"

His narrowed eyes found me through the rearview. "Why? Which side you on?"

Christ, whichever side eats you, pal. "Neither. Don't want to see anyone hurt."

He grunted. "They say the guard's got it under control."

Right. I remembered the liveblood panic when a single skeleton was loose in Buell Park. The police were using elephant guns for a mosquito and they still couldn't hit it. The guard was the same, only with less college required.

The fastest way to Colby's zip code was through town, so I'd soon see for myself. I figured it was over before it'd gotten started. The suburbanite with the gun was just paranoid and trigger-happy.

Within twenty minutes, though, we passed some searchlights and stiff-backed guardsmen. There were no rioting dead I could see, so this was all show to keep the LBs calm. Calm about what?

In the retail district, things were a little more exciting. A major box store was in flames, its windows smashed, black smoke curling against the dark interior. Figures faded in and out among the aisles like tricks of light. They were chakz, moving as fast as they could, meaning not very. I spotted one carrying a flat-panel TV. Dead men looting, now there's something you don't see every day.

I was a little surprised there weren't more ferals around, but the big orange-and-black detour signs likely took us around the main action. Once we were on the road that followed the train tracks, there was nothing to see. The rest of the ride was a quiet forty minutes.

Green kept his sanctuary safe through a combination of distance and clever landscaping, though it seems an insult to call rerouting a river and planting a few acres of new forest landscaping. You can't even see the wall surrounding his property until you're practically on top of it.

Front gates that could stop a tank opened noiselessly, but we weren't there yet. The winding driveway went on half a mile before the mansion came into view. It was huge, but a gangly chimera, a little of this, a little of that, like it never could decide which style it belonged to.

All in all, I hadn't worried about Nell's health while she was with Green, especially since she'd become a TV star. Sure, he'd sold her to a serial killer to get back some incriminating photos, but how often does that kind of situation come up? Experience had since proven there were worse fates for a chak than being the favored pet of an überwealthy reprobate.

Not that I'd call Green compassionate. He'd hold big festivals with scores of chakz, then let them go feral after they'd outlived their usefulness. He even helped the process along by locking them in a pen in his ample basement, but there are monsters, and there are monsters. At least he didn't cut them up.

The limo stopped out front, the entrance for honored guests, which I'd used by accident during my first visit. The driver idled the car, but didn't look like he planned on getting up. I let myself out.

Up some marble stairs, the two Stonehenge-sized slabs being used for doors swung in. A short fellow greeted me with a curt nod and a nervous rubbing of his gloved hands. His face was covered with white pancake, giving him more than a passing resemblance to the emcee from *Cabaret*. I remembered him from last time, too, but didn't remember him this anxious.

"Nice night for it," he said.

For what? The lights in the House of Gaudy were dim, the place so quiet only the air was echoing. The usual bacchanal wasn't taking place. Cancelled on account of insurgency? Sure. Even if they didn't take the danger seriously, it wouldn't do for a congressman or chief of police to be found away from their desks engaged in necrophilia.

Wordless, I followed the agitated emcee. Green's security dogs, all in black with thin ties and white shirts, dotted our trip, but it seemed like there were a lot fewer than I remembered, and some weren't exactly in shape. His standards were slipping.

Last I'd met Colby Green, we'd spoken in a small office, the only normal-sized thing in the joint. I guess this time he wanted to make a different impression, because I was led to the dining room, which was anything but normal.

Green, fifty-something with bat-black eyes, sat at the head of what would've looked like an aircraft carrier if it hadn't been made of wood and covered with linen and dishes. Behind him, a series of marble busts sat on a mantel. Among them, I recognized Dionysus and Epicurus, natural favorites for any hedonist.

He wore a white robe over T-shirt and sweats. On

someone else the outfit would've looked informal, but it made him look like an ancient king. He reminded me of a Tarot card, the two of something or other. It shows a lone figure, Alexander the Great, looking out at the world he's conquered, filled with an existential sadness at having finished everything in life he considered possible, or desirable.

Only this king wasn't alone. Nell Parker stood behind him, wearing a revealing gown whose green color matched her eyes as closely as the folds of fabric matched her white curves. Her eye color was a present from Green's more modest chak-experiments. Now she had another gift from him: a golden collar around her neck, with a chain leading to a latch on an arm of Green's chair.

I got the point. It wasn't exactly subtle.

"And they say you can't tell a thing from chak-eyes," he said. He didn't move much, almost like a chak. His darting pupils did all the work.

Seeing as he didn't get up to shake hands, and Nell wasn't in any position to move very far without ruining her chain, I stayed at the far end of the table.

"And what do you see in mine, Mr. Green?"

"Hatred."

I flipped my palms in a noncommittal gesture. "You know chakz don't feel anything that deeply. Nice collar, Nell."

"Thanks," she said, touching it with her fingers. "It was a real surprise. Matter of fact, the whole night's been a real surprise. I'm usually at work."

Green held up his hand like a cop directing traffic. "At first I didn't believe you still had the vials, but your ghost-ninja followed you halfway here before my driver lost him."

Good. That meant it was less likely she'd double back to recheck the warehouse.

"Sure you lost him?"

"Reasonably."

He grimaced as if recalling something unpleasant. "I'd be lying to say I've lost sleep over it, but again, let me express my regrets at what happened to the officer and your assistant."

"Then, at least you're well rested."

"I average about three hours a night. Never needed more."

"It's true," Nell put in. "He's a regular night owl."

"Just like Caligula. As I recall things didn't work out too well for him. Assassinated by his guard, wasn't he?"

Green leaned forward like he'd spotted a brand-new bug. "You remember the name of a Roman emperor and how he died. I sometimes wonder if your memory really is bad or simply convenient."

"I'm good at Beatles trivia, too, but mostly it seems pretty random. Otherwise I'd have recognized your smell in this a long time ago."

He idly played with Nell's chain. "Could be old, scattered patterns in your nervous system. Engaging in patter with me, for instance, or looking at Nell, and your brain tries to comply with the situation, dancing without being really aware of the tune. I'm an amateur compared to Rebecca Maruta, but I'd love to run some tests on you. Nonintrusive. We both might learn something."

"No thanks, I stopped taking tests when I graduated from school."

"Except the chak-test, no? I helped ChemBet design it, you know. We do cooperate when our interests coincide."

"Well, there's another reason to hate you, isn't there? If I did hate anyone, that is."

He narrowed his gaze. "This could've been over days ago. I told you, the man who kidnapped your assistant was a bad hire. I thought he may have been one of Rebecca's moles, we're always spying on each other, but he was too stupid for that, an addict who lacked basic impulse control. What's the use of a sadist who has no control? It's so hard to get a good S and M man these days." He shook his head. "Do you realize how little research has been done on sadism beyond guessing at possible causes: parental condemnation and shaming leading to a desire for superiority; a response to feeling disgust for anything sexual; acting out from a hidden fear of castration. What does that tell you? Nothing."

"Is there a point hiding in there somewhere that's afraid to come out?"

He smiled a little. "Perhaps. Given your history, I know your propensity for violence is triggered by a sense of righteous betrayal, probably some childhood trauma. I've been trying to figure out if Rebecca Maruta is simply a sadist, or something else entirely."

"Oh," I said. "That's an easy one. Trust me. She's something else."

"Then consider the possibility that *Project Birthday* would be in better hands with me."

I shook my head. "You're also something else."

He rapped his fingers on the table. "I could've stopped you from finding your wife's killer, but I didn't."

"It didn't suit you."

"I could've let you rot in jail, but I secured your release."

"To get Nell back."

He put his palms up. "Nevertheless, like my work with ChemBet, our interests have coincided in the past. They could again, if you'd let them. I want the vials. What do you want in exchange? I destroyed the body of the man you murdered, so there's no evidence of your crime."

"Forget it, I already confessed to the head of homicide. Aside from erasing the last week the only thing I want is that shit safely destroyed."

He acted like he hadn't heard me. No, he acted like he shouldn't *have* to hear me. He tugged on Nell's chain. "You miss having company? Helping Misty isn't enough? I'll give you Nell. I'll even see to it she keeps her broadcast career. She could support you both."

She stiffened. I wasn't sure if that meant she liked or didn't like the idea.

I shook my head. "I don't buy and sell human beings."

He grinned. "Isn't that a line from *Casablanca*? Marvelous. What are you afraid I'll do with it if I get it?"

"Use it."

"I'd take every precaution. And if it works, if it really brings the dead back to life, I wouldn't keep it for myself. You want assurances? Give me one vial, keep the other. If the testing pans out, use it on yourself. You'd be alive again. Think about that. *Really* alive. Depending on the efficacy, O'Donnell could be brought back, too, maybe even your *wife*. We're talking about immortality. We'd be *gods.*"

I'd seen red when Jonesey or Misty suggested bringing back Chester, but Green was smart, and a better talker. I admit I imagined seeing my flesh pink again, Misty happy with Chester, seeing Lenore rise from the grave, everyone singing that old song based on the Book of Ezekiel, *Them bones, them bones, them dry bones . . .*

But the pretty pictures ended with Dad, scotch balanced in his remaining fingers, giving me one of his snippets of advice: "If it sounds like it's too good to be true, it *is* too good to be true."

I nodded at the busts on the mantel. "Gods, right, like the ones who killed their father, sometimes ate their children, and had a habit of turning people into animals."

"This is all semantics. Tell me what choice you think you have. The rumor is, *Project Birthday* is some kind of virus that can spread airborne, meaning you can't safely destroy it even if you wanted to. If it turns out to be dangerous, I can."

I pointed at him like he was a pair of car keys I'd been looking for. "See, that's it, Mr. Green. *That's* what I don't trust. You say you'll let Nell go, I believe you. You say you'll find Misty and get her into rehab, I believe you. Destroy Kyua? No, I don't think so. If something grosser than chakz came crawling out of those vials, you'd name it, dress it up, train it, and add it to your collection. I don't care how much money you . . ."

Money. The lack of guards, the flatulent limo driver, even his hired goons. They were all second rate, like he was cutting corners. On the phone he'd been bitching about how much the assassins and the drone cost him. It hit me.

"You're strapped for cash, aren't you? With the chakcamps scooping everyone up, you've been losing money and influence. Now you think you can get it back with whatever's in the vials. If it works, you keep it. If it doesn't you sell it back to ChemBet."

He threw his hands up in the air. "I tried the nice way . . ."

CLUNK!

Colby Green went forward, he forehead-smashed the plate in front of him, cracking the expensive china right down the middle.

Nell stood behind him, holding the small marble pedestal she'd grabbed from the mantel. One white edge marred with a bit of blood.

She turned her green eyes on me. "He's got some new drug he thinks will prevent a chak from going feral temporarily. If you didn't cooperate, he was going to shoot you full of it and cut you up into little pieces until you talked. I want to get out of here. You wanna help or what?"

26

Unlike whatever made me and Booth ankle buddies, Nell's chain was for show. I was going to snap it off, but she stopped me, stuck her hand in the pocket of Green's robe, and pulled out the key.

Before she could use it, he moaned. A welt was growing on the back of his head, but even so, he had a way of moaning that made unconsciousness seem dirty. The collar unlocked, she pulled it off and tossed it at his groin, like she was hoping it would do some damage.

Then we stood there a second, face-to-face in the quiet.

"So, you gonna kiss me again?" she asked.

"You want me to?"

"I . . . don't know. Yeah."

We gave it a go. It was a little longer than last time, she making more of an effort. Prepubescent kids press lips sometimes to see what all the fuss is about. This wasn't exactly like that, but it didn't feel the way it did when I was alive, either. There was a lot less moisture. I wouldn't say it felt bad. I liked the sense of approval, and something else stirred . . .

. . . until Colby Green moaned again, long and low. His eyes were open. I was afraid he was enjoying watching us, but the pupils were vacant. Still, it ruined the moment.

I pulled back from Nell. "What's the best way out of here?"

"Didn't work out that part," she said. "Kitchen leads to the basement, from there we can get to the garage."

"How much security, you think?"

She gave me a little smile. "You were right. I don't know the details, but he's been cutting back on expenses. Between here and the garage there may be five at most."

"Better than fifty, but we'll still need some insurance in case we run into them." I pulled a groggy Green to standing. "Do you know where any weapons are? A knife? Something we can threaten their paycheck with?"

She pulled open a drawer and pulled out a Walther P99, one of the few guns I can fire without risking my hand. "This do?"

"Geez, marry me. Point it at him."

"No, you take it," she said, shoving it in my pocket. "I'm afraid I'll shoot him for the hell of it."

I eyed her hand in my pocket. "I appreciate the attention, but you either have to hold the gun or Green."

She pulled it back out. Before I could ask if she knew how to use it, she had the safety off. "Fine."

Holding his arms behind his back, I aimed Green at the door. His head lolled. I don't know how aware he was, but somewhere in that overheated head, a very smart, very angry man was fighting his way back to consciousness. I wanted to be far away when he won.

The kitchen staff backed off at the sight of Nell's Walther. A maid in a skimpy outfit even held the basement door for us. The stairs were tricky. A quarter of the way down, I lost my grip and Green skittered down to the poured-concrete floor. I was surprised that didn't snap him out of it. When we yanked him to his feet, he was still disoriented.

The basement was a cinder-block labyrinth, but Nell knew the way. The only thing I recognized was the open door to the chak pens. Last time I was here it was standing room only. Now, they were empty. A sign of the times.

Green rustled and opened his eyes. I motioned for Nell to aim the gun at him, but he took one look at her and started *sobbing*. Tears rolled down his cheeks. Thin mucus poured from his nose.

"Nell . . , Nell . . . Nell . . ." he said.

"Now you feel guilty, you son of a bitch?" Nell said.

I grabbed his hair and pulled his head back. His eyes rolled in the sockets.

"It might not be his conscience talking. You whacked him pretty good. I think the bawling is a symptom of concussion. Inappropriate emotion."

She sneered. "You can't get more inappropriate than tears from Colby Green. He gonna die?"

"How the hell should I know? How much farther to the garage?"

"Down that way and to the left."

I expected some guards in the carport, but the only one there was my chubby limo driver. When we came in, he was balanced in a chair, sitting in the middle of six

stylish rides. Coat open and flopping along his sides, he
was reading his e-book again.

Seeing us, he bolted up and reached for his own gun.
Then he saw the one Nell had aimed at his gut.

"I don't see how I could miss you, Tony," she said.
"Put it down."

Green's head steadied. When his eyes took in the fat
man as he laid his gun on the floor, he cackled like the
Crypt Keeper, only in a much deeper voice.

"Did you drug him?" Tony asked.

"No," I said. "He's just happy to see you."

I pushed him toward the befuddled driver. While he
collapsed into the man's arms, I scooped the gun off the
ground.

Nell grabbed a set of keys from a Peg-Board and
pressed the button. The lights on a Tesla Roadster Sport
flashed and the door locks clicked open. As Nell and I
climbed into the car, Green's laughter grew frantic. It
was like he'd forgotten how to use words and was trying
to order his man around with laughs.

I shot Tony a look. "If you want to keep your boss
alive, call him an ambulance."

"Okay, he's an ambulance."

Everyone's a comedian.

A minute later, we were speeding away on the tree-
lined road that brought me here. Much as I admired
Nell's ecologically minded choice, I worried that the
Tesla's battery-powered electric motor would max out
around sixty, making it easy for a gas-guzzler to catch up.
But we were doing ninety, and the needle kept climbing.

No one seemed to be following, but that would be a
first. Couldn't do much about what I couldn't see, so

when the curves in the road started stressing my system, I took it down to sixty.

All in all I thought the meeting with Green had gone pretty well. At least now I didn't have to worry about what he might do to Nell if I didn't fork over the vials.

I looked at her, her black hair mussed, her green chak-eyes focused on the road, maybe worried I'd hit something. She looked better than she did on TV.

"You swing a mean marble bust."

"Thanks. It's how they thought I killed my husband, Mitch, but I only knocked him out, too."

That's right. She'd been executed like me, ripped when they figured out the evidence wasn't as conclusive as they thought. We had a lot in common.

"Ever feel bad about it? Your husband, I mean."

She shrugged. "Sometimes I'm sorry I'm not the one who killed him, if that's what you mean."

Wouldn't say I was disappointed to hear that, just surprised. Hell, I felt bad about Flat-face, and we weren't even married.

"What about Green? Why'd you clonk him?"

"I didn't have a gun. What is this, a therapy session? Green's a thousand times worse than Mitch. He didn't beat me, but he made me . . ." her voice trailed off. "I told you he was going to cut you up, isn't that enough?"

"Yeah, more than enough, and I owe you for that. Believe me, I know how sometimes it's as hard to do the right thing as it is to figure out what it is."

She grit her teeth and looked around uncomfortably. "You're as crazy as he is."

"Then why are you with me?"

She bit a polished white nail and spit out the torn bit.

"I figure it's safer to be with the crazy guy who thinks there's a right thing to do. I didn't think there'd be this many questions."

Speaking of the right thing to do, I pulled over.

"What're you doing?" Nell said. She looked behind us to check for other cars.

"Paying back the favor. There's a train station an eighth of a mile ahead. A lot of people will be coming after me because of those vials. It's not safe. You're better off on your own."

She slapped me across the face, hard. "Stupid dick, think you're hot shit? Did you forget my show? My face has been all over the country every night, and I just gave Colby Green a concussion. You're the one who should be worried about being with me. And if we were splitting up, I'd keep the Tesla."

I rubbed my cheek, though most of what she'd hurt had been my feelings. "I take your point. So what do we do now?"

"Just . . . keep going north," she said. "Until we're out of the country."

"They have chak-camps in Canada, too."

"Yeah, but in the northwest they run them more like wilderness refuges, no guards except on the borders. You want to come out, you take a test, and get a pass for a week. Otherwise they leave you alone. The smart ones are trying to build like a society up there."

"How do you know all that?"

"I'm in broadcasting, surrounded by liveblood reporters. I read e-mails I'm not supposed to. I keep my mouth shut and listen when they get drunk. We don't cover it because our government doesn't want people pressuring them to follow suit and the Canadians don't want a rush of corpses heading north."

She put her hand on my leg and said, "So, dead Mann, there is someplace we could go. How about it?"

I was thinking it over when the next curve put us in a small town, no more than a post office and a strip mall. The soundproofing in the Roadster was so good I didn't hear the gunfire until we were on top of the scene.

Six armed livebloods stood outside a pharmacy, two wore khaki guard outfits, one had a flamethrower. A dark-skinned, sweaty man, bald up top, but with hair on the sides, was screaming and trying to yank the flamethrower out of the guardsman's hands.

Lit with the greenish tint of fluorescents, about the same number of chakz were inside the store. They were trying to hold off the LBs, and so far, they were doing it. I wouldn't say they were a well-oiled team, but they were sort of organized. Of course the big thing in their favor was the sweaty guy who wouldn't let go of the flamethrower. Most likely it was his store and he didn't want to see it go up in flames.

I slowed down. Nell, watching too, didn't object. A weird expression came over her face.

"Is that a sign they're putting up?" she said.

I thought she meant the LBs, but three of the chakz were holding up a big banner as a third struggled with a roll of duct tape, trying to paste it to the front window. In a barely legible scrawl, it said:

FREE CHAKZ

I didn't think it meant they were giving themselves away. It reminded me of the march at the mall, but it wasn't like the old days. The middle-level chakz had been weeded out by the tests. Sure that left a lot of goners around, but it also left the crème de la crème, too, chakz smarter than Jonesey who kept passing the tests, some of whom probably even remembered what it was like to be alive.

Maybe Jonesey was still on the roof of the lab, organizing this with his cell phone, or maybe not even a chak believed the pictures of Hudson were a hoax. It looked like the rebellion wasn't over yet.

Good as the Canadian refuge sounded, Misty was still out there somewhere, Booth was under arrest, and our part of the world was burning.

Nell watched the scene, shaking her head. "You know *that's* not getting any press coverage."

Press coverage. The photo was out. ChemBet also didn't want anyone to know about the vials. What if everyone did? Hard to believe, but I was actually thinking of taking a cue from Jonesey.

"Nell, the studio you broadcast from, where is it?"

She answered with a worried look. "Thirty Centre, overlooking the plaza, why?"

"Because you're the chak with the knack."

I spun the car around and headed for Fort Hammer.

27

I'd either had an idea, or my brain had split into chunks. If it was an idea, it went like this: Nell gets in front of a camera and explains the rotting, dirty truth: ChemBet's lab experimenting on LBs and chakz in a way that'd make Mengele proud, their security forces murdering police officers, the lost blue vials, Colby Green angling to steal them, resulting in the death of a police officer and the false arrest of the head of homicide, the investigation stifled by no less than Mayor Kagan.

I didn't even think we'd need proof. After all, it was television. Once the data-starved twenty-four-hour news cycle picked up on it, the whole country would go berserk. I'd hand the vials to the station with the most viewers or the Web site with the most hits, and let them worry about it. There'd be mass protests. It'd be the sixties all over again, only with zombies and better drugs. Those hippies did stop that war, didn't they? I never remember how that worked out. The trick was making it happen.

"Fuck," Nell said, after I gave her the short version. "Just fuck. I'm a stripper, for Christ's sake. All I do is read off a teleprompter."

"People pay attention to strippers."

"Not to what they say."

I gave her a smile. "You weren't always a stripper. You were a women's rights advocate. You must have given a speech or two. Remember any of that?"

She rolled her head and blew some air through her nostrils. "Shit, I thought hanging with you'd be *safer*."

"Sorry to disappoint you again. We do have two things on our side: Near as I can tell, Maruta has no idea where we are, and with any luck, Green's still in la-la land."

I had her attention. "And once this gets out, that'd be the end of him, pretty much?"

"And Maruta. Not sure about ChemBet."

"If I do this stupid thing, *then* can we go to Canada?"

I nodded. "You drink, I'll drive."

She let out a long sigh. "Maybe it'll make up for past sins."

Assuming she was referring to things Green had made her do in his pleasure dome, I decided not to ask for details.

A lot had happened since I passed through the city an hour ago. Fort Hammer's silhouette was never much to look at, more a feeble Christmas tree than the stars at night, but even from a distance we could see it was much darker than usual. Most of the office buildings were down to emergency lights. There was no reason the guard would cut the power on purpose. Maybe some chakz had damaged the grid by falling into a power station and incinerating themselves?

You'd think two zombies in a Tesla would attract attention, but the guard was so busy, as long as the car kept moving, Nell and I passed. With no flatulent limo driver trying to skirt the trouble, we also had a tour of the uprising dead.

There wasn't a civilian LB in sight, most having locked themselves in their homes. There were plenty of chakz though, moving about the fires and broken windows. Some were feral, some were just pissed, and it wasn't always easy to tell which was which.

The bulk of the "revolution" was a moveable feast. Trying to herd the restless departed, the guard cordoned off a street here and opened one there. Simple strategy. Once they had enough chakz in a concentrated area, they could open up with maximum firepower and minimal property damage.

Without realizing it, the ferals cooperated, gnashing their teeth as they shambled along the path of least resistance. The smart ones were the troublemakers, understanding the plan and doing their best to thwart it. They tried to steer the ferals themselves, using everything from hot-wired cars to two-by-fours to veer them any place but where the livebloods wanted them to go. When they had the numbers, they slammed through roadblocks. When they didn't, they rushed through the buildings and came out the other side.

I wanted to root for them, but didn't see a good end coming. The whole thing was ridiculously hopeless and stupid. But maybe that was the point. Dad was never much of a reader, but whenever Mom asked what he was so pissed about "this time," there was a Dylan Thomas poem he'd quote, though you have to swap "chakz" for "old age" to really make it work:

Do not go gentle into that good night,
Old age should burn and rave at close of day;
Rage, rage against the dying of light.

And, after all, I had my own ridiculously hopeless and stupid plan.

The first we saw of the plaza was the scaffolding surrounding the memorial Mayor Kagan had commissioned at the site of the last riot. I'd seen mock-ups of it: a brave police officer with a flamethrower, three citizens—man, woman, and child—cowering behind him as he squirted bronzed flames at a leaping bronze corpse.

Past that lay the ruins of a medical center, where Nell and I had our first date as captives of a psychopath. No memorial there, just a pile of hazardous cement, a buried lunatic, and the heads of his victims. If I was headed into a reverie, Nell pulled me out by shaking my shoulder and directing me onto Centre Street.

We headed toward the studio, a five-story brick building. When I pulled up to its underground parking lot, the electronic gate recognized a transponder on Green's car. The place still had power. I drove in and parked in his spot next to the elevator.

I turned to my celebrity pal. "What're we going to find up there?"

"They have to be covering the riots. Nick, the director, was real unhappy when Green pulled me away. I can probably take over for whoever they've got subbing. If I get that far, what am I supposed to say exactly?"

"Uh . . ." In the glove compartment I found a pen but no paper. Improvising, I pulled out the registration and scribbled on the back. "I'll give you the bullet points."

"Write large and use small words."

The list got longer and longer, the handwriting as tiny as my uncoordinated fingers could make it.

"Enough!" she said, jerking the paper out of my hands. "They're going to cart me off after the first minute."

"I was thinking I'd hold them at gunpoint."

"Oh, so we get two minutes? You think ChemBet and the police don't watch TV?" She scanned the list. "You want me to say the blue stuff is deadly? You don't know what it does any more than Colby."

"Having seen what ChemBet's capable of, I expect more of the same."

She looked at me, green eyes almost as piercing as a liveblood's. "But you don't know, and you want me to lie?"

"A minute ago you're a stripper who reads off a teleprompter. Now we're debating journalism ethics? What if you say it's experimental and possibly dangerous?"

She either twitched, or gave me a wink.

Once Nell gave me the gun, we took the elevator to a tastefully decorated, but empty, reception area that was standing guard over a locked door. Most of the lights were off, making me wonder whether they were broadcasting at all.

Nell grabbed the phone and dialed an extension. "I'm back, Nick."

An over-caffeinated voice answered: "Fan-fucking-tastic!"

Half a second later the door burst open and a slightly balding man with a goatee flew out like he was attacking. He swooped a hairy arm around Nell and pulled her back toward the door.

She pointed back at me. "Nick, this is . . ."

"I don't care who he is, I don't care where he stands. All I care about is having you in front of that camera. I'm trying to cover this decade's 9/11 and that idiot Morton keeps pronouncing the "z" in chakz like it's three syllables long. He's screwing my Pulitzer like a dog in heat," he said.

Good old Nick pushed her so fast he nearly took her off her feet.

"Easy on the talent!" I snapped. "I don't care if she is just a chak to you."

Nell raised an eyebrow. Nick kept pushing but looked back at me. "You're crazy. I *love* this woman. I live for her. I'd die for her. She pays my mortgage, she's paying for my kid's college. We've got a once in a lifetime situation—the chakz and the guard are going back and forth, the police are stuck on the sidelines, and . . . why the fuck am I telling you? Becky!"

At the end of the pencil-thin hall it was bright as day. There were three cameras and a set that looked much smaller than I'd imagined. A liveblood I assumed was Morton sat behind Nell's desk, looking like he'd swallowed a bottle of sedatives. He was struggling to keep his head straight as he looked into a camera and squinted at a rising series of words on a transparent screen.

I'd already passed beyond the veil, now I was entering

TV-land. Something in my head vibrated between what I was seeing, and a vague sense that it should all be up on a screen, and I should be watching from a distance, with my butt in a broken recliner.

A final "loving" shove sent Nell teetering in the direction of Becky, a bespectacled woman with strong arms. With the intense gaze of an irritated librarian, Becky shoved a transmitter down Nell's low-backed evening gown and a microphone up along her chest. It would've been easier if she'd waited, because the next instant, she and a second woman, who'd either hopped out of Becky's pocket, or appeared out of thin air, pulled off the gown completely.

Nell was left standing there, dressed only by her panties and the highlights the studio kliegs made on her snowy skin. The camerapersons didn't blink, and Morton kept reading like nothing was going on. And I thought *I* was dead.

Working on her like she was a life-sized Barbie doll, they threw a blouse over her head and struggled to get her legs into a pair of black slacks. Balanced on one foot, Nell looked at me, more worried about what was coming next than whether I was gawking at her.

She aimed her nose over my shoulder. "First door on the right's the control booth. That's where you can, you know, try to control things." The LBs didn't even notice her choice of words.

I turned to see Nick disappearing into a shadow behind an open door. Before it swung shut, I slipped into a darker, smaller space, crammed with apparatus and monitor banks. Most of the light came from the wide window looking out on the set.

Nick flopped into a central seat flanked by two thirty-something techies, raised his hand like Captain Kirk, and said, "Gimme street feed three so we can make the switch."

The image on the biggest monitor changed from Morton, to a reassuring view of the guard standing in formation, their riot shields forming a shiny bulwark against any threats. Morton's voice came over the speakers.

"Guard spokesman Derek Freeman reports that clear progress is being made in the midtown retail sector, but more chakzzzz . . ."

Nick groaned. "One syllable! One syllable!"

". . . have made their way into the financial district."

Though the audience didn't see it, in the middle of his next sentence, Morton was pulled from the seat and Nell shoved into it. It happened so fast, it was pretty funny.

"Cut Morton's mic. No, *burn* Morton's mic. Get ready to cue Nell. We still have that Command Sergeant?"

"He's on five."

"Nell, with me? You're going to do a live interview with . . ." He snapped his fingers repeatedly.

Becky came in and announced, "Command Sergeant Stanton Maldonado."

"Right. Nell, his group had to pull back from the financial district. CNN reported there were casualties. He'll say they're all alive, he's fine, it was just some scratches. Try to get him to repeat that the chakz are deluded, confused by the fake photo and . . ."

Before he finished, Nell's voice came over the speakers.

"This is Nell Parker. The photo circulating among the

chakz depicting a grotesque vivisection at a ChemBet facility has been verified as true."

Nick pumped his fist into the air. "Yes! She's on! Wait . . . what's she saying?"

"Moreover, the ChemBet facility laboratory where the picture originated has been performing similar experiments on liveblood subjects."

"Shit!" Nick said.

I pulled the Walther, kept the safety on, but pointed it at the back of his head. "Nick? Can I get your attention for a sec?"

Becky saw me and raised her hands like it was a bank holdup. When the guys at the controls did the same, I waved the gun in their direction. "No. You boys keep doing what you're doing. Nick, a moment if you don't mind?"

He was still staring at Nell. "She's off the prompter."

"Nick? Nicky? Buddy? Over here. Look at me. Now."

"Why is she off . . . ?"

I tapped the top of his head with the barrel, not too hard, but hard enough. He spun, angry, maybe thinking I was someone he could fire. The second he saw the Walther all that crazy energy sailed right out of him.

He sighed, spun back, and pressed his forehead down into his fist.

"Shoot me," he said. "Just shoot me."

"Relax," I told him. "Do as I say and you may actually get that Pulitzer."

28

Nell's two-minute estimate was generous. She'd barely made it to the part about Tom Booth being unjustly accused when all the lights and the equipment croaked. Everyone looked at the dormant ceiling fixtures like they were stars on a cloudless night. If I had a heartbeat, I would've heard it. In fact, I think I heard Nick's heartbeat.

"That broadcast went out live, right?" I asked.

He nodded. "Nationwide. Our first time, ever. Was any of what she said remotely true?"

"Even the stuff we should've lied about. Now, get your people out of here."

"Why? Who's coming?"

"ChemBet, Colby Green's men, maybe a short ninja. No idea who'll get here first, but they're all killers. Move quick enough and they won't give a shit about you." The door open, I called to Nell, "The underground parking will be the first thing they block, so we're on foot. Back stairs?"

She tore the mic from her body like it was a leech. "This way."

She grabbed my hand and took me through a rear door. At our backs, the crew rushed and bumped into each other on their way to the front elevators.

I followed the tug on my hand away from what little light was left.

"How was I?" Nell asked.

"I'm prejudiced. How'd it feel, making up for past sins?"

She squeezed my fingers. "Same as before. I'm still running, only now I have less a chance of getting away."

She took us into a stairwell. After ChemBet, I was sick of stairwells, but what can you do? A dull glow illuminated the rubber padding on the edges of the concrete steps, guiding us down. We'd hardly reached the next landing when I heard someone coming up. Having gotten so many people into so much trouble lately, I tightened my grip on the gun, hoping to prove Nell wrong about her chances.

A blur of movement appeared between the railings. Bracing the gun against my chest, I fired. My wrist hurt, but nothing broke. I heard shoes stumble on the cement steps, the quick rustling of someone diving for cover.

A deep voice called, "Hessius Mann?"

I motioned for Nell to keep quiet. "Who wants to know?"

"Officer Mark Davis, Fort Hammer police."

"Police? That supposed to make me feel better?"

"It's not doing much for me lately, either, but I got a personal request from Chief Detective Booth, asking me to get you out of this building."

That was news. "I thought he'd be dead or in jail."

"I heard both, but I guess not. Officially, I'm not even here, I just owe him. I thought it'd beat directing traffic for the guard, until you shot at me."

"Sorry about that. Lots of powerful forces arrayed against us. Trust no one, that kind of shit."

A half flight down we met a helmeted man in a uniform and a Kevlar vest, carrying a riot shield. His raised visor revealed dark skin and a friendly enough face, but there was blood on the shield.

I pointed at it. "Chakz don't bleed."

"Things were calming down until about five minutes ago. Then all hell broke loose. Real people, no offense, started coming out, smashing windows and throwing bricks. I don't even know whose side I should be on anymore."

Nell's broadcast, already? A weird sensation took the back of my neck. Maybe there was something to hope for. Not that I thought the revolution would succeed, but maybe we'd get one of those commissions that meet for a year then make recommendations that everyone ignores.

"Any second this place'll get very crowded. How far is your car?"

He shrugged apologetically. "Haven't got one. An RDV dropped me off at my designated corner with nothing but what you see and my good looks to protect myself. Booth said he'd try to get here as soon as he could, so we should stay nearby."

I clicked my tongue against my teeth. "If he's using words like 'try' we're on our own. Manhole nearby? Hate to ruin your studio clothes, Nell, but we could head into the sewers."

She raised an eyebrow. "After what I've been through, the sewers will feel clean."

But our new tour guide shook his head. "Sealed since the last riots. Take a blowtorch to open one back up."

"Shit. How about a safe spot with lots of exits?"

He made a face. "Safe? Not a word I'd use, but there's a bowling alley across the street with all the windows smashed. It's big and empty, nothing to take, unless the looters like bowling shoes. From inside we could probably see who was coming."

"Any port in a storm," I said.

Opening the door at the bottom of the stairs let in the thick smell of putrefying garbage courtesy of a closed Chinese restaurant next door. Every building over two stories tall still had emergency lights. Only the studio was jet black, putting to rest any crazy thoughts that the blackout was a coincidence.

I didn't have to inhale, but I couldn't keep from hearing, and the noise was worse than the smell: screams and sirens on the high end, cracks and crackling from guns and fires in the middle, and desolate moans and dull explosions filling in the bass.

Davis' arm chopped the air, pointing. Even with the electricity out, you couldn't miss the huge red and white Booby's Bowl sign looming four traffic lanes, five guardsmen, and a dozen shambling chakz away from us. The storefront was a wall of windows, an effort to lure customers with the exciting sight of overweight citizens hurling heavy balls into equally pear-shaped pins. Davis hadn't exaggerated—every pane had been smashed, and Booby, if that was his real name, had never heard of safety glass. The aluminum frames were lined with glass teeth.

"Hurry it up," Davis said.

I guess Nell and I were moving a little slowly through the alley's putrid garbage for his taste. I was going to explain how we like to avoid getting rotting meat on our skin when I saw three black SUVs sitting in a familiar formation in front of the studio. ChemBet had arrived. A little rot not being the worst thing in the world, we picked up our pace.

It looked like Maruta's little men were in the building, so I was hoping we might actually make it. But, by the time we braved the rioters and crossed the street, three sedans were peeling down Centre Street. Green's men, the reckless, cut-rate dogs, were here, too.

Occupied with their own battle, the guards and the chakz moved on, but a teen liveblood carrying a stolen Xbox ran in the other direction and didn't see the lead car coming in time. It hit him and he wound up flying halfway across the street, just like an incidental character from a violent video game.

The *trust no one* thing hadn't registered deeply enough with Davis. Seeing the hurt teen, he waved his hands to stop the speeding car.

"You don't want to do that!" I shouted.

Too late. The driver saw us and headed for Davis. The cop was alive and well-built, both of which made him heavier than me, but I threw myself into him, got lucky and hit him low. He fell out of the way and I rolled toward him, the sedan's tires pinching my clothes to the street as it zoomed by.

As I got up, it skidded sideways to a stop. Winded, Davis was still down. Nell and I pulled him up and the three of us dove over the broken glass into the bowling alley. In all the excitement, I didn't realize that since we'd been spotted going in, it wasn't much of a hiding place anymore.

We'd reached a row of pinball machines when the first of Green's dogs fired. A .38, I guessed, given the delay between bullets. Davis positioned himself behind one of the support pillars in front of the lanes and returned a few shots. Nell and I ducked behind the main counter, where my head was pressed hard against a pile of used bowling shoes.

The other two sedans arrived, and the new dogs didn't use .38s. Automatic weapon fire sprayed the place, shattering what was left of the windows, tearing fists of plaster from Davis' support pillar. I covered Nell's head with my arm and put my forehead to the floor. Bits of Formica counter and wooden frame splattered us.

Moments later, the gunfire paused. Like an idiot, I picked my head up to see what was going on. Something hot and fast sizzled a quarter-inch-deep line into my cheek. Before I could duck, Nell pulled me down.

Twisting, I got a good look at breaking pins and exploding score monitors. A bowling ball cracked in half. The amateurs didn't know how to aim, but with that many bullets it didn't matter. Through all the dust and powder vapor I counted six exits, not one free of flying lead. It was one great big dead end.

Time was when knowing Project Birthday's secret location could be a bargaining chip, but we'd essentially destroyed both Green's and Maruta's careers. There wasn't anyone left to negotiate with, making me think this was probably the last time I'd have a whole body to myself.

It would be like Butch Cassidy and the Sundance Kid, or Bonnie and Clyde, only, unlike them, Nell and I would stay conscious during and likely after. I was happy to escape being dumped in acid once, but now I wondered if it would've been better than being minced.

I leaned over and kissed her forehead, sort of to say good-bye. When I pulled away, a flake of my dried lip clung to her skin. I stared into her two, angry, dismissive emerald eyes, expecting my field of vision to splinter at any moment. Then it dawned on me, the Formica rain had stopped. The gunfire was fainter.

Whatever they were shooting at, it wasn't us anymore.

This time when I raised my head, nothing hit me. The dogs were yelping, running for the cover of their sedans. There were staccato flashes against the black studio building. Maruta's linebackers and their submachine guns had taken positions behind their SUVs and were shooting at Green's men.

Maybe *she* still wanted the vials? Or was she just crazy angry at Green for trying to steal them?

The sedans were covered with gray welts, but the bulletproofing had yet to be pierced. Nothing's bulletproof forever, though. While they were busy with each other, I grabbed Nell, planning to run, only to have a stray bullet bore another hole into my shoulder. Nell yanked me down again. She looked like she wanted to slap me even harder than last time.

"My mistake," I said.

A sickeningly familiar voice piped above the gunfire. "Don't let them escape!"

Through what was left of the counter, I saw the source. A Kevlar vest was wrapped tight around her yellow lab coat, and her black gloves were missing, but the demon-woman, Mistress Maruta, hadn't changed otherwise. She was here to prod her little men by hand.

At her order, half the machine pistols pointed back our way. The counter shrank as we crawled its length. Rebecca either wasn't interested in the vials anymore either, or she was planning to ask whatever was left of me.

A nearby rack collapsed. As the bowling balls in it bounced and rolled, a metallic squeal snapped my eyes to the street again. A fourth black sedan had pulled up.

I suppose the emergence of what looked like a shaved gorilla in a black suit carrying a rocket launcher should've been the big surprise, but it was the fifty-something man with the bandaged head that really grabbed my attention. Colby Green was here, too, his habitually placid face twisted in rage. I had to wonder if the wound had driven him permanently emo.

I knew they'd come for us after the broadcast, but I was thinking it'd be by proxy. Maruta and Green should be on private jets, fleeing the country. Instead, having their schemes revealed had thrown them into some sort of final tantrum. And the public thinks it's the chakz who're dangerous.

Green patted the gorilla and pointed at Maruta. Without so much as a hello, a smoky trail from the rocket launcher covered the distance between them. They say gorillas are smarter than dogs, but his aim was off. A white hot sphere erupted as the missile hit the front end of an SUV. The blast shed all sorts of sparkly shit and sent Maruta ten feet through the air and into the studio building's façade. She landed flat against the fake marble, hung there an instant, then fell face forward into the sidewalk.

That got everyone's attention. Green smiled like he'd won with a single shot. I figured that the Marquess de Sade was dead, unconscious at least. But she hopped up with a look of total rapture, gave the world a throaty laugh, and redirected all her firepower at Green and his gorilla.

I pulled Nell to her feet. "Now!"

She snatched her hand back. "That didn't work so well last time."

"Staying put won't work either," I told her. The counter was only about a foot tall and still smoking. Through the haze, Davis waved us over to his pillar, but that looked worse than the counter.

I was about to try to drag Nell out when the howl of piercing sirens announced that the cavalry, or something like it, had arrived. When I'd told Davis back in the stairwell that this place would be getting crowded, I wasn't kidding. Two squad cars, lights flashing, pulled up ten yards south. Seconds later, they were joined from the north by another two cars and an armored van. Six policemen, wearing all there was of Fort Hammer's body armor, piled out of the van.

Better yet, a voice came from the crackly loudspeaker: "This is the fucking police."

It was Booth, that beautiful son of a bitch, somehow back in charge, and smart enough to box in Maruta and Green. On another planet, where the sky is always blue, that might've been the end of the movie. But, this wasn't that. Not even close.

Nobody moved as the cops fanned out in a semicircle

to tighten the net. Even the Lady Maruta froze, maybe looking forward to getting shot.

But then Green called, "Rebecca?"

She shook off whatever trance she was in to respond in her best cheery business voice, "Yes, Colby?"

"I believe we have them outgunned. Temporary truce?" Green said.

Head wound or not, he'd done the math. Her eyes flashed with admiration. "Done, Colby."

Bullets flew again. This time, Booth and the police were ready. They gave as good as they got until a second missile from the shaved gorilla headed for the armored van. Seeing its smoky anaconda trail, the police dove. When it hit, the explosion blew them along the street like so many leaves. As far as I could tell no one was seriously hurt until the little men opened up with their machine guns.

We'd blown our chance. With ChemBet security no longer shooting at them, Green's dogs didn't have any reason to stay outside the bowling alley. Seven silhouettes appeared at the empty window frames. The shifting shadows told me Nell and Davis were still alive. Knowing I was the main target, I fell flat and dragged myself away from them, along the smooth floor. I braced the gun against a ball dispenser and waited for a shot.

One dog, on his way in, tripped when his foot hit a bowling ball instead of the floor. When the other six turned to look at their fallen pal, I fired in their direction until the clip was empty. One collapsed, his right leg buckling. Another twisted at the waist and dropped. Davis, wherever he was, followed suit, and a third dog went down.

The four still standing aimed at the flashes from my gun. Splinters flew from the floor. Hoping Nell and Davis were better off than I was, I pushed myself backward down one of the lanes.

The dogs advanced. My gun was empty. No further return fire came from Davis. It was time to try negotiating. I inhaled, got a mouth full of wood and plaster dust, then half coughed, half shouted, "Can I surrender? I do still have the fucking vials."

The shooting stopped. One of the dogs, ugly as a chak, his long fingers and equally long face making him look partially melted, like Droopy Dog, walked toward me, a hand cupped to his ear. I kept expecting him to say something, but he didn't. He got closer until his black shoes were inches from my face. The barrel of his AK was right above my skull. He stood there for the longest time, hand to ear, listening.

As the seconds stretched, my leg started vibrating. When I couldn't stand it anymore, I looked up at him and said, "Well? I'm right here. What's it going to be? Your boss still want the precious secret of immortality?"

He nodded, then turned my way. "Mr. Green wants me to cut your head off and bring it to him. We're just trying to figure out how to do that. I don't think bullets alone would work, do you?"

"Probably not," I told him. "Hacksaw? I think there's a hardware store around the corner. Give me a couple of bucks, wait here, and I'll go grab one for you."

He cupped his ear again. "Oh, okay." He looked back down. "Mr. Green wants to hurry. He says the bullets will be fine." Droopy Dog aimed the gun. "Stay still, I want to try to make the line as clean as I can."

"Hey, why not? I like a clean line as much as the next fellow." I stretched my neck like I was going to cooperate, but I'm a zombie, right? Why not give the people what they want? I yanked his pants cuff up and bit into the meat of his lower calf as hard as I could.

Don't let anyone tell you human flesh is tender. Maybe when I was alive my teeth could cut through meat, but it felt like I'd snapped off both incisors. My jaws didn't close, but I did get past the epidermis. Leg skin pressed into my tongue as the dog's salty blood dribbled into my mouth.

Yowling, he tried to yank his leg free. When I held on with my teeth and both hands, he wound up dragging me along the floor. I wanted to tell him he should've let me surrender, but my mouth was full. I clamped down harder, driving my teeth in deeper.

I don't know what George Romero was on about in those movies. It tasted god awful.

"Get him off!" Droopy screamed. His three remaining pals aimed our way, but didn't want to risk hitting him.

Next thing I knew, someone lifted my legs high enough to get my chest off the ground and tugged. I bit and kicked. The three of us danced that way half a minute, me praying I didn't tear a chunk of Droopy's leg free. Once he was loose, I'd be a really easy target.

I'd given whoever was behind me a decent kick when an agonized groaning erupted. I thought Droopy Dog was yowling again, but the voice was too dry. A feeling of dread pulsed through. Had Nell gone feral? No, it wasn't her, and there was more than one set of cords at work, making a sound like a pile of sad autumn leaves swirling in the wind. My teeth still busy, I twisted my eyes and saw the new arrivals.

Chakz. At least a dozen. I'd forgotten we were smack in the middle of a zombie revolution. I figured they were ferals, drawn by the pretty lights of the explosions, or Droopy Dog's wet screams. When I heard a few fire-cracker pops, and realized they weren't from the dogs' weapons, I noticed something different about them.

The chakz were carrying guns. And they were using them.

They weren't very good at it. One shot himself in the leg. When a second pulled the trigger on a shotgun, I winced as the kickback tore his hand off. I don't know which one fired the shot that hit Droopy, but his head bucked forward and his body crumpled.

More came in from the rear and the sides. Thirty? Those who didn't have guns held baseball bats or two-by-fours with thick nails. By the time I pried my mouth off the dead dog, chakz were swarming in and the last three dogs running out.

I got to my knees, spitting gory chunks out of my mouth, but thankfully, no teeth. The moaning quieted. I heard an arid chuckle.

"Mann, I gotta ask, does it taste like chicken?"

I got to my feet, still spitting. It was Jonesey. He was the chak who'd lost his hand. He was rubbing the stub against his ear like he was scratching an itch.

"No, not like chicken. Not at all." I wiped my pants and looked around for his missing appendage. "How the fuck did you get here? And don't tell me Kyua provides."

"He did, but, if you prefer, I saw the broadcast. Who else knows about those vials but you, right?"

I spotted the shotgun, but not his hand. "That much I guessed. I mean, how'd you get off the roof at Chem-Bet?"

"Long story. Give me a sec, Hess," he said. He pointed his stump at the front of the room. "Everyone! Make a line at the windows, guns up, like we practiced. You're all doing fantastic!"

They obeyed, sort of.

I motioned toward the stub. "You should find the hand."

"What for? Can't repair the nerve endings with Krazy Glue. Kyua will . . ."

"Shh!" I said.

"I know you don't believe, but you don't have to. . . ."

"No. Listen. No one's shooting. . . ."

I rushed up to the haphazard line of chakz and looked out. The armored van was a cinder. Bodies, the dead kind, littered the street. Green was alive, but nearly alone. His gorilla lay in a heap at his feet and his last three dogs didn't look like they had any fight left in them. A lot of the police and ChemBet security were standing, but they were all facing the chakz in the bowling alley.

"Tom!" I yelled. "Don't shoot! Jonesey brought them."

"You think that's a good thing? Shit! I want my man out," Booth said.

I turned back inside. "Davis, you still with us?"

"Yeah," he said. He limped forward. His face was covered in blood, but I didn't see the source. He tried to leave, but the chakz stopped him.

I eyed Jonesey. "Let him go, J. Officer Davis saved two

chakz, me and Nell. Booth is on our side for a change, or as close as he can get to it."

He nodded, the chakz parted. Davis hesitated and looked at me, like he was worried about leaving us behind. I shook my head. "It's okay, I know him. Thanks."

Once Davis left, a weepy Green called, "I want Nell out of there, too. Nell, I won't press charges, I swear. I just want to see you."

When no one objected, I turned to Nell. "Go."

"No," she said.

I pushed her. "Go! I'm safer here than I've been in weeks."

She pushed back. "It's not about you, dick." She walked deeper into the building and sat on a ball return. "I'm not going near him again."

There was something in her expression, but I couldn't quite tell what it was. "This still about selling you to a killer or did Green come up with a whole new level of awful I don't know about?"

"You have no idea."

"Why don't you tell me?"

"I'm saving it for my biography," she said.

"Come out, Nell!" Green called. "Please!" He sounded like he was crying again.

Maruta giggled. "Colby, did you get rough with that poor dead girl?"

"Jesus," Booth said. "I don't know what to throw up about first. But I'll have plenty of time to decide later. There are fifty guardsmen on their way. It's over for all of you."

Green sniffled and shook his head. "Not exactly. On

the way here, I spoke with the governor." He wiped his eyes and turned to Maruta. "Thanks to a number of ChemBet files in my possession, a plea deal has been arranged in exchange for my testimony. I'm afraid our truce is over, Rebecca."

"That's all right, Colby," she answered. "You were always a terrible partner anyway, and an amateur, despite how highly you thought of yourself. You might want to wipe some of that snot from your nose, or order one of your men to do it."

Looking hurt, Green wiped his nose on his sleeve, then told his surviving dogs to lay down their guns. I wasn't thrilled that the hand behind O'Donnell's death and Misty's kidnapping might get off scot-free, but that made it one armed group down, two to go.

Booth eyed the chakz next. "Mann, tell Fidel Zombie over there that if he has his cadavers stop pointing those guns our way, I'll arrest Maruta first."

Having heard him, Jonesey nodded. The chakz didn't drop their guns, but they lowered them, then stepped so far back into the darkness of the bowling alley, it felt like they weren't there anymore.

Booth ordered his men to train their sights on Rebecca Maruta's linebackers, but they did it before the words came out of his mouth. And when Booth said, "Drop the guns," the little men did.

He stormed up to Maruta, whirled her, and slapped some cuffs on. "You're the sick fuck I wanted most anyway."

She giggled girlishly, as if she really, really liked being handcuffed. Booth tightened the cuffs, thinking that'd hurt her, but when she gave off a pleased, trembling sigh, he shivered and stepped back. She knew it would get under his skin, and if there was one thing she did like, it was getting under someone's skin.

"I appreciate the heat of your desire, Chief Detective, but you really don't want to arrest me."

"Really? 'Cause I sure as hell feel like I do," Booth said.

Her smile got so wide her eyes disappeared. "You won't when I tell you what's in those vials."

All our ears perked up at that. Green stopped sniffling. Jonesey whispered, "Kyua." Booth kept his distance, but said, "Talk."

"This very evening, right before that unfortunate broadcast, I discovered a note from my late husband. He had the tiniest handwriting, like an insect! It turns out he was very naughty before he died. He created a mycoplasma, not a virus, not a bacteria, something in between. It loves water, even the moisture in the air. Once released, it will infect anyone who comes in contact with it." She sniffed excitedly. "It's also self-replicating, growing all along. It will probably burst the nutrient containers anytime now. And my people are the only ones who know how to destroy it."

Green's and Jonesey's lips moved at the same time. *Destroy.* Booth caught the significance, too. "You trying to say this myco-crap will kill livebloods?"

She laughed. "No, no, no. It's much better than that! We'll be completely fine, so long as we live. It's afterwards that's the problem. At death, the mycoplasma will automatically reinvigorate each and every cell. Each and every cell. Do you understand, Chief Detective?"

She watched the furrows form on Booth's brow and

thicken, then waited for realization to sink in. When his eyes went wide, she nodded happily.

"Yes, there it is. That's it. *Everyone* comes back . . ." She tipped her head first at Booth, then at every live-blood in sight. "You, and you, and you, too! Everyone! Everyone will come back as a chak! I told you he was a naughty boy!"

29

Happy fucking birthday.

I stepped from the bowling alley with Nell. All around our gaudy pocket of light, the riots continued, destroying what it could with flames or fists, guns or stubs. It seemed like only the buildings had real shapes, and everything else was tired of pretending. Maybe that's what a world full of chakz would look like: gray trash, shifting around, forgetting what it used to be.

My foot hit something heavy. A .38 lay a few inches from the openmouthed body of one of Green's dogs. I picked it up, almost wishing I could use it to blow my own brains out.

"Uncuff me," Rebecca Maruta said. "Or I'll let it happen."

Booth was torn between rejecting what he'd just heard and deciding what to do if it were true. "You can slide further on bullshit than concrete," he said.

Maruta looked puzzled, so I translated. "He's calling you a liar."

She spoke as if we were boring her. "I'll prove it, then. I'll give you my system password. My husband's notes and whatever footnotes my staff has added in the last few hours are on the hard drive. That is, if you have anyone who can read them."

"I can," Green said. "My laptop's in the car."

After hearing how the new toy he'd wanted might actually work, he was looking worse for wear, unsteady on his feet. Eyes wet again, he looked around for someone to command, his gaze settling to my right. "Nell, would you please get it for me?"

"Fuck, no," she told him.

Since this didn't seem like the best time to sort what etiquette he did or didn't deserve, I headed toward his sedan. The door, bent and dented from the gun battle, groaned like an elephant. I grabbed the computer off the backseat floor where it'd fallen, flipped it open, and whirled it toward Green.

Unable to keep his emotions hidden, his expression wavered from one to another. I saw an arrogant contempt for Booth, a boyish sadness about Nell, bitter disappointment that Maruta might be telling the truth, and some more I couldn't name. It was strange, not satisfying, to see him so helpless. He'd spent so much time trying to figure out what chakz were, now whatever he'd known about himself was slipping away.

He coughed, swallowed, and managed a pitiful semblance of his game face. "What am I looking for, Rebecca?"

"The most recent file from R & D Sector 6, Colby. It has a high-alert tag. By now the molecular analysis should be attached."

Once he found it, we gathered around, but the document had so many big words it may as well have been hieroglyphs. He read, twitching at parts, swallowing sobs at others, and we waited.

Somewhere on the third screen, the prince of perverts lurched. I thought he was going to have a seizure, but what came out was more like a sob. Then there was another and another. Colby Green went to his knees, wailing like a lost child.

"I take it she's telling the truth?" Booth asked.

Green nodded. Funny he'd be the only one who had it in him to weep for the fate of the world.

Maruta seemed pleased by what she thought of as his weakness. "The extent of the emotions are likely a side effect of his concussion. But I take it you get the point? Tick-tick-tick?"

Booth looked like he was thinking about letting her go.

"Tom," I said. "You can't. She's not magic. Get the stuff to the CDC."

He nodded. "Yeah."

Maruta shook her head. "Bad boys. Bad, bad boys. This isn't a dirty needle. If so much as a few drops get loose there'll be contagion."

Booth's eyes grew darker, but I was the one who growled, "You're not getting near those vials."

Confident she could ignore me, Maruta took a smooth step closer to Booth. "Are you actually willing to take . . . ?"

I leveled the .38 at her forehead, not caring if it took

my hand off. She looked around, if not for sympathy than for some semblance of shock at what I, a chak, was doing. Finding none, the Queen of Hell blinked, then deigned to look at me.

"Detective, you wouldn't be here if it wasn't for Travis Maruta and myself."

"That's kind of the point, isn't it?" I said. I cocked the hammer.

Finally, she looked down. "Very well, I'll allow the cuffs to stay. But let my people destroy it."

Tom crunched his molars, then said, "Fine. I'll have the CDC and the army meet us at the site. Charlotte Manson here can alert her staff. It'll make it easier to arrest them all. Now give me the gun, Mann, and tell me where we're all going."

"Sure. It's . . ."

A keening, low, but strong as a mournful gale, erupted from the bowling alley. The chakz had reappeared. Only now there weren't thirty, there were more like a hundred. Every liveblood, police, dog, and little man, reached for their weapons.

"Sorry to interrupt," Jonesey said, stumbling over one of the empty window frames, "but as representative for a certain group of aggrieved citizens, I should be there, too."

I tried to cut him off. "Right. You heard Booth. The guard will be here in under a minute and turn your constituency to cinders."

Jonesey nodded and held his cell phone up. "Probably, once they get through our roadblocks. But even when the fifty show up, I already outnumber them two to one. Then there's the few thousand waiting to hear back from me." He walked past me and headed for Booth. "Yea, though I walk through the valley of the wretched living, I shall fear no evil. Kyua is why I'm here. Let me bear witness and they'll stand down, provided the guard does the same."

Booth's face trembled. He rubbed his chest and leaned back against a squad car. "Christ, either your head or my chest is going to explode any second. You want me to believe you control *all* the chakz?"

To his credit, Jonesey softened. "It's not about control, it's about empowerment. I tell them to trust each other, they trust me. I guarantee you on my word, at least seventy percent of the rebels will pull back. If they *don't* hear from me, well . . . things get worse before they get better. What do you say? Cuff me if you're afraid I'll eat someone. All I'm asking is that you let me see this through to the end."

He held out his arms. I nodded at his stub. "Not much point to the cuffs, Jonesey."

He looked at it. "Well, whatever."

Booth kept rubbing his chest. "Somebody call Kagan or the governor. This one's their call. They were quick to get me out of holding after that broadcast, so I can guess what those cowards will say. Shit. I should have hired a fucking school bus. Can we please try to get out of here before the vampire union or someone else shows up?"

Someone else. Damn. Maruta, Green, the chakz, the cops, it was like the end of a stage play, everyone here except . . .

"Tom, put us in a car. Everybody if you have to, just make it fast. I'll drive."

Booth's eyes flared. "You making demands now, too?"

"No. But someone's missing from this picture, don't you think?"

He thought about it, rubbed his chest some more, and nodded. "Yeah. You're right. Let's move. Crap."

Disarmed, the hired goons were cuffed. With the police van destroyed, they sat in a line on the curb. State witness Colby Green, in protective custody, and Maruta were unceremoniously shoved in the back of a squad car. With an okay from our corrupt governor, Jonesey was put in a second car with two cops.

I'd hoped Nell would slip in with the dead and wander off, but, acting like she had some backstage pass, she got in the car with Jonesey. Her expression dared me to try to stop her. No one else said anything about it, so I didn't mention it. Like a lot of situations, if I'd thought it through, I might have done different, but at the time I was thinking it wasn't like the mycoplasma could hurt a chak.

By the time we were ready to roll, the guardsmen arrived, reporting that aside from some liveblood looters, things had suddenly quieted down. Booby's Bowl looked empty, but I knew the dead were all around, waiting in the shadows for their phones to ring.

I got behind the wheel of the first car. Booth, swilling some Mylanta supplied by one of the guardsmen, took shotgun. Once he confirmed we had the CDC tracking us and an entire army regiment being deployed, we were on our way. I headed down the main drag, followed by a car with Jonesey and Nell. Within a few blocks, two more squad cars joined us.

The broken windows of our bloodied city looked like blackened eyes, the shredded doors like missing teeth. The LBs we passed were more about videotaping for

YouTube than vandalism. There were still fires, still ferals, but without a guiding force, they wandered aimlessly. The patches of quiet grew longer until finally that's all there was.

The silence made me antsy. Booth was busy talking on the radio and nursing his gut. My head was full of puzzle pieces refusing to make a picture. I didn't know if that was because I was too crappy at puzzles to make it happen, or the biggest piece, Bad Penny, hadn't turned up yet. Common sense said if she'd been listening in and heard what the birthday surprise was, she'd tell her bosses the bad news and stay clear. But ever since this began common sense had been an oxymoron.

I didn't want to talk to the Hell Queen, but she was the only one who could fill in some blanks. If she wanted to. I looked at her in the rearview.

"Colby already told me he has no idea who the ninja is. How about you?"

If she was surprised Green didn't know Penny, she didn't show it. She didn't show anything. Serves me right for trying a direct question.

"How will you destroy it?"

Without a gun to her head, she might even have ignored that question, but there was nothing else going on. "Acid or superheating usually works. We just have to be sure we get it all."

"And if it gets out, no cure?"

She looked idly out the window. "It takes up to two years of antibiotic treatment to eradicate the known mycoplasmas, and this is something new."

"Why would your husband even make something like this?"

She met my eyes in the mirror. I knew she thought of chakz as less than dirt but something about my question amused her. "You'd be better off asking why he'd make something like *you.*"

That rattled me a bit. I wasn't sure why. "So the stuff in the vials was another mistake. Good thing we caught it before you started marketing. But why was it in that briefcase?"

"He was being a very bad boy," she said. Her smile faded slowly, giving me the weird impression she missed her partner in crime.

"In what way? Was he trying to sneak it out of the lab himself? Working with someone like the ninja?"

She made a vague effort to keep from laughing too loudly at me. "No. He'd never do anything like that without permission. That wasn't the way he liked to surprise me."

Good lord, if this was his better half, what was Travis like? The rumor mill pegged him as the submissive partner in their little S and M game, a workaholic who reveled in being out of control. But this went far beyond bedroom fun and games. Their work put the species at stake and they knew it. Did they already see themselves as the sort of god Colby Green imagined he might become?

When we reached the warehouse district, I made a left and saw the gargantuan tin box I'd called home. Before I slowed, I scanned the alleys and roofs for our missing player. Nothing. The brakes gave off a final mouse squeak. I took a long last look before stepping out.

"End of the line, end of the world," I said. "Everybody out."

Booth exited, but not wanting to touch them, waited for his men to yank Green and Maruta from their seats. Trucks and a few cars appeared down the road. A helicopter swooped over the warehouse, its light shining down on us.

Booth answered the question before I could ask. "They're ours. All of them."

"Can I call my people now?" Maruta asked. "This is not the sort of operation you want to delay any more than absolutely necessary."

Booth shook his head. "We'll wait for the CDC to unpack. A Dr. Alice Dixon will be coordinating."

"Dixon's second rate!" Maruta said, her voice like the bark of an annoyed lapdog. "Tell them, Colby, tell them she's no good."

But Green was sniffling and peering guiltily at Nell. He looked . . . hollow.

As the rest of the good guys pulled up and Maruta's protests fell on deaf ears, I walked over to Nell. "You want to tell me exactly what happened with you and Colby? Some new perversion didn't sit right?"

"Just leave it," she said.

Nell wasn't talking to me, so I went up to the leader of the chakz. Jonesey had taken to watching and chuckling. Between that and Green's quiet sobs, we were running the gamut of human emotion. There'd been something bugging me about him, anyway.

"Hey, I've got a sense of justice, or at least revenge, that keeps me going. You already know there's no cure in those vials. What's keeping you from going feral?"

He raised his eyebrows, a fleck of something fell off,

hair or skin. "You already know the answer to that one, Hess."

I gave up. "Right. Kyua. Look, Nell says they've got like chak refuges north of the border. Doesn't sound like a bad deal. Maybe when this is done you can herd your merry rebel band up that way."

He shook his head. "Thanks, Hess. But Kyua will not disappoint."

He reminded me of the guy stuck on his roof during a flood. A raft, a boat and a helicopter came, but he refused their help, saying God will provide. After he drowned, he went to heaven and asked God why He didn't provide, and God said, "What are you talking about? I sent you a raft, a boat and a helicopter."

By then the CDC trailer and mobile lab had arrived. They put plastic sheets, inflatable tunnels and filters over the outside of the building. It was hard to tell who Dr. Dixon was, since they were all wearing the same heavy bio-safety suit with hood and gas mask. They even forced the rest of us into those suits—chakz, too, for fear we might be carriers. Every time someone pointed Dixon out I lost her in the crowd until I realized she was the one with the big red X on her back.

ChemBet's boffins were on their way, but Dixon didn't think it was a good idea to wait for them. Once Maruta and Booth were suited up, I was given the nod.

I entered the puffy plastic bubble covering the entrance, then pulled the door open along the wheels. The metal squealed long and loud. All sorts of lights pierced the interior.

"Welcome to Shangri-la," I said.

Inside, the only guardians of humanity's destruction were some water rats. They scampered into the remaining shadows, their fat bodies followed by flashlight beams.

"We'll have to exterminate once we're finished," one of the suits said. "The whole block at least."

Looking like the Pillsbury Doughgirl in her suit, Maruta shoved her way next to me. "I hope you didn't just leave them lying around, Detective. You did use some sort of cushioning?"

Rather than answer, I made my way to the cinder block where I'd left the vials. I tried to stick my hand in, but the gloves made it impossible. Dixon handed me a set of tongs and cautioned me to go slowly. I poked it in, felt around . . .

And found nothing. My eyes popped wider than they'd been since I'd died.

"Gone?" Maruta said, sounding genuinely flummoxed.

Booth stared at me. "You sure this is the right place?"

"Yes!" I said.

Booth grabbed Maruta, loosening the seals on both his suit and hers.

"Did you take it?" he said. "You bring us here to ambush us?"

"Excellent idea," she said with a girlish giggle. "If I'd known the vials were here, I might have thought of it."

He spun back my way. "Who else knew about this place?"

"You, me, Penny, and Green, but I doubt he'd have shown up personally to kill me if he had the vials to play with. Bad Penny followed me to Green's thinking *I* still had them."

"Anyone else? Anyone who knew you well enough to guess how you'd play it?"

I thought about it. Flashes of my long-lost assistant stepping from a taxi outside this very warehouse appeared in my head.

"Just . . . Misty. She could second-guess me easy. But why would she . . . ?" She wouldn't, unless someone lied to her. And then I realized . . . "Penny was hiding with me when she called. We struggled over the phone. She could have seen Misty's number, called her to try to get to me."

I felt for my cell phone, but didn't have it anymore.

Booth pulled out his. "What's her number?"

"I don't know . . . I can't remember," I said.

"You *have* to remember!"

"I can't."

"Wait a minute," Jonesey said. "I've got it."

The bio-safety suit pointless now, he pulled it half off and fished out his phone. His face was lit an eerie blue by the screen as he checked his contacts. "Whoa, haven't used that one in a while. But it's still three on the speed dial."

He pressed the number, then tossed me the phone.

Two rings later, a shaky voice answered. "Jonesey? I heard what you've been doing. I want you to know you're right. It's all going to be okay. I've got it. I've got the cure. I'm going to see Chester again."

"Misty . . ."

"Hess?"

"Where are you?"

"Where am I? Where have you been? You abandoned me!"

"Long, long story. Listen carefully. That blue stuff is not a cure for anything. It's *extremely* dangerous. Put it down and get away from it."

She gave off a tired laugh. "Too late for your fairy tales, dead Mann. Kyua already warned me you'd say something like that."

The line didn't go dead, but a thud told me Misty dropped the phone. That tired laugh came again, then grew fainter. I screamed her name until the sound of her laughter faded completely.

30

You've got to love resources when people know how to use them. The CDC had been tracking the call since Jonesey dialed. Misty's cell was located before Booth ripped the phone out of my cold dead hand. Dixon handed Booth a touchpad with a map grid. Misty was a blinking red light in the middle.

"Where is she?" I asked.

"Looks like the woods," Dixon said. "The closest building is labeled Tuke's. I'm not from around here. Does that mean anything to you?"

I knew the name, but before I could answer, Rebecca Maruta gasped. She slapped a smile on her face and tried to pretend it hadn't happened, but her lips twitched as if she were working hard to keep the grin in place.

We all stared at her, but I asked the question. "Something you want to tell us?"

She gave a single quick shake of her head, no.

"You really think this is a good time for keeping secrets?"

No reaction. I doubted torture would work. She might enjoy it. Regardless, there wasn't time to get it out of her. The longer we waited, the farther Misty would get from her phone.

We ran back to the cars, Booth driving this time, speeding actually. Green hadn't moved fast enough, so Jonesey wound up stuck next to Maruta in the back, making for an even more awkward couple. Booth had one hand on the wheel, using the other to radio commands to whoever would listen.

I wasn't going to stop him, except to say, "Make sure they understand she doesn't know what she's doing, Tom. It's Chester, it's the drugs. Go easy on her. We both know who Kyua is."

"Fucking ninja midget. You were with her how long before you finally figured out she was a liveblood?"

Maruta shivered again and this time spoke up. "The raggedy you brought from the overflow camp? She was with you in the lab?"

I wheeled back. "What do you know? You really want a world full of chakz? Help us!"

Her face went blank, her eyes defiant. I started fishing, hoping to hit a nerve. "You didn't even know she was a liveblood. Too many subjects to look each one over? She knew the lab well enough to think she'd get in and out. Disgruntled employee? Do you have any *gruntled* employees? She military? A lover? Part of your bedroom antics with Travis? One of your experiments?"

Nada. I listed back into the passenger seat, my gut vibrating like it was filling with boiling oil. I looked long-

ingly at Booth's half-full bottle of Mylanta, wishing ant-
acid could work on the dead.

Once we left Fort Hammer, the road was lightless.
Everything else, like my body, was a shade of gray.
Maruta had closed her eyes, pretending to sleep, but not
doing a good job of it.

There were two possibilities, one bad, the other worse.
Either Penny didn't know what the vials were, or she did.
What was her angle in this? What was she?

An experiment. I'd said it by accident, but it made
sense. Penny was sure as hell unusual. Was she one of
those liveblood volunteers Maruta said was so hard to
come by? Had they turned her into something in between dead and alive?

Jonesey'd been remarkably quiet, probably focused
on *bearing witness*. He was looking curiously at the end
of his arm where his hand used to be, his eyes filled with
the opposite of my father's shame.

Please don't look at it.

"Tuke's mean anything to you, J? Some kind of Kyua
holy spot like Stonehenge?"

He rotated the stub into a new position, fascinated by
the dangling shards of dry flesh. "Nah. Kyua works in
some fucking mysterious ways."

Minutes later, two tapered columns and the angled
roof between them broke up our view of the stars. When
I first heard the name I thought Misty was planning on
committing herself, but the Samuel Tuke's Psychiatric
Hospital would be a pretty weird choice for a lower-class
city girl.

Pilgrim State in New York was the world's largest.
Tuke's came in fourth or fifth, booking ten thousand pa-

tients in its heyday. New drugs, coupled with the personal-responsibility ethos of the Reagan era, reduced Tuke's population to a few out-of-their-mind relatives that the wealthy wanted to keep out of sight.

Ahead and to the right its weighty shadow loomed, but before we reached the grounds, Booth, following the signal, pulled off the road. He grabbed the touch-pad and I snagged a flashlight from the glove compartment. As Jonesey and Maruta exited, a weaving line of lights and vehicles stopped behind us. We didn't wait for them.

He walked. I followed. The water vapor from his mouth was thick as cigar smoke. We climbed over fallen trunks and branches left over from the last storm, and crunched the frozen leaves that had the blessing of being allowed to turn back to dirt.

A large entourage developed in our wake: police, the CDC, and all our special guests. Maruta glided along stiff-backed, exhaling in regular puffs, obviously struggling with something inside. I guess every pain fascinated her equally, including her own. Green's breath dribbled from closed lips. The cold seemed to have braced him. At least he wasn't sobbing anymore. Nell was a graceful ghost, her skin the same color as the stars. Jonesey could've been a Boy Scout on a hike. Like me, no vapor came from their mouths. When we chose to breathe, it went out as cold as it went in.

The woods ended with a vengeance in a flat, open area bordered on the far end by the massive bulk of the hospital. The space was cleared on purpose and kept that way. I couldn't figure out why the hospital would need such a large field until my foot landed on something hard and rectangular. Aiming the flashlight I saw a small stone etched with a date and a number. A burial marker. Looking around, I realized it was one of thousands. We were in Tuke's graveyard, its disenfranchised patients buried without names.

Booth stopped, bent down, and scooped up Misty's phone. He pressed some buttons on it.

"Anything?" I asked.

"Last few were from an Unknown Caller, otherwise, Jonesey, you, O'Donnell, and a Mary Sanford."

"Mary was her sponsor," I said. "I don't see her knowing much about any of this."

He dialed a number, asked for a trace on the line, and got an answer in under a minute. "The unknown calls are from a prepaid phone, purchased three nights ago at a convenience store back in Chambers. I'll have some men get ahold of the owner and check the security cameras, but we already know who made the calls."

Most of the hospital windows were dark, but a few were glowing yellow, so I trudged toward the light. When everyone hesitated, I called back, "Where else would she go?"

The nearer we got, the more Maruta slowed. I slipped from the lead and went dead until she passed. Coming up from behind, I gave her a shove I hoped would startle her.

"Hello, Detective," she said without looking.

"Afraid you'll wind up a patient, or is there someone in there you don't want to see?"

"Push me harder," she said.

I did, nearly taking her off her feet, making her lab coat and blouse bunch up. "The sadomasochistic foreplay may make Booth uncomfortable, but I'm a chak, remember? No sense of shame or sex, thanks to your late husband."

"You'd be surprised how little you know about yourself," she said.

Before she could finish adjusting her clothes, I shoved her forward again.

"Wouldn't be the first time, but there's lots of chakz and only one of you. Makes you the bigger mystery. Does cutting up chakz get you off because it makes you feel in control, or is that dominatrix thing a mask for something else?"

She sighed. "When a child tears apart a bug is it cruelty or curiosity? Maybe I think if I keep peeling things back, I'll find something worthwhile." She spun to face me. "Want a peek under the hood?"

All at once there was something different in her eyes, something deep, old, and dark, like those gods Colby kept on his mantel. It felt like her gaze was cutting me up as surely as any blade. Much as I tried not to show it, she'd gotten to me. I had to walk away.

A stone archway, part of the original construction, hung over the front steps. It was undergoing repairs, or a politically correct makeover, but a few words still visible said it all: LUNATIC ASYLUM. An ambulance and some guard vehicles pulled up to meet us. Good thing the driveway had plenty of space. Two medics grabbed Green and steered him toward the ambulance. He stared dully at the sky and building.

"So sad and beautiful," he said.

A salt-and-pepper-haired tank of man in a khaki uniform came up to Booth. From what I could make out, the tank was in charge of the guard and Tom wanted them to cover the perimeter and search the building.

The newcomer, not grasping the gravity of the situation, laughed. "It'd take two hundred men at least," he said, pointing at the stone behemoth.

"Then get them."

We went in. Someone had phoned ahead, because the staff had already gathered in the reception area. Even so, the doctors, nurses, and interns were surprised by our small army, more so at the sight of chakz in their private hospital.

Booth slapped his hands to get their attention, then looked at me. The crack echoed in the wide space.

"Describe Misty for them."

I made one last guess. "I think it'll be faster if we ask if they have any patients named Maruta."

"No!" Maruta said. Pay dirt.

"Do it," Booth said.

The Queen of Hell shivered. "Please . . . don't look."

"Who is it?" I asked. "Got a mother hidden away in here? Father, sister, brother?"

The receptionist clicked some keys, and keeping her eyes on the screen, read, "Asteria Maruta in the dementia ward. She's in a private isolation room."

Furious, Maruta lunged for the receptionist. I wrapped my arm around her neck and pulled her back. "There a picture?"

After a nervous glance at Maruta, the receptionist turned the screen our way. The girl in the photo wore a vaguely diffident expression that made her look like a healthy teenager, except for having half her face missing.

Fun facts from beyond the grave: Asteria's the name of a Titan, mistress of, among other things, necromancy— magic from the dead. I could see why she preferred Bad Penny. A live feed to the security camera in her room showed a small figure curled up in a bed.

Seeing the face, Maruta broke her silence. "She was my b-..."

At first I thought she was going to say something uncharacteristically affectionate, like "baby" but the shape of her mouth quickly changed. The word that came out was "daughter."

"She's my daughter."

We headed for the room en masse. A doctor called after us, weirdly asking all sixty of us not to upset the residents. The corridors were mostly empty, but a few patients with long gowns and vacant stares wandered freely. They froze when they first saw us, but as we passed, they howled. Moisture aside, the sound was different from feral moans, more tense, not quite as sad.

At the stairs, Maruta tried to fall behind again. I grabbed her by the scruff of the neck. "I'm not even going to ask why you kept your secret daughter locked up here. A lot of mental illness is genetic, but you want to tell me about the chemical burn on her face? That happen before or after you and Travis experimented on her?"

She stumbled on the steps barely bothering to pretend it wasn't an accident. I put my foot into her back and held her there.

"Does she even know what that stuff will do?"

"You'd have to ask her. I'm sure I don't know. Tell me, Detective, are you going to eat me before or after you kill me?"

Not trusting myself, I let two officers drag her the rest of the way.

"Private isolation" sounds like something you'd do voluntarily at a Buddhist retreat. This was closer to solitary confinement. We went through so many empty halls and passages modified with thick, locked doors, it looked like Penny had the whole floor to herself.

The only time I slowed was when we passed a gun case. Through the glass I saw handguns, rifles, and small boxes. The name ASTERIA MARUTA and a date were scrawled on the top of each box. They were tranquilizer darts, just for Penny.

A peek in a stinking garbage bin near the last door told me at least a week's worth of meals had been stuffed inside. As we entered her room, where the figure on the monitor lay, old movies and cheap novels flit through my head. I thought we'd find a dummy, makeshift, like Penny's weird weapon, but there really was someone there.

Just about the right size and shape, she shivered as we crowded in. When I flipped her over and the wig tumbled off, it wasn't just half her face that was missing, it was her nose, both her ears and part of her skullcap.

A raggedy was in Asteria's bed. A real one.

Booth screamed into a phone, demanding security camera footage.

I knelt and looked her in the eyes. "What's your name, kid?"

"Don't know if I should say."

"Okay, let's try something else. I happen to know the usual tenant's been out for a few weeks. How the hell did you pull this off for so long?"

"She said they were afraid to come up here, so they

stayed away, and if I kept throwing the food out, kept my back to the cameras it'd be fine." She looked around at the crowd in the room. "It was until now. I only wanted a bed. You're not going to put me in the camps, are you?"

"Not up to me. Do you know where Asteria is?"

"She was here a while ago, waiting for someone. I have to stay under the bed when she's here. But when she saw all the lights she left early."

"Lights? When we showed up, maybe a few minutes ago?"

"No, out there." She waved at a barred window. "Same way she always comes and goes."

The curved bars looked formidable, but there were scores of little scratch marks in the cement where each bar met the wall, covered over with what looked like white crayon to match the paint. The whole thing would probably fall off if I pulled on it. But I didn't, I was too busy taking in the view. Maruta said the blue stuff loved water.

Cupped by trees, still as a mirror, maybe half a mile away, was the center of the conservation area, the Fort Hammer reservoir. Even if the local authorities were idiots, the feds weren't. Like I said, an army regiment had gotten involved, and they knew which potential targets to cover. Choppers hovered above the water, klieg lights illuminated the troops patrolling the area.

If the raggedy was telling the truth, the previously scheduled meeting had been interrupted. But Penny was smart and fast, and Misty wanted to see Chester again.

31

The road to the reservoir had more curves than an intestinal tract. No time for seat belts, I was thrown around so hard only dumb luck kept bones from breaking. Outside, flashlights carried by the guard sliced up the woods. We'd made good time finding the cell and reaching the room, but it'd been at least half an hour, which meant Misty could have walked to the reservoir and back by now. As for where Penny was, that was anyone's guess.

I turned to Maruta and tapped my wrist. "Tick-tick-tick. Can your baby see in the dark?"

"No," she said dismissively. After she thought about it a moment, she added, "At least I don't think so."

"You don't know?"

Avoiding my gaze, she looked at the light show outside the window. "Asteria was my husband's doing."

"What, so you had nothing to do with it?"

"He was being very naughty."

Again with that stupid word. "Like an affair? She was someone else's kid?"

"Nothing so crude. She's mine, genetically, but I didn't participate. When he wanted to be punished, he'd tell me by doing something naughty. That time ... he crossed the line."

"You mean like *he stole an egg* from you?"

"He wanted to surprise me. I was surprised."

No wonder I couldn't figure them. The Marutas were a species all their own. In Penny's case, literally.

The beam from a helicopter searchlight passed directly above us. It seared the cabin of the car, then burned the dark ahead just in time for Booth to avoid colliding with a tree. As he cursed, a voice came over the car speakers.

"We've got an adult female near treatment center six. Blue Raven has a clean shot."

Adult female. Misty.

Tom shouted, "Don't shoot! You could hit the vials! Tell your commanding officer to coordinate with the CDC. Take us there."

The search beam steadied, then led us a few hundred yards off the road. Its harsh light penetrated my feeble eyes like a strobe, freezing a still image in my brain: We were along the edge of the reservoir. A small concrete building sat below the line of earth that held back the water. Misty, the contours of her form washed nearly to nothing, her hair and clothing whipped by the chopper blades, was crawling along a stone floor toward the building. The foam and duct tape had been torn off. The blue vials glowed naked in the crook of her arm.

I saw the image for less than a second. Booth slammed

the brakes and I nearly went through the windshield. He was already out of the car while gravity was still throwing me back into my seat. I fumbled with the door lock and fell out after him, my dead hands and brittle knees hitting dry twigs and cold earth.

I pushed myself up. The second copter had joined the first, making the scene too bright for me to see a thing. I squinted as I forced myself forward, blinking rapidly, hoping that might help my chak-eyes adjust.

Forms wavered in the light. Smoky edges seeped into rough shapes. Misty was no longer alone. As if by magic, a hooded figure had appeared a little more than yard away from her.

Booth reached the edge of the circle. His gun was out and aimed. Misty's back and Penny's chest were both clear shots. "Don't shoot, for God's sake!"

He hesitated, but then said, "Fuck this."

As he squeezed the trigger, a glint of silver flew into his ribs. He grabbed at the wound and fell.

A rifle crack rose above the rush of the chopper blades. A sniper in one of the helicopters had fired, but Penny had stepped sideways, and now a puff of concrete dust rose at her feet. Another glint of silver appeared in her hand.

"Misty!" I screamed. "She's not Kyua, she's Asteria Maruta, a genetic freak and a killer. A psychopath raised by psychopaths!"

Penny hmphed loudly, reminding me, for the first time, of her mother. "I like to think I adapted to my parents experiments rather well."

"Yeah? Show me. Stop this now. Those vials will turn everyone into chakz."

She laughed. "Did Rebecca tell you that? She's lying. It's the Cure. Her final present from my father. Everyone will be alive again. All that we love will be restored."

She reached her hand toward Misty. "I'll prove it." She wriggled her fingers. "I'm not a chak dead, am I? Look how pink and supple the flesh is." She raked her makeshift blade across her palm, leaving a line that wept red. "See? Real blood."

Misty looked astounded. "You were dead?"

"I died when I was born. I died at home. I died in a lab strapped down to a table. My mother tried to destroy me with acid, but my father brought me back. It wasn't perfect, it wasn't painless, but *that*," she said, pointing to the vials, ". . . *is*."

I stepped toward the light. Penny raised the blade in warning, aiming not at me, but Misty. "She's lying. You can't ever see Chester again. That's what death is."

Misty's lips curled. Even in the spotlight her pupils were dilated. She was high as a kite. "You really going with that, Hess? If death was death, you wouldn't be standing there at all."

"Good point. But you've glued enough of us back together to know what we're like. That stuff won't let anyone die, but it won't let them live, either. Misty, please, don't trust her. She's crazy, she's . . . she's *the reason Chester died*. He swerved the car so he wouldn't hit her."

I thought I heard her gasp. "That was a raggedy."

I shook my head. "No. Costume. It was her."

Misty turned her head sideways like I'd slapped her. Two fat tears fell, disappearing into the whitewashed ground. Misty wavered. Maybe it was from the freezing wind, or maybe she was about to back away from Penny. I'll never know.

Shaking her head in judgment, Asteria threw the second blade. Misty grabbed at her neck and fell. By the time she hit the ground, both vials were in Penny's hands. She sidestepped another rifle shot.

I rushed up to Misty, tore off a chunk of my shirt and shoved it at the deep wound. The blood had waited for me. Now it was everywhere.

At the edge of the light, Penny said to the air, "Wish it had been you, Mom."

"You know what it is, don't you?" I said. "You've known from the start."

She nodded. "Oh, yeah."

"Why?" I asked.

Something whooshed past my head. I ducked, then heard the muffled crack of gunfire. Booth had fired at Penny and missed. Sneering, she ducked a third sniper shot, then vanished from the light like a liquid shadow slithering down a drain.

I put Misty's hand on my balled up chunk of shirt. "Press down hard. I don't think she cut the jugular. There are paramedics. They'll be here in a second."

She grabbed me. "Chester left me, Hess. Don't you leave me, too. Not again."

I cupped her hand then forced it onto the wound.

"Misty . . . I have to . . ."

I left her behind to run in the dark. If she died and I didn't stop Penny, she'd be back.

32

I ran alongside scores of people, but felt completely alone. Worse, keeping track of Penny was like chasing a new moon, dark against dark, always out of reach, showing only a shy edge if you happened to look at the right spot at the right time. Despite all that, I did see her, often enough to keep heading in the right direction, often enough to call to the others when they, much faster, headed the wrong way.

If *I* was leading the way, something was wrong, but it wasn't until the seventh time I spotted her that I realized what it was. She was waiting for me, letting me catch up. Did it mean there was some hope I could get the vials back, or was she, like her mother, enjoying any little extra pain she could cause?

Either way, I didn't slow down.

The helicopters fanned out ahead, their white eyes riding up the treeless, tiered mounds in front of the main reservoir dam, a hundred feet of stone ending in grassy hills on either side. A walkway, held up by Romanesque arches, water visible beyond their curves, sat astride the stone. In the center was a Gothic tower, the tall windows on its highest floor above the waterline.

Unless Penny planned to chuck the bottle thirty feet over the wall, and I wasn't sure she couldn't, the tower was the only way up. At the ground level, the entrance was sealed by a hinged metal grate. A copter beam flitted across it, revealing a rounded shadow just beyond the tower's threshold. It was Penny, swinging the grate to show me it was open.

Satisfied I'd seen her, she moved deeper into the tower. I'd never stopped running, but the guardsmen barreled ahead of me easily. Before they reached the entrance, the grate shut with a loud metallic clunk. A second, lighter click announced that the lock was in place.

The helicopters steadied over the scene, their beams tracing the spot where the tower met the walkway. They hovered low enough for me to see that the rear hatches were open, snipers in place, bracing themselves against the craft's jarring movements and the cold.

Four men reached the gate before I did. Three tried to yank it open. The fourth, the thinker of the group, was on the horn.

"Get the jaws of life up here, stat!"

It was the right idea. Invented to free victims from the mangled wreckage of car accidents, the jaws' gas-powered hydraulics would get through those bars in less than ten minutes. But, given how fast Penny moved, by then the mycoplasma could be in the water, and she in the next state.

Praying there was a reason she'd waited, I called her name. "Penny, what is it you want to have happen here?"

The blackness in the tower's guts sucked away any sense of depth, but the answer came echoing. "Tell those men to back off a few feet."

I nodded at them. They hesitated, unsure if it was the right thing to do, not wanting to take orders from a chak. Judging from the row of lights moving toward us, there'd be plenty of livebloods to call the shots in a minute or so, but for now there wasn't anything else they could do, so they moved back.

Penny didn't move, she just appeared, like the shadows had decided to stop covering her. She opened her mouth as if about to speak, so I came closer. She rushed at me with such speed, it looked as if my eyes had suddenly developed the ability to zoom in. I heard the door unlock, felt her pull me in and off my feet, then heard a slam and a locking sound before I hit the floor. By the time I flipped onto my back, she was gone again, and the guards were pulling at the bars.

"Did you see where she went?" I asked.

Looking like they'd just seen Big Foot rape Elvis, they shook their heads. Except for me, the space was empty.

Two stairwells led up into the tower. I took the one on the right and reached a floor with some sort of chugging pump that took up most of the space. By now, I realized I'd see her only if she wanted me to, so when nothing appeared, I headed farther up.

On the next floor, the damn chopper lights spilled onto the stairs, threatening to blind me. I held my arm over my eyes and kept climbing. The last floor was nothing more than a big open platform, four stone columns holding up a roof. Beyond the edge, it was a ten- or fifteen-foot drop to the water.

The searchlights wreaked havoc with my vision, making the shadows opaque. I stepped toward the water, only to have a chunk of plaster explode at my feet. As I threw myself behind one of columns, a voice called out.

"The snipers are very antsy, don't you think? But if you can't stay still, who can? Then again I've overestimated you before. I didn't think you were stupid enough to hide the vials in the same place you'd hid your clever decoy. But Misty assured me you were."

My flashlight beam was pathetic against the searchlight, but I aimed it toward the sound. I think I caught a glint of blue liquid.

"You don't have to see me. All you need to know is that I'm close enough to the water to toss the vials in."

"You could have done that before I got here."

"I'm not sure I want to. I am surprised you're trying so hard to stop me. What do you care how many chakz there are?"

"Because I know what it's like and wouldn't wish it on a dog. Thing I can't figure is, what do you care? You let me in. I'm here. What's this about?"

"I want to hire you, Detective."

I almost laughed. "Hire me? What for?"

"To prove my father was murdered."

I blinked. "Murdered? Really? Kind of a shame if it wasn't suicide. It was the only thing he ever did I liked."

The rattling sound of a gas engine from below told me the jaws of life were in place. Penny understood what it meant, too.

"Might want to keep the jokes to a minimum. The moment I hear anyone coming, oops."

"Okay. Who do you think killed him?"

"My mother."

"And you want to bring her to justice? I can almost understand that, except for all the corpses."

"Fuck justice. I want an excuse to kill her."

"Get in line."

"Remember what I said about jokes."

"Right. As far as I know, she controlled the guy completely. What's her motive?"

"I believe my father was on the verge of a breakthrough, a way to bring chakz *truly* back to life. I think he felt so guilty about his mistakes, he'd decided to give the most valuable secret on earth away for free. Project Birthday was a decoy. He hid the real cure."

It sounded like a kid's fairy tale, but I nodded. "Which would have put it totally out of her control. And she couldn't stand for that. Got any evidence?"

"That's what I need you for. You're a detective, *detect.*"

The words sounded familiar, even the tone. It was something like what Misty said back at the office when we first opened the briefcase. Had Penny been listening even then?

I put my hands up. "Happy to. Give me the vials and I'll do everything I can. I'll even halve my fee. It'll be easy with your mother in custody."

She laughed, but it wasn't at my joke. "But then killing her *wouldn't* be easy—especially since I'm not likely to survive this. You'll have to solve the case *before* they get through the gate."

I took an angry step toward the voice. "Are you fucking crazy? I have trouble solving cases on a good day! I can't just . . ." A sniper shot sent me tumbling back.

"Tick-tick."

How the hell was I going to . . . ? Maruta. She was here at least. Maybe I could get her to confess, or at least *lie* about killing her husband.

"Can I have your mother brought over so I can question her?"

"How you do it is up to you, but the gate stays locked."

As I raced down the stairs, I heard the slow groaning snap of the first bar. As soon as I reached the bottom, I waved my arms and shouted, "Stop!"

I had to say it twice to get them to pay attention. Then, I had to explain the situation three times before they started to understand. Not that I understood it myself.

"Just get me someone with authority."

They looked at one another, confused. "Booth?"

"He's still breathing? Get him on a radio, now!"

A walkie was shoved in my hand. "Tom? Is Misty . . . ?"

Maybe I should've asked how he was His voice was garbled. It wasn't easy for him to speak. "With the paramedics, not conscious last I saw. Lucky you got out of there. They've got a launcher on the chopper with a thermobaric grenade and orders to fire the second they've got a clear shot."

"What? That could blast the stuff right into the reservoir. If one drop survives, it's all over."

"That's what Maruta says, but I've got an army general insisting that as long as they hit dead-on, the heat blast will burn it all right up."

"And if they miss by a foot? Can you get him to change the order? Delay it at least?"

"Doubt it. Not unless you got better."

I couldn't believe I was saying it. "Asteria's my client

now." When I explained, he laughed, but it melted into a cough. Once he stopped hacking, he agreed to bring Rebecca over.

"Better hope they don't miss," was the last thing he said.

I lowered the walkie, feeling even more hollow than usual. Acid juices bubbled all over my insides. I sat on the concrete floor, wanting to stay there until I rotted. There was always the chance Maruta would hand me a confession, maybe insist on a presidential pardon in exchange for information confirming her guilt, like they did in *24,* but something told me it wasn't going to play that way. And aside from asking if she was guilty, I had nothing to go on. Less than nothing.

Even if I had any clues, odds were I'd screw things up, adding two and two and getting five, everything crashing down because of it. On the other hand, I did remember that the name of the doctor at the camp was Steven.

A van drove up, Maruta in the passenger seat, Nell and Jonesey in the back. Jonesey probably insisted, but why was Nell still tagging along? I hope it wasn't a misplaced sense of loyalty.

Booth, side patched, arm in a sling, lumbered out. He made a lame but stubborn effort to yank Maruta from her seat, but she eyed him with palpable disdain and exited on her own.

You don't even know how to hurt me.

She marched up to the closed grate. "The situation's been explained. I'd be happy to lie to her, but there's only one problem. I didn't kill him and she wants *proof.* I can't give you what doesn't exist. She'd spot it. Intelligence runs in her genes."

"So does a lot of other shit. Why does she think you killed him?"

"I don't know, but I understand why she wants me dead. I was the one who kept her locked away."

"Once you realized she was a monster."

"A monster? Hardly. The child is superhuman. That had nothing to do with it. I hate children. Travis knew that. I'd quoted *Mildred Pierce* a thousand times: *alligators have the right idea—they eat their young.*"

"But . . . then, why did he . . . ?"

She gave me the same withering look she'd given Booth. "Must I spell it out, *again*?" She sighed and closed her eyes. "He *wanted* to be punished, he wanted me to punish him. So he'd give me . . . presents he knew would upset me."

There was a weird pause before the word *presents*, but I didn't know if it meant anything. "And you killed him for it?"

She sniffed. "No. He often asked to die, but I refused."

I bought about half that. Who wouldn't be suicidal after inventing chakz? And maybe there were rules to their little game, but rules could be broken.

"You said he crossed a line when he created Asteria. Why shouldn't I believe you crossed the line with your punishments?"

"Because, you fool, that's how it worked! He was weak, he crossed lines. I was not weak. I did not cross lines. It would've ruined everything. Death was the ultimate punishment. More than anything, he wanted to deserve it, so of course *I* couldn't give it to him."

God help me, I was starting to understand. It's an old joke. The masochist said to the sadist, hit me, and the sadist said, No, I won't.

"Not even by accident?"

"I . . . don't . . . have . . . *accidents*. Not like that."

"And your daughter's idea that he planned to give the cure away for free?"

"Ridiculous. If there even were a cure we wouldn't be here, would we? The mycoplasma wouldn't matter."

"Then . . . you're certain it was suicide?"

She pursed her lips. "No. Travis never hurt himself. He needed to be punished by someone else, *me*. I can't believe he'd do *anything* like that without my permission."

"But he did."

"Perhaps."

A stronger, younger version of Rebecca's voice echoed down the stairs.

"Tick-tock," Penny said.

"If you were listening," I called back, "Then you know she didn't kill him."

"If *you* were listening, you know someone did."

Maruta repeated her daughter's words, "Someone did. She's right. He might be naughty and play with someone else a little. *That* could have gotten out of hand. But he was never even alone with anyone without my say-so."

"Who'd you give permission to?"

She shrugged. "No one with the nerve for anything like that. Wimpy little lab assistants and a rare press interview."

"Wait . . . press interview?"

I turned toward the van. Nell was leaning against it, listening. She'd managed to be here all along. Past sins. The last piece clicked into place. I wished the hell it hadn't.

"Nell?"

She flashed her green eyes at me. "Should've just gone to Canada."

"If it were anything less than the end of the world ... I'd ..."

"I bet you say that to all the girls."

Maruta twisted her head. "Parker. The chak with a knack. Colby vouched for you. I did say Travis could be alone with you."

Nell looked down at her nails. "Yeah, you did, didn't you?"

"Why wouldn't I? You're just a chak. A groveling thing less than human."

"Your husband and I had a lot in common."

I gripped the bars, wishing I could reach her. "Travis Maruta was having an affair with you. That's why you were so pissed at Colby. What could be worse than turning you over to a serial killer? Forcing you to chak-up with the man who stopped you from resting in peace."

She pushed away from the car, walked up to the grate, and stroked my fingers. "You know how Colby loves chakz and chemicals. It was a way for him to snoop on ChemBet. I begged him not to make me do it, but that never did any good. Whenever I was with Maruta I never made it a secret that I hated him as much as any chak would, but that only turned him on more."

I held her hand. "It was a masochist's ultimate thrill, being submissive to a chak. And his wife would never give him the satisfaction of dying, but you didn't have that problem, did you?"

"No. The first time he asked me to kill him was the only time I did exactly what he said. I jabbed him with the hypodermic he gave me and pushed the plunger. Now ask if I feel bad about it."

I didn't. I just held her hand.

"See that?" Nell said. "You're a much better detective than you think."

Rebecca's face, meanwhile, had turned beet red. She spoke quietly at first, but got louder as she went along. "It's not right. He wasn't yours. You can't own anything. And he . . . he didn't have permission! He didn't belong to you! It's not right!"

Cuffed hands held in front of her, she jumped at Nell. I let go of her hand just in time for her to avoid the lunge. Nell pulled back, but Maruta grabbed at her blouse, tore it, then tried to scratch the skin.

"Not yours! Not yours!" she cried.

Locked behind the grate, I called, "Tom . . ."

He'd been watching so intently it was like he'd forgotten he was there. He grunted and the guardsmen pulled her off.

Maruta kept screaming. "He wasn't yours! You had no right! He didn't make all the naughty presents for *you*!"

Presents. The card on the office desk, World's Best Boss. I thought my brain was having a little ironic moment for itself, but my body put the meaning together before I did. My insides clenched. She wasn't about to say *baby* when she was talking about her daughter. She was about to say *birthday present*.

"November twelfth, the day he died, probably the same day Asteria was born. Project Birthday. *Your* birthday. He's been giving you *birthday* presents. He designed that blue crap on *purpose*, to get you to punish him. But that means . . ."

Couldn't be. I didn't want to believe it, but it was staring me in the face. November twelfth was also the day the RIP was announced to the world.

Everything spun. I grabbed the bars to keep myself from falling. I was never a pious guy, but there I was, saying, "Oh, my God!" and "Jesus Christ!" over and over. "The RIP. He *knew* it was faulty when ChemBet released it. He *designed* it that way. It was part of your game ... another one of your birthday presents. ..."

I wished it had been greed. I wished it had been stupidity. I wished it had been politics, or even love. I wished it had been anything else. But it wasn't. I thrust my hands through the bars, screaming: "That's why we're all so fucked up! That's why we're freaks! Just so he could get you to hurt him!"

Jonesey, who'd been listening all along, went to his knees, clasped his hands, and started muttering, "Kyua, Kyua, Kyua ..."

Rebecca Maruta was unable to suppress a slight smile. "That was a *very* naughty gift."

I swear I would have pulled her *through* the grate to get to her, but she stepped back an inch, putting her just out of my reach.

A pained, abysmal shriek told me Jonesey had stopped praying. He was on all fours, heaving. He picked his head up, moaned, and wasn't pretending this time. Chakz don't usually cry, but his cheeks were stained with gray ooze.

"Hess, man, remember when you were wondering how I could keep from going feral? I think ... maybe ... all I needed was something like ... this."

They say that when you go feral, intent vanishes. If it's

true, Jonesey may have had just enough time to point himself. His body bolted to its feet, faster than a chak has a right to, and threw itself into Maruta. A guttural sound erupted from his throat.

Her low center of gravity kept her from falling, but she staggered sideways. Jonesey, or his body, or whatever, acting as if it were in a Romero movie, bit into her neck, enough to make a little tear. He used the fingers of his remaining hand to widen the hole, then tore out a chunk of her throat, which he proceeded to stuff into his mouth and chew.

As her screams turned to gurgles, a chopper light veered to cover the sudden uproar. The funny thing is, even with all those cops and guardsmen standing around, no one moved a muscle to stop Jonesey until long after everyone was sure she was dead.

33

Not wanting to see what they did to Jonesey's body before it hurt anyone else, I was almost grateful I had one last bit to play. There'd be time to mourn him later, maybe an eternity. I was still woozy as I ran back up the stairs, wondering how long I'd stay standing.

"You heard it," I called. "Your mother's dead. It doesn't matter any—"

The searchlights were still pointed at the fracas below, but there was enough light for me to see a small hand extended over the water, pouring blue liquid from an open vial.

She'd done it.

"Why? I did what you asked."

The hand let go of the empty vial and slipped back into shadow.

"I imagine my father asked that often when my mother punished him. She called him weak, but I don't think she ever understood him. She couldn't. It's like that black wall you run into when you try to remember something. But if you think about it, he never invented anything that wasn't used. He invented this thinking she would use it."

The choppers rose and twisted back into position, making wild abstract shapes in the tower, all white or all black, no grays. They didn't even realize there was no point anymore.

"But you hate her," I said. "Now she's a power of example?"

"Not her, my father. He believed in surrender, submission. That no matter how much willpower you think you have, things move on their own. He must have thought my mother a fool, spiritually at least. It finally dawned on me that trying to bring her to justice made me a fool, too. So, this is how I surrender."

I think I wanted to understand, but so far, it wasn't happening. The best I could come up with was that the child of Travis and Rebecca was now playing her parents game all on her own. Afraid she might run, I took a step forward.

"Don't move," she said. "I really don't want them to fire before I apologize."

I was stunned. "You release a plague on humanity and you're sorry?"

"Oh, not for that, but for what I did to your father."

I don't know how I managed to look surprised anymore, but I guess I did.

"He was in the lab as a volunteer. *You* gave him the case."

She nodded. "I'd been inside often. It was easy to sneak in and out. It was the first place I headed when I learned my father was dead. I found the briefcase he'd left wrapped with a pretty bow for mother's big day. I wanted to prove she'd killed him. Having her present would give me leverage. But I was afraid it had some kind of tracking device, that they'd catch me. So I gave it to your father, along with the fake ID. He didn't know the name Kyua, so I explained it was the Cure. He wanted very badly to give it to you, so I showed him where to run."

"You used him."

"I wasn't the first, but I think I was the last. Once I thought it was safe, I met him there. I gave him every chance to give it back, I even told him what it really was, but he thought I was lying, that he had a way to save you. My mistake. It hadn't occurred to me that someone could care for their child that much. Can't blame me for that, can you?"

The folds of her hood dipped in and out of the light, black squiggles on a snowy field. Over the reservoir, metal clicks mixed with whirring blades.

"By then I was in a hurry. Mother knew her gift was missing, Colby Green found out about it, too, from one of his moles. We fought. I actually had to take your father apart, and thanks to whatever my father had done to him, he *still* got away, part of him, anyway. That's what I'm sorry for. But at least you knew your father for a while."

A sliver of color appeared in the ebony wall. Blue. She was holding the other vial.

"I didn't know mine, not really. In all my life he only wrote me one letter. My mother tore it up, but let him send me the pieces. She told me it was an apology for creating me, but there was only one line I could make out. Do you want to know what it was?"

She stepped into the searchlight beam, holding the remaining vial in both hands, as if it were a chalice. I heard the hiss of a launcher firing.

"We are the stuff of stars. Remember?"

The grenade hit. I had no choice but to submit. I flew backward down the stairs, seeing all those stars Travis Maruta had written his daughter about.

34

Humanity's fondest dream, immortality, was about to come true. Frantic warnings were issued, pipelines clamped shut, but even without the riots, there was only so much they could do. Even if people didn't have a tendency to drink water, Project Birthday worked just as well airborne. Evaporation would send tons of the stuff into the air.

That didn't stop people from trying. Every LB in the area, Misty, Booth, Green, the guard, the police, the army, the hospital patients and staff, all of us were placed under quarantine. The CDC and a horde of penitent ChemBet boffins worked us over around the clock.

When they told me Misty survived her throat wounds, I wanted to see her, but they wouldn't let me. I was kept in a separate room, submerged in a vat of some shit called Plasmocin. I heard Nell got the same. It wasn't as bad as it sounds. The vat had a window with a TV on the other side, so there was something to watch, and they let us out every few hours so we wouldn't lose it.

Speaking of losers, judging from the cable news, after the ferals were rounded up, the rebelling chakz, with no further orders from their glorious leader, became more interested in watching all the excitement rather than causing it.

Once I was pronounced clean, they let me visit Misty. Sort of. She was behind a thick glass wall and I was carrying a bucket to catch the Plasmocin still dripping from the various cracks in my body.

She'd been off the drugs a few days. Her eyes were clearer, but that only made the sadness in them clearer, too.

"You look like shit," she said.

"For a chak, that's an improvement. You working your program?"

She made a face. "It's a psychiatric hospital. Half the staff are addicts. We have meetings every six hours."

"How's it working for you?"

She bobbed her head and swallowed. "I miss Chester. But I'm glad he's not coming back. I don't want to either. I'd hate to be like you, Hess, no offense."

She held her hand against the barrier. I pressed mine to the same spot. The glass probably felt better than my skin.

"None taken. At least it gives you a good reason to stay healthy, huh?"

She nodded. "If they let us out, and there's ever a case you don't want to take, I won't argue. We can both watch television all day."

"Deal."

To get on my good side, or keep me from joining the long line of people suing them, ChemBet sent me the volunteer application my father filled out, the one that gave them permission to do whatever they wanted and keep him as long as they liked. In the little space where it asks why he's signing up, he says, "My son's a chak. I want to do right by him."

Had a hard time wrapping my head around that one. I couldn't blame him for being duped by Penny, but I still didn't forgive him for kicking the dog.

Nell was declared clean about the same time I was. In her case, she was immediately placed under arrest for the murder of Travis Maruta. Booth, cursing his head off in quarantine, took the time to arrange a meeting for me before they transferred her out.

We sat in a small windowless room for half an hour, holding cold hands and not saying much until it was almost time for her to go.

On the way out, she asked, "Canada?"

"Sure," I said.

We both knew it wasn't going to happen. Not that I thought she'd get jail time. With the truth out, or as much reality as mankind could bear, her broadcast made her more popular than ever. It'd be to the state's advantage to drop the charges and have her take the stand against ChemBet, or Green, or both. Even if the case went to trial, I doubted any jury would convict her. People were getting more sympathetic to chakz now that they knew they'd be one someday.

The reason Canada was out was because we couldn't get there from here anymore. Fort Hammer and the surrounding county had been sealed off. More troops manned the borders every day. And you had to figure that if they didn't find a vaccine quick, someone up the chain was already planning to nuke the place.

How long before that? Like the poet said, April is the cruellest month. That's when the CDC figures the mycoplasma will be too entrenched in the general populace to stop the spread.

Judgment Day? More like Misjudgment Day. Not that graves would burst open and the dead rise, but when any infected LB died, in an hour or two they'd be on their feet. Then again, since the body wouldn't have much time to decay, most of the newcomers would be smart, at least for a while.

After Nell was shipped out, I was told I'd be free to wander Fort Hammer again, provided I agreed to keep mum about certain facts I'd learned regarding the inspiration for the invention of the RIP, the revelation of which would likely cause more chakz, and some livebloods, to lose it. I agreed. With the evil geniuses behind it all dead, what was the point?

After a few days back in the office, the first snow started to fall, some of it into the hallway. As I was busy trying to sort the trash into different piles, I got two more surprises. The first was that a liveblood FedEx man was actually delivering in the Bones. The second was the contents of the package.

Inside a small white box there was a plastic bag containing, according to the label, the ashes of my father's arm. An enclosed letter said the CDC had all the samples they needed to reverse engineer whatever Maruta had done to him. Meanwhile, ChemBet was suing to get the remains back, insisting my father's cells were their intellectual property. Rather than let that happen, they'd cremated what they had. Satisfied that 1900 degrees Fahrenheit would take care of anything communicable, as "surviving" heir, they decided the ashes rightfully belonged to me.

I took the little bag to the roof and looked at the Bones and the city. I still wasn't sure he got the meaning right, but I had to say something as I tossed the ashes into the wind, so I muttered the last few words of that poem Dad liked:

And you, my father, there on the sad height,
Curse, bless, me now with your fierce tears, I pray.
Do not go gentle into that good night.
Rage, rage against the dying of the light.

Funny thing, as I watched the snow fall on the living and the dead, I was struck by a rare *optimistic* thought. If everyone gets the virus, maybe someone with half a brain and a healthy attitude really will try to find a cure. And then, who knows?

A cynical view of humanity? Maybe. Or maybe you just have to be dead to think that way.

Life is wasted on the living.

Praise Kyua.

ABOUT THE AUTHOR

Born in the Bronx, **Stefan Petrucha** spent his formative years moving between the big city and the suburbs, both of which made him prefer escapism. A fan of comic books, science fiction, and horror since learning to read, in high school and college he added a love for all sorts of literary work, eventually learning that the very best fiction always brings you back to reality; so, really, there's no way out.

An obsessive compulsion to create his own stories began at age ten and has since taken many forms, including novels, comics, and video productions. At times, the need to pay the bills has made him a tech writer, an educational writer, a public relations writer, and an editor for trade journals, but fiction, in all its forms, has always been his passion. Every year he's made a living at that he counts as a lucky one. Fortunately, there've been many. *Ripper*, which is sort of like the Harry Potter books but with no magic and with a serial killer, is available now.

New in the Revivalist series from

RACHEL CAINE

Two Weeks' Notice

After dying and being revived with the experimental drug Returné, Bryn Davis is theoretically free to live her unlife—with regular doses to keep her going. But Bryn knows that the government has every intention of keeping a tight lid on Pharmadene's life-altering discovery, no matter the cost.

And when some of the members of a support group for Returné addicts suddenly disappear, Bryn begins to wonder if the government is methodically removing a threat to their security, or if some unknown enemy has decided to run the zombies into the ground…

Available wherever books are sold or at penguin.com

facebook.com/AceRocBooks

R0119

Kat Richardson

The Greywalker Novels

A detective series with a supernatural twist,
featuring PI Harper Blaine.

<u>ALSO AVAILABLE IN THE SERIES</u>

GREYWALKER
POLTERGEIST
UNDERGROUND
VANISHED
LABYRINTH
DOWNPOUR
SEAWITCH

"The Grey is a creepy and original addition
to the urban fantasy landscape."
–Tanya Huff

**Available wherever books are sold or at
penguin.com**

R0113